I0637447

Ski Mask Money 2

Renta

**Lock Down Publications and Ca$h
Presents**
Ski Mask Money 2
A Novel by *Renta*

Renta

Lock Down Publications
Po Box 944
Stockbridge, Ga 30281

Visit our website @
www.lockdownpublications.com

Lock Down Publications
Like our page on Facebook: Lock Down Publications @
www.facebook.com/lockdownpublications.ldp
Book interior design by: **Shawn Walker**
Edited by: **Cassandra Barrett-Sims**

Stay Connected with Us!

Text **LOCKDOWN** to 22828 to stay up-to-date with new releases, sneak peaks, contests and more...
Thank you.

Submission Guideline.

Submit the first three chapters of your completed manuscript to ldpsubmissions@gmail.com, subject line: Your book's title. The manuscript must be in a .doc file and sent as an attachment. Document should be in Times New Roman, double spaced and in size 12 font. Also, provide your synopsis and full contact information. If sending multiple submissions, they must each be in a separate email.

Have a story but no way to send it electronically? You can still submit to LDP/Ca$h Presents. Send in the first three chapters, written or typed, of your completed manuscript to:

LDP: Submissions Dept
Po Box 944
Stockbridge, Ga 30281

DO NOT send original manuscript. Must be a duplicate.

Provide your synopsis and a cover letter containing your full contact information.

Thanks for considering LDP and Ca$h Presents.

Dedication

This one is for *every* man or woman trapped within the belly of the tarantula! Prison— the place where abandonment and heartache rob us of the last good piece of heart we have left. For all those who've experienced broken love and had no other choice but to fight back—*alone!* This one is for you! The ones trapped in that cell, wishing time could be rewound or sped up! Hold ya head, family, there's Beauty in the Struggle! I'm 17yrs in! Still won't break … won't fold … won't bend!

—Renta and Red

Renta

Part I:
A Talk with God

'Sup, nigga? Long time no see and I just wanna catch a vibe with you. I've been goin' through some shit ... and it's been a hard pill to swallow, especially for a nigga of my caliber.

I'm trapped inside the belly of the tarantula ...
Praying you deliver me from this animal!

I'm searching for sunshine throughout the rainstorm ...
The devil's in my line of vision and I don't know which way he came from!

God, I need you! Hard times got me lookin' at niggas crooked, even though we've ventured down the same roads...

Broke bread amongst the same folds ... and even tossed up some of the same hoes ...

'Cause when money's in the equation, there's no tellin' how the game goes...

And when a knife's against your throat, it ain't no tellin' which way the blade rolls!

Being lost within my hustle, I never knew I could cry like this ... Lord, she's the only woman I've ever loved ... why she had to lie "like this?"

Being lost within the abyss, it's the broken wings that makes it hard to fly "like this!" And I know it's not proper to question you, God, but it's the struggle that got a nigga askin' why ... why, "like this!"

And for the nigga that crossed me? I wish we could go back to the beginning of our chapter... before jealousy and envy ever tainted our picture ...

I'd pause our movie at the scenes that made our hearts so bitter!
Say, nigga! I don't fault you for fuckin' that hoe ...

But after ya dick had spit and you grabbed ya shit to split, I fault you for not "crushin'" that hoe!

Say? "How" you fall in love wit' "my" hoe? I admit she had some fire head! Pussy so wet, she could fill up water beds, I just expected you to have a tighter head!

*To Ms. Lady who had me chasin' after her gushy?
I met another bitch who's just ... like ... YOU! She trying to
entice me with the depths of her pussy! But I can't fault you, for
havin' a nigga sweat ya... 'cause you "are" the same bitch that you
was since the first day that I met ya!*

*Lord, have mercy on your ghetto child, I ain't been to church in
a long while ... but the reason I'm standin' before You is 'cause he
shook my hand, but had the wrong smile!*

*And Dear God? I would've given "my spine" for this nigga!
All in the name of loyalty ... signed 99 for this nigga!*

*It was partially my fault, 'cause I was bred by this street shit ...
taught to look in the toilet; I ain't gotta smell it, 'cause I can "see"
shit!*

*Peep this ... God, I saw the double cross before it hit me, but
overlooked his intentions 'cause this real shit is really in me!*

*Went from a friend to an enemy — Greeed clouded his vision
... Now, I'm aimin' at his shower cap until he pays me my pennies!*

*That's why I'm standin' before You, Lord, a gangsta beggin'
forgiveness—but the streets gotta be a witness!*

— Gambino

CHAPTER 1
First Name Basis

The dayroom on G1 Pod was lively as the large group of men crowded around a back table, bobbing their heads to a jailhouse beat. 180, the convict creating the beat, expertly created the melody using his knuckles, a pencil, and harmonizing almost inhumanly as Gambino fell in love with the vibe:

♪ *"Pole on me, lil nigga, the H and K black and gray/ I was raised during times of hate, by shacks and crates/ where headhunters swallow ya face/ and my bitch will suck your dick just to stake out ya place ...*

I hail from the slums, me and my dawgs squabble for sport/ mama kicked me outta the house/ I skipped over the porch/ and dived in that water where the weak gets swallowed, can't have no heart when swimmin' with sharks, I keep mines hollowed...

Used to look up to Tony, he had every bird you can mention/ till the federals put the Rico Act in his face, and turned bro to a pigeon/ now when them dolphins goes swimmin' across the Pacific/ can't jump too high outta that water, the coast guard too deep in his bidness ...

So I don't fuck with these niggas, I stick to the laws of the jungle's trees/ seen an ape whack an ape, and even witnessed the snake whisper in her ear to humble Eve ...

I've braved zero degrees/ brodie nem ran down on the plug, secured the bag when they drilled em/ when it was time to split up the dough, the nigga bro considered a bro up'ed the burna and killed em!" ♪ He spat the lyrics to the roar of the crowd.

***

After disconnecting the call, Oshaya sat frozen on the loveseat, staring absently into nothingness— *"I've been having nightmares of our past—when we were young girls."* Patrese's words plagued her, and without forewarning, a storm converged in her eyes. She remembered that time in her life, a time when her body wasn't her own ... a time when her mind was dark, and she remembered the time of the *Deadly Rose*. She remembered it all, though she tried her best to forget it all. And as she sat with her pedicured feet tucked beneath her, the throw pillow she'd reached over and pulled close to her body became her only anchor to the life she now lived.

"Once upon a time in Mexico," she whispered as her mind carried her back to that exact time ...

Down! Get down! Policía! Policía!" someone shouted as the door flew off the hinges. Shay was stunned and she hugged her clothes to her naked body as the swarm of agents invaded the room and aggressively secured them.

"No, move! No, move," one of the Mexican officers demanded, as he manhandled her to the bed— *"naked!"*

"Wait-I— No, I didn't—" She tried to explain.

"¡Cállate!" He cut her off and told her shut up in his native tongue.

As Hector was dragged out of the room kicking and screaming, Shay was snatched from the bed.

"Wait, my clothes, I need my clothes," she cried. The deviant man smiled wickedly as he handled her roughly. His vision fell to her perky breasts before trailing to her paradise, and though sex had been her life ever since she'd been a child, his predatoriness sent a chill down her spine.

"Tú looky better with no clothes, señorita," he chuckled in broken English. *"Te gusta follar, si?"* Realizing she hadn't understood the question, he smirked and translated— *"Tú likey to fok, yes?"* Shay frowned before spitting in his face so unexpectedly the man jumped in surprise, yet shock quickly melted into rage. His anger

12

mounted as saliva dribbled down his face, and in a blink, the officer's hand reared back to slap her. Shay tensed against the assault, and just as the blow descended toward her face...

"What the hell is wrong with you, man?" Her savior arrived in the form of a tall, black man in a double-breasted Celine suit. He'd caught the officer by the wrist in a firm grip and was glaring down at him from a heated gaze. "I'll take it from here."

"No, she's one of the—"

"I said"— her savior gritted before tightening his grip and stepping into the shorter man's face— "I'll take it from here!" he spat menacingly.

The two men allowed testosterone to dance in the air, as their eyes danced the tango of wolves when a challenge was made. A moment passed before the officer released Shay and snatched his wrist free of the other man's grip. Spitting on the floor, he spoke rapidly in Spanish, and whatever he'd said caused the other Hispanic officers to glare at the tall American in contempt as they slowly trickled out of the room. The tall gentlemen returned their glares until a slap to the back caused him to tense in defense.

"Good job, Givens, you've successfully pissed off one of the crookedest men in Mexican law enforcement!" A mutually tall Caucasian man chuckled. The black man relaxed when he realized the other man was a fellow American Federal Agent.

"Yeah, whatever, Jordan, —these motherfuckers didn't like America before I pissed off their sergeant, so fuck 'em!" Agent Givens declared.

The other agent nodded his agreement before his sharp eyes took in the protective stance his comrade had taken in front of the naked girl. "I'll see ya outside, partner," he announced with a quick, sneaky smirk.

After he'd departed, Agent Givens turned to Shay and stepped around her. She tensed, not knowing his intentions.

"Relax, I'm only going to uncuff you so you can get dressed," he revealed, and triggered the cuffs to slide free from her wrists. For some strange reason Shay felt comfortable around him, and didn't rush to get dressed. Being naked before a man was nothing new to

13

her, but turning to find the man had turned his back to give her privacy was. She frowned in confusion as she got dressed, but when realization dawned on her, she paused, with her dress midway down her body.

"You're the man who was at the table with Rosa, right?" she asked, not truly comprehending the events of the night. Figuring she was already dressed, the man turned to face her, only to find her bare from the waist down. He quickly reverted his eyes and received a girlish giggle from her. It seemed outlandish to her that he wanted to respect her.

"Yes, that would be me," he answered, eyes still averted.

"You bought me and now—"

"I was doing my job."

"Job?"

"Yes."

"Job?" she reiterated, before pulling her dress the rest of the way down. The man's eyes returned to her young, but experienced eyes,.

"Yes, my job. I'm Agent Givens when professionally addressed, but my name is Nigil Givens, and you?" His question seemed foreign to her and the expression on her face told the tale.

"I-I don't remember," she whispered, shame blossoming within her downcast eyes. That's when it dawned on him that the girls who had been snatched into the white slave trade became someone entirely different from who they once were. The realization stung him.

"Choose a name," he offered, with a soft smile. Shay thought on it before her eyes lifted to find him. He was different from the many other men she'd met; who only wanted to mount her. To fuck her!

"Oshaya, just call me Oshaya." She was born.

The Present

The crowd had calmed enough for the next convict to show his skills, and the boy Klutch stepped forward with that Dead End, saucy swag, as if he had something to say that had never been heard before. The jailhouse beat slowed a bit and had a different vibe than the one Gambino had spit over, and the change seemed to fit the young boy's vibe as he spit from the gut:

♪ *"I'm RNO Klutch-A-Mill/ a lot of real with a touch of skill/ Gangsta/ step on niggas like soda cans, "crush ya ears"/ Gangland/ plottin' on my team without a game plan/ will get you dabbed up and smoked with the same hand/*

"You lame man/war ready, my blows goin' in/ Sticks will poke ya neck for a check and bend ya shoulder in/ I'm colder than a polar bear/ heart dark as Moses hair/ we the reason ya hoes will stare/ and baby, loyalty will get you chauffeured on some foreign wheels/ real bitches only give my heart to a Lauren Hill/

"So if she not a Nubian, I leave her with the crew she in/ bleed for my flesh like a blood set, "UBN"/ 4real/ what's blessin's Flesh, what the fruits is/ pour my 40 in the dirt for dead homies, call it root beer/ convertible foldin' stock get your rag top roof peeled/

"Or I'll have your Adam's apple hangin' from an apple tree/ unless my Flesh rather bust your head for dem apple seeds/ Real Niggas Only, not a gang, just a way of life/ can't balance fake with the real, just don't weigh up right/

"Homie" ... niggas feel I switched up on em/ it is what it is, Klutch-A-Mill fuck with real niggas only." ♪ He spat to the roar of the crowd. Even Gambino had to give it up to the young bull—playboy was raw talent.

"That boy going somewhere," someone raved.

"Naw, for real for reeeal!" a second seconded.

As the crowd gave dude his flowers, Gambino's attention was captured by a convict waving frantically at him. Excusing himself, he made his way to the bars of the dayroom and dapped homie up.

"What's good, Lil Chester, tell me somethin' good, playboy," Gambino greeted.

"Damn, nigga, you boys lit in that thang." Chester nodded toward the crowd at the back of the dayroom. Gambino shrugged.

"You know how it go down. We just freakin' out on the beat, but fuck all that, you get that for me?" he cut to the chase. Chester laughed, knowing how much Gambino wanted the info he had for him. Nodding his confirmation, he reached inside his pocket and came out with a folded piece of paper.

"Yeah, this gonna cost ya a few knots of that gas you boys been pushin' around this bitch." Chester smirked as he handed over the info. Gambino nodded his agreement before again bumping fist with the man. Chester laughed— "Yeah, ole buddy y'all put that work in on, Funk, he workin', bro, it's all on the paper." He nodded to Gambino's hand. Gambino chuckled before bidding homie peace in their departure. He already knew Funk was a rodent, but he was more concerned about the other info on the paper.

Glancing around to ensure no one was looking, he unfolded the kite and smiled at the name inscribed across it. A week ago, he'd found Chester in the law library and had him look up Givens' *first* name, and as he allowed it to brand his mental, he smirked— *Oshaya Givens.* He liked the way it sounded in his mind— "Oshaya," he whispered and liked it even more rolling off his lips.

Chapter 2
30 Minutes Later

"Lawson, hurry your ass, motherfucker, unless you're trying to stay in Hotel La Estelle with us for just a little more time, huh?" CO Stevens shouted from the first tier. Gambino chuckled as the cell door rolled and Pierre grabbed the only thing, he was taking with him when he exited the prison.

"Bruh, why the fuck you are taking a Ramen noodle soup to the world with you?" Gambino laughed.

"My nigga, the reason most of us ends up back in this bitch is 'cause when we touch down, life happens, and we forget these cold nights. Bleed, I'm taking this soup 'cause it's gonna be my reminder that they got a place for my ass if I trip over my shoelaces." Gambino nodded his understanding as he and his mans faced off. When you've lived with a person for years, and learned their habits, their strengths and weaknesses— the good, bad, and the ugly, it builds a camaraderie amongst men. Neither man was weak, but the love was thick. They clasped hands in a soldier's embrace, eye to eye. Pierre hated to leave his mans behind, and Gambino overstood. He nodded toward the open cell door.

"Fuck outta here, guy, what?"—Gambino chuckled— "you on some emotional shit now?" They laughed. "You can't do shit for us here; caged up. You can make it happen from the other side of that gate though." He gave it up. Pierre nodded his overstanding. Real niggas respected real niggas. They embraced once more before Pierre turned to leave. "Pierre?" Gambino called.

"What's brackin', fam?" Pierre paused and glanced back.

"Fuck them niggas out there, bruh, don't get out there and get lost in the sauce. We know what broken love feels like, and I know it's been a minute since you had some pussy, but tame ya dick, playboy. Don't go out there fuckin' wit' the same hoes who ain't put no loot on ya account when your piece was off the board. Get ya bag right."

"I'm on it, big bro, and I'ma make sure I fuck wit' yo fam— your daughter is my daughter, family, I got you."

"Lawson, get the fuck down here! Now!" the officer demanded. Pierre gritted his teeth, on the verge of spazzing on him.

"I ain't gon' miss this shit, dawg. I'm thinkin' 'bout slidin' down through this country ass town and whackin' some of these hoe-ass CO's for the hell they take us through."

"Nigga, you sound like a lame," Gambino spat irritantly. "Screw ya head back on tight, repay 'em by gettin' your bag up! Pull back up at viso in something foreign! Come back and run dick in they wives ... fuck these hoes who up here actin' like they corporate bitches when all they are, are regular females wearin' a uniform." They shared another laugh before Pierre saluted him and made his way toward his freedom.

"Ridge, you have a celly!" CO Timmons declared, snapping Gambino out of his reflections.

When his eyes focused, Gambino's vision locked into the hardened gaze of a big, country, cornbread fed White man. The pointed thunder bolt beneath his left eye revealed the man's *Aryan Circle* association, and when their eyes locked, neither man blinked as the door rolled. Gambino slid from the bunk as the man stepped in with his property, and they automatically sized each other up.

"Say, homeboy, I'm assigned to that bottom bunk." His new celly's voice was raspy and deep. Gambino looked him up and down with that animal shit reflecting in his eyes.

"Is there a problem?" CO Timmons eye'd them suspiciously.

"Yeah, I'm assigned to —"

"Naw, we good." Gambino cut him off, and the muscular White man cut his eye's toward him. "We good, T, you can go do you." Gambino gave CO Timmons *the look*. She shook her head with that *"boy-you-pitiful"* expression on her face, before nodding and making her exit.

The Caucasian man mumbled something beneath his breath as he sat his bags down and stepped toward the back of the cell. "So, what we gonna do about this bunk situation, 'cause I'm way too big to be climbing up there." He nodded to the top bunk.

Gambino sized him up to be about six four in height, two ninety in weight, and he had tattoos covering every inch of his exposed

18

arms, neck, and bald head. Without the verbal, he reached down and took hold of one of the man's bags of property and hefted it up onto the top bunk. As the white man stared with a feral expression on his pale face, Gambino reached down and took hold of the second bag, but the man slapped his hand away.

"Now look here, goddamit, I—"

Bam! That was as far as his words made it before Gambino fired off. The punch busted the man's lips, but Gambino learned quick that ole buddy was with *the shit. Bam! Bam! Bam!* The punches flew from both men. *Boom! Boom! Pissssh! Pisssh! Pisssh!* The sound of knuckles against flesh echoed off the walls as they showed that work. Gambino weaved backwards out of reach of a wild haymaker, and though he was raw in his defense, the cell was too small for the penitentiary fighting style he was bred with. The *Helter Skelter* technique had been mastered at the Telford Unit in Texas, but with cages and blocks of the technique, one needed room to play.

"Come onnnnn, motherfucker! That's all you got?" White man roared. Blood poured from his lips and nose and dripped down his chin from the blows traded.

Bam Bam Bam! Bam! Pop! Pop! Gambino dipped in with a left, a hard right, and another left. A hook, followed by two jabs rocked the man sideways, but it didn't sit dude on his ass.

"Come onnnnn!" *Pish! Pishhh! Pishh!* The big man went all the way, *White man,* and began to punch *himself!* "I'm gonna kill you, you black piece of shit! Arrrugh," he roared when he rushed Gambino.

Damn! Gambino thought when the man slammed him into the bars. Somehow, the man had gotten him in a bear hug and seemed to be squeezing him for dear life.

"Say, fam, whoop that hoe, Gambino!" Tay shouted from two row.

"Nigga, you bet not let that White boy whoop you or I'm gon' crash him *and* check in wit' you next!" Lil K was hot he couldn't get at ole dude—" Say, when these doors roll, all you White boys betta have it on ya mind!"

"That ain't got nothin' to do with us, but ain't no White *boys* over here, homie, I'm a White *man!* When these doors roll, we can get that! I'm talkin' to Texas!" A White cat named Thomas Ashford, known simply to the streets as *T,* rose to the occasion. He was one of the *few* White men on the unit who boys recognized as a gangsta.

The three tiers were alive as the sounds of war emitting from Gambino's cell fed the danger in the air. The tension was thick, and to add to the madness, one of the other inmates began madly shaking his cell door, causing unnecessary ruckus. All the while, in Gambino's cell, he was attempting to break the man's hold on him, but to no avail—

"Let me go, bitch, let's get it in blood . . . on some gangsta shit!" he growled.

"Fuck you!" the man spat, and before Gambino could reciprocate the sentiment, the big man reared his head back, and with the speed of a striking serpent, headbutted blood from Gambino's nose. Blood exploded onto the man's forehead as Gambino went limp, out on his feet. Feeling him go slack, the White man released him, and allowed him to slouch against the bars, but after running a hand beneath his bloodied nose and seeing the harm the Black man had done, he heartlessly punched the shit out of him. The impact woke Gambino from his nap and caused a groan to ensue from him as he shook the cobwebs off.

"Fuck?" he mumbled as he zoned in. The floor was slippery with their blood, but in that cell, where they were held captive and trapped with nothing but anger, resentment, and those four walls, shit had turned dark. Both men huffed and puffed, fighting to catch their breath.

"I want my bunk, Dude!"

"A'ight, bruh, a'ight, damn!" Gambino relented.

"Get your shit, *boy!"* The White man saw the defeat in his eyes and fed off its power.

Gambino nodded before finding a towel to clean his face. "That's a bet, homie, you earned my respect." He relented.

"What's brackin, G?" someone shouted from down the tier.

20

"Say, cuz, you straight, Gambino?"

The Bloods and Crips were ready for that action. A lot of them had White men for cellies, and they merely awaited the go-button to be pushed by Gambino, and it would start pure mayhem. Gambino knew it, and he also knew how ugly shit could become, so after a moment's glare, he smirked evilly.

"I'm Gucci! Y'all boys chill. We just had to get an understandin', it's no pressure," he shouted, as he eye'd the White man. "You good?" he asked. The White man's face was wet with crimson liquid as he nodded.

"I just want my bunk, dude, that's all. I'm no hoe, homeboy."

"Gambino." Gambino introduced himself with a bloodied smile. "You fight hard as a mu'fucka, White boy." He chuckled.

"I'm an Aryan *man*, not a boy," the White man corrected, but extended his hand, nonetheless. "I'm Big Country." He returned the smile as they shook. Gambino nodded, but as soon as their hands separated—*Bam!* He hit dude with a powerful jab that landed square on his nose. Big Country's eyes shut naturally—*Bam! Bam! Bam!*— a left, right, and another right, slumped him against the wall and Gambino wasted no time getting to the business. He rushed to the table and snatched up his hotpot and went to work.

Clunk! "Pussy"—*Clunk!* — "Ass"—*Clunk-Clunk!* "White boy!" *Clunk!* Every time the hard plastic made contact, blood shot from the man's scalp like water from a geyser. Big Country crumbled to the floor. Sleep! Gambino leaned down before arching the pot back as far as it would go.

Finish him! He could hear the Mortal Combat voice in his head and just before he obliged—

"Hold up, Gambino, don't do it like that, my G. Them hoes gon' bring the electric chair back just for you if you do him in. Let dude make it, big bro." J-Bo's voice snapped him out his blood lust. When Gambino's eyes focused and he saw what he'd done, he slung the bloodied hot pot against the wall.

"Fuck, mane," he growled before pacing the floor. *I can't let this boy die in here,* he thought, as his eyes lifted to find J-bo's reflection staring back at him from the handheld mirror he'd positioned toward Gambino's cell. They eye'd each other.

"Nigga, clean the cell and get that boy some help," J-Bo reasoned as Gambino glanced back at the unmoving man."Big bro," J-Bo called to him, and when their eyes met, he leaned a little closer to the mirror so he could get a good look into Gambino's eyes, "you gonna have to come up with a hellafied tale of how that boy got like that."

***

"You good, hump?" Ms. June, Gambino's mom asked the man she'd just walked to the door.

Hump was five years younger than her, and he was a successful hustla from the South Park section of the city. He finished zipping his pants before turning to flash her a gold-toothed smile. Though he'd just allowed Ms. June to *orally* compensate him for the capsules of heroin he'd just supplied her, the man knew he was out of bounds for serving her. When Gambino was free, he'd warned Hump that it was a no-no, but as soon as the man had gotten cased up, the money overrode Hump's desire to live. Yet, Dunte, Gambino's younger brother, had become their mother's protector, and the man-child had the city shook up. If Gambino was the boogeyman, Dunte had to be Lucifer incarnated.

"I'm Gucci, just know those lips of yours not no Black Card, I like money, June."

"I know, baby, I know, but my check ain't came in yet. Next time I'll come proper." She smiled as he made his exit. Hump paused on the porch of the shotgun house, and just when he turned to respond, he was greeted with the door slamming in his face.

"Bitch!" he growled, before laughing. *Dopefiends,* he thought, while pulling his keys from his pocket. Hitting the automatic start, the Benz came to life as he swaggered to it and slid behind the wheel; life was good for the hustla. He eased the whip out of the driveway, and at the same time, a forest-green Buick Lacrosse turned onto the block—the devil behind five percent tint.

***

♪Fuck what they talkin' 'bout, keep gettin' scrilla/ My hittas don't play, when I say they gon' get ya/ Blood gang bleedin' from the concrete…♪
The fifteen-inch speakers in the trunk vibrated the car as Dunte bobbed his head to MO3's, "I Get It", track". He was slouched down in the passenger's seat as his gal drove toward his mother's crib. The slab was a beautiful machine, especially with the gleaming Orangoutangs poking and the gold flakes shining in the paint of the car. Just as Dunte cracked his door to empty the contents of a cigar he'd just busted open, Hump's Benz sped by and froze the blood in his veins. Dunte smirked crookedly as he came to a homicidal conclusion.

"Say, bae, turn this bitch around and follow that Benz," he demanded after tossing the cigar, and easing a FN Five-seven from beneath his seat. It was a pretty weapon with a thirty jutting from its ass, and Dunte was anxious to make it vomit.

"Dunte, you promised! We ain't on the bullshit today," Mya whined, but spun the car around nonetheless. She was a Rida—a jazzy, five foot three, chocolate, who resembled a darker version of Lori Harvey. Out of her peripheral, she watched Dunte pull a burgundy bandanna out of his right pocket, before tying it so it covered the bottom half of his face. "Papi, who is that and why you maskin' up? Nigga, its broad day, I know not! You not 'bout—"

"Bitch!"—Dunte spazzed, voice muffled behind the bandanna—"Shut the fuck up and just drive," he spat, with a murderous glare. Mya rolled her eyes with a suck of her teeth before giving him the finger. He ignored her as he clutched the steel, keeping his eyes focused on the cat and mouse chase. He'd warned Hump about playing his mother close, and seeing him leaving her block only confirmed that the man valued a dollar more than he did breathing.

I'm 'bout to burn this boy face off! Dunte's thoughts were homicidal as he watched Hump stop for a red light. It was one car between them, and he knew time was of the essence.

♪I had to take some time to realize that I'm not/ who y'all want me to be/ I apologize for not tellin' no lie/ I'm just a street nigga/ would I be wrong to feel like I'm always right, you can't blame me 'cause I've been left alone, to do it on my own/ That's why I gotta get it, get it, I get it, get it... ♪ MO3's lyrics played low as Mya eased the car to a stop. She rolled her eyes when Dunte crouched low before pushing his door open. He ducked down when he slid from the car and Mya could only shake her head as she witnessed the devil dance.

***

♪Operator- it was like a bad dream/ ohhh, you should've heard, the way he shouted, the way I screamed/ I regret it 'cause I was so unfair/ I took it out on him, just 'cause he was there/ ohhh! When the rollin' gets ruff, you say some things you should not say/ I never meant, to treat my baby that way/ I... apologize/oh believe me I doooo/ I... apologize/ 'cause I know I was wrong... ♪ Anitia Baker's, "I Apologize", classic played softly as Ms. June sat on her living room sofa. The flame from her lighter reflected in her eyes as she held it beneath the spoon she held. She watched in fascination as the heroin melted into a brown liquid before the little piece of cotton soaked up the impurities.

After she was sure *her escape* was proper, Ms. June gently rested the spoon on the table and propped it atop the ashtray to insure none of the tainted liquid spilt. Carefully, she dipped the tip of the needle into the liquid and slowly used the plunger to suck the drug up into its belly. She watched, fascinated as her Heaven was swallowed by the devil's eye. *♪Believe me I doooo/ I apologize/ Honest and true/ 'Cause I know I was wrong ... so I sing you this song... ♪* Anita Baker's melody was the balm to internal scars that the woman yearned to forget.

Holding the needle up to eye level, she began to flick it with her finger to clear any chance of air bubbles before she reached for the leather belt beside her on the couch. Her body craved and cried for the tainted bliss of that brown-skinned demon. It ached for the course the narcotic would swim through her veins. Ms. June carefully looped the leather strap right above the crook of her arm before holding it up for inspection. Her arm was marred with track scars, and it was a treasure hunt for that one good vein that would allow her to ride the giant wave of heroin's waters.

She began to tap her arm. "Come onnnnn, I know you ain't tapped out on me ole gal," she spoke to her veins, and not in vain. As if her body wanted to prove it had a little bit more fight, a thick, juicy vein arose. Queen smirked. Her addiction wasn't her *want*, but wanting a divorce from her addiction wasn't enough will power for her addiction to want a mutual separation. With a steady concentration, she placed the tip of the needle against the small lump her vein formed beneath her skin, and slowly . . . as she watched . . . the devil's eye sunk into her flesh. The inside of the syringe turned a devious color as her blood mixed with the drug, and as if resentment and regret had waged a short war against her need to get high, her eyes watered as she chose the victor.

"Auuuhhh..." She sucked in a deep breath as she pressed her thumb down on the plunger. The brown demon laughed as it entered her veins, and she cried as her eyes drooped. The demon swam. Queen floated, and just as she rose and fell between the distances between Heaven and Hell, life added its own addition to the crooked picture.

"Nanna, what you doin'?" Khloe, Gambino's daughter asked. Ms. June's eyes were glossy when they lifted to find her grandbaby standing there, staring curiously at the needle as it hung lazily from her arm— a long trail of blood running a streak down toward her elbow.

"Awww, baby, Nanna j-just t-takin' her medicine. Gone and play now, baby. Nanna 'bout to take a nap now, okay," she whispered hoarsely.

♪ *Believe me I doooo/ I I I I apologize/ Honest and true.* ♪ Anita Baker apologized for the last time as the song ended, and Ms. June fell into a nod.

***

"I don't give a damn, Marco, you betta have my bread when I get there or it's gonna be some shit! I been waitin' on you to pay up for months and—" Hump was raging into the phone as he waited at the stop light, and just as it turned green, he noticed a shadow appear on his window as if some sort of black magic had been practiced. He jumped in surprise, and as soon as his vision captured the evil glint of Dunte's glare, the phone slipped from his hands, and he attempted to cheat death. "Oh shit!" he screamed, before his arms shot out as if they were attempting to block the bullets.

Boom! Boom! Boom! Boom! Boom! Boom!

The first two shots pierced his chest and knocked his heart loose. The third and fourth slugs hit his neck and lower jaw, but the last one rocked him sideways with its impact. The Benz rolled slowly forward as Dunte took off in a sprint, burner clutched tight in his right hand.

"Pussy boy, told you to stay away from my T-Jones, rest in piss, bitch nigga!" he gritted. Back in the Benz, Hump lay slumped toward the passenger's seat with his eyes open.

"Hello? Hump? Say, OJ, I think something bad done happened to Hump!"

"I hope it did so we can split that loot right there."

The phone was still connected to the call, and the reaper decided to play. Hump gargled on the blood filling his lungs. As the Benz slowly drifted into traffic, Mya drove by with MO3 still vibrating the trunk.

CHAPTER 3
You Play Chess?

Christmas Day

God, forgive me for my untamed ways. . . My nature is crooked. I know I've done things that You may find hard to forgive, and just on some G shit, if it was you doin' it to me? I probably wouldn't know how to forgive either. Yet still I pray. Hoping You can understand that my heart's been cracked so many times that it's turned me cold. I'm not Jesus, God, and I'm not too sure if who the Bible says He was, is solid or not, but for the sake of argument, I come to You in the name of "every" real nigga who's ever wanted to believe that there was something better than this. I need you, OG, to show me "how" to believe. I've lost my ability to have faith.

They say faith is the evidence of things unseen, but God, how can I place faith into what's unseen when it's the unseen that's hurtin' me the most? My daughter needs "me" to show her a man's view of a woman, yet, my nothin'-ass baby mama is so lost in life that all my seed knows is my absence—that her daddy ain't shit. I know my actions led me here, God, but they say You'll never leave nor forsake me. Where you at, God? I'm on my knees, OG, waitin' on a blessin'. I'm fightin' for my life even though I've lived a crooked path. Don't turn yo' back to me, Lord, fore I've never bowed to no other man, but You. Hear me with your heart, Lord, even gangstas need mercy.

In the blood of every real nigga, I pray, Amen.

Gambino's eyes cracked open at the sound of his cell door unlocking. He was on his knees in the prayer position when his eyes found his celly standing there with two CO's and a sloppy built Lieutenant whose last name was *Cook*. He climbed to his feet and his eyes bounced back and forth from each man, before settling on the stocky White man whose eyes had big black rings around them. His head had strange designs created from the sixty stitches he'd had to get to hold his scalp back in place. *White boy squealed on me!* he thought.

"This must've been a helluva fall this here boy took, Mr. Ridge. I ain't ever heard of a man falling from the top bunk and obtaining lacerations to the front, sides, *and* back of his noggin'." The Lieutenant whistled after the statement. "And you? How'd you get those cuts on *your* face, you must've fallen off *the bottom bunk*, asshole, he spat—*literally.*

That's when Gambino's glare noticed the thick lump behind his lip. Most of the White officers kept them a lip of bacca stuffed in their mouth even though it was illegal. *Country ass White boy!* Gambino's thoughts were spiteful as the cell door rolled.

"You got away this time, *boy*, but next time me and my guys gonna teach your little pink ass some respect. Keep your fuckin' hands off my White boys, you hear me, you coon?"

"Suck my dick cracka," Gambino growled. He took a step toward the group of officers, but to his surprise, his celly spun around with a dangerous tension exuding from his stance.

"Watch your fuckin' mouth before I teach *you* some respect," he spat, as he and the Lieutenant eye-wrestled. The two CO's took a step forward, ready to show the big man who was in charge when Lieutenant Cook held up a hand. He'd read the man's travel card and knew the inked-up convict was held in high regards in the Aryan Circle family.

He chuckled to camouflage his fear. "Any more out of you two and I'm locking *both* of your asses up! Come on, Jackson. Brown." He nodded to the two officers.

After they'd left, the cell's door rolled shut and locked. The big white man turned to face Gambino. They glared at each other ... two lions prepared for the showdown, but Gambino respected real.

"'Preciate that, but I coulda handled them suckas."

"You tried to kill me." The white man looked as if he wanted smoke.

"If I wanted to snatch your soul, it would've been on its way to Heaven already. Real "G" shit," Gambino spat.

"You hit me wit' a fuckin' hotpot, motherfucker!"

"You weigh 'bout three hundred pounds to my one ninety and you tried to wrestle." They allowed their eyes to dance and the tension was rising as Gambino prepared for the tango, but the other man absently rubbed his hand over his scarred scalp before bursting into laughter. Gambino relaxed subtlety but stared at him in bewilderment.

"Look, man, we can either kill each other in here or find some common ground. You got my respect, homeboy, and I'm tellin' you now, if you don't wanna be cool because I am what I am, we can keep our space. I see it in your eyes, and you don't like my tattoos. And I'm sure I got a few more you won't find too appealing, but I'm *AC,* and I'm gonna rep this shit *hard.* Just as I expect you to do with whatever you *believe* in," Big Country gave it up as he extended his hand to declare a truce. Gambino frowned, but one *has* to respect what another is willing to die for. Their hands locked in a tight lock as they shook.

"Bet, but I'm keepin' my bottom bunk." Gambino smirked.

Big Country nodded his acceptance before breaking the handshake. He pulled his shirt off and Gambino's face instantly balled up at the sight of a huge Swastika, inked so big it covered his entire stomach. Big Country chuckled. Gambino glared.

"You play Chess, Gambino?"

"You need to put your shirt back on, homeboy."

"Gambino, you good, my nigga?" someone shouted from two row.

"I'm straight, fam." Gambino acknowledged but couldn't take his eyes away from the racist symbol on dude's stomach. "You racist."

"Never have been, never will be—a little prejudice, maybe, but far from racist."

"Fuck is the difference, and how you not racist when you walkin' 'round wit' a fuckin' Ku Klux Klan symbol on your stomach?" Gambino was tempted to take off on dude again.

"See, I think we both have some misconceptions about our races, so how about you enlighten me and I'll enlighten you. Iron sharpens iron, Gambino, and there is a *big* difference between racism and prejudice. Racism is solely based off one's perspective of their race being greater than the next, and prejudice is a universal hate which can be directed toward religion, race, or *any* social group." Big Country tossed his shirt on the top bunk. "You play chess?"

Gambino stared at him before placing judgement to the side. He nodded. "Yeah, I play."

"Let's run a few games as we talk. I'm quite curious as to why you and your people call each other *niggers*." Big Country's words caused Gambino's eyes to turn to slits.

"*Nigga*, White boy, with an *A*, not an, *er*."

"What's the difference, G, when the *true* definition is derogatory to your people? How is another race supposed to take the word out of their vocabulary if your own race has poeticized the term? No matter if it's said with an *A*, or an *er* at the end, when the opposite race hears it, all they hear is *nigger*."

***

It had been days since she'd taken the vacation across town, and Patrese seemed to have found peace there, at Hotel La Casa Oshaya. Her and her friend had cried and laughed, cried some more, and forgot how to laugh at the same time. Oshaya had admitted to having dreams about their younger years in Mexico as well. It wasn't until she assured her that it wasn't a sin, did Patrese find peace within the pieces of her broken parts—Oshaya helped her understand that having been forced beyond their will didn't make them any less than women. Patrese even returned to work.

♪"*Back up on my bullshit, back upon the scene…*"♪ She sang along with Jhene Aieko and H.E.R as she made the bed in Oshaya's guestroom. She had her wireless ear buds in and slightly danced as she hummed with the melody of the beat. Nigil was passing by the room when he heard her singing, and his curiosity caused him to peek in. Patrese had her back to him and it must've been the part of the song she really liked. She was bent at the knees with her hands down by her shapely hips, and she snapped her fingers as she made her booty convulse.

30

Nigil was *stuck*. His eyes digested the feminine creature as she did her thing, and the gray sports bra only made the cotton boyshorts seem more wicked to his libido. She'd done that little sexy thing women do when they were on their low-key attention seeking mission. She'd pulled the already too little shorts up until they imprinted her ass cheeks, her hips, her camel toe, and to make matters worse, she'd rolled the waist of the material down until it bunched up, low on her hips. Nigil's eyes bore into the deep ravine of her ass crack before they fell to the smoothness of her legs. And as if his stare had become physical, as if she could *feel* it, Patrese glanced behind her.

"Oh, my God, Nigil, I'm soooo sorry!" she exclaimed, before snatching an ear bud out of her ear. She'd spun to face him and instantly became uncomfortable under his lustful gaze.

"You good, woman. I was just on my way out and wanted to let you know to lock up." He gave her a reassuring smirk, but Patrese wasn't an ordinary woman. She was more familiar with the power of lust than she was with breathing. She saw it in him and rolled her eyes.

"Where's your *wife*? You know, my best friend?" She crossed her arms over her small breasts with the question. Nigil chuckled at the silent message before raising his palms in surrender.

"Chill, Patrese, it isn't *that* type of party. I was merely passing by and didn't want to disturb your little"—he paused—" um…" He rolled his hand as if attempting to come up with a word for her little dance.

"Dancing? Cleaning up?" She aided.

"Yeah, that." He smirked lasciviously. "My dear wife is at work."

"On Christmas Day?"

"Hey, what can *I* say? She loves her job."

***

Gambino studied the board intently before positioning his bishop, and Big Country smiled at the setup before queen side castling.

"You never answered my question, *brotherman* ... why do your people use the *"N"* word so *passionately?*" he inquired, as he watched Gambino push his own queen behind his bishop.

"Bruh, people turn *everything,* that derives from a negative, into a trend. It's not only *my* people. See, White folks called us niggers because of their own stupidity. They couldn't pronounce the word *Niger* which is a plant in Africa. It's also a country in Africa, along with *Nigeria,* so they pronounced it *nigger,* pronouncing it, er, instead of, *jer. We* poeticized the term because *slaves* had become so accustomed to the title, they adopted the mindset and began to call themselves niggers *out of spite!"* Gambino opened his mental to him before studying the board. He saw Big Country's strategy was to line his rook up with his queen, so he moved his knight into position to defend the pawn directly in front of his king.

"Yeah, but why do *modern* Blacks keep the term alive, but get offended when other races use it?"

"Again, Big Country, it's become a trend. Like how Blacks call Whites *crackas* or *peckerwoods.* Guess what *your* people do? They create a gang called *the woods!"* Gambino's point was proven when Big Country burst into laughter at the absurdity of the truth. Gambino shook his head in shame. "People in general take derogatory shit and mold it to their liking. Like, it used to be disrespectful to call a woman a bitch or a hoe, but now, that's how they carry themselves, and call it expression. Back in the day, eatin' pussy or suckin' dick wasn't somethin' a mu'fucka walked around broadcastin', but now you'll know if a bitch sucks dick before you learn her name. A nigga will let a female know he'll give her an *oral* hysterectomy before he even asks her name. Shit crazy." Gambino chuckled before taking the man's pawn with his bishop. Big Country nodded as if he expected the move. "So, what's the bidness wit' this Klansman shit on your stomach?" Gambino asked, finally verbalizing his thoughts.

"It's a Swastika and the symbol has *nothing* to do with the Klan, Gambino. The Klan is a hate group that was created back in 1866, just four months after slavery was abolished. Those boys were formed to stop Blacks from voting but became more vicious as Blacks began to realize their freedom."

"I don't get that ... why though? Why would your people be so fucked up over a man finding his own?" Gambino's expression was tainted by frustration.

"Because, even back then, my people knew *the power* of the vote, but this symbol"— Big Country paused to point to the Swastika— "it's not a Klan sign. It has many meanings! The Swastika has been a symbol used for *thousands* of years, G, *before* the Nazi party, and especially before the Klan was formed. Gambino, this symbol has been used in Tibet, Greece, India, and even *Africa*," he schooled, before reaching down and placing his knight on the thirty-first square of the chess board, seemingly unprotected. "Brother-man, this symbol wasn't adopted by the Nazi party until 1900's. Though it's merely a symbol formed by a Greek cross, Adolf Hitler adopted it in 1935 and it's *his* use of it that's become so infamous."

"Yeah, the cock sucker hated Blacks,"

"No, he hated *Jews*."

"Fuck Hitler!" Gambino spat, before pushing his bishop up. "Check," he called.

Big Country laughed as he watched, he'd placed the knight as a sacrifice, but Gambino was too sharp to fall for a move so elementary.

"Look, man, I admit that *most* White families were created from a racist perspective, but ... it's the same in Black culture," Big Country spoke, while pushing his queen down to the thirty-second square. "Bloods, Crips, the Panther party? All those groups were created from racism."

"Yeah, to protect *us* from *your* hate."

"And in the end?"

"Fuck that mean?" Gambino glared.

"Whoooaaa, cowboy, peace"— the white man held up the peace sign—"listen, Gambino, yeah ... your people created protection from the days of old, but in the end, all those protections turned on you. Didn't the Panther party become the Crips and Bloods? Aren't the Crips and Bloods sellin' drugs to your own people? The same drugs my people introduced? Come on, man, Blacks are killin' more Blacks than any other race ever has."

Gambino wanted to argue. He wanted to deny. He wanted to punch the White man in the face for his truths. Big Country saw it and smirked. He was forty years old, and ten years older than his celly. He'd lived a Black-and-White life his entire life, and he understood both ends.

"*Yeah*, G, there's scars our races have inflicted upon one another that may *never* be forgiven, *but* everything ain't about Black and White. Man, your people always speak of lookin' forward, but they're always lookin' back— a centenary back. It's the past that always keeps our future ugly. I—"

"Everything is about color! Black and White, Big Country," Gambino seethed, before standing to stretch. "Why you think people made God out to be a *White man*? A *pure* White man? But made the reaper and the devil dark ... evil ... and most times, *Black?* Why you think we have the conception that *black* clothes are meant for funerals and mourning, but *White* clothes are suitable for weddings! Symbolizes purity?" Gambino laughed as he watched Big Country study the board. Stomach growling, he went to his locker and got a bag of chips. Tearing the bag open, he reclaimed his seat. "Think about the game of pool, Big C. There are sixteen balls, bruh, but only *one* white ball, and only *one* black ball, yet the white ball is used to push all the *colored* balls out the way ... down the hole, a *grave!* The black ball, the *eight* ball, is meant to be avoided because it signifies the end of the game. It's the notion of black and white, White man." He smiled before stuffing his face with a handful of chips— crunching noises ensued as he gave the man a superior gaze. "The *eight* ball, fam, *eight* letters, Big Country. Eight"—he paused to show eight fingers— "B-L-A-C-K-M-A-N"—he counted off each finger— "the white ball kills all the other balls until it's the only ball left on the table. *Genocide!"* he shouted, "just what Adolf attempted."

Big Country chuckled before moving his Knight forward. "Check! And, *White man* is eight letters as well, Black man." "Yeah, but the ball is *black*, White man. "Just like *all* lies are negative, but a little *white* lie ain't so bad. *All* sheep are ugly, but the *black* sheep is considered the fuck up. Oh, dig this—" Gambino put the chips down before holding up six fingers. "The pool table has six holes, for six letters! E-U-R-O-P-E! Germany, where Hitler's bitch ass from!"

"Hitler is an Austrian. Have you not read his book *Mein Kampf?* Hitler didn't give a damn about Blacks, it was the Jews he detested."

"Yeah." Gambino laughed before pushing his queen down. "Check, next move checkmate," he declared, before glancing up at this celly. "They got Black Jews, too."

***

The midday breeze was a mixture of hot and cold, and though the sun was nowhere in sight. The sky was still bright as Oshaya strolled through the center of the park that surrounded downtown Houston.

She was gazing up at the sky scrapers when—

"Excuse me, excuse me, sweetheart, I don't mean to interrupt your vibe, but I was just wondering if you've been vaccinated?" someone called from behind her.

"Come again?" She frowned as she turned to find a handsome gentleman jogging to catch up to her. He was a latte-hued brotha, dressed casually in a white button down, and a tan pair of slacks. He smiled, and though he didn't have a drop of sweat on him, he ran the back of his hand across his forehead theatrically.

"Whew! You sure moving fast, beautiful, so I know you're in a rush. So, look"— he paused to dig in his pocket— "I was asking if you'd had your Covid vaccine? I know all the hype behind it and why our people are skeptical about taking it, but the death tolls in urban communities are far greater than others." He spoke common knowledge as he pulled out an ampule—*the small bottle doctors withdrew vaccines from.* He held it up for her to see. "I'm a RN and"— he paused to glance around suspiciously before his vision recaptured hers—"I'm selling vaccine shots for five hundred bucks, all you have to do is meet me at—"

"Uh-uhhh." Oshaya cut him off as she leaned closer to get a better look at the small inscription on the mini bottle, but dude quickly pocketed it. Glancing around for the second time, he dry sent off warning signals.

"Listen, love, this that Johnson and Johnson vaccine everybody fuckin' wit'. I'll show you some love since you're beautiful and—"

"Brothaman," Oshaya gave him the hand. "That ain't say no damn Johnson and Johnson." She giggled before crossing her arms over her chest. "That shit said *Johnston and Johnston!* With a *T* after the *S*, negro!" She laughed.

"Naw, see ..." Dude did that fishy little glance around. "Don't get all starstruck, 'cause this shit is F13 classified!"

"*F13*? Fuck? *And* vaccines are free now!"

"Hold up! See-see, you ain't even up on that F13 shit. Look, Larry *Johnson* and J-Rock *Johnson* are my cousins!" He put emphasis on the last names. "See, *my* last name is Johnston, and my cousins knew everybody didn't have the money to get the Johnson and Johnson, so we made the Johnston and Johnston for the broke mu'fuckas. It's the cousin of Johnson and—"

"Boyyy, stop!" She laughed. "You tried it." Oshaya had had enough. She shook her head in shame before turning, and without a word, walked away.

"A'ight, when yo' ass catch that Rona, you gon' wish you had copped a dose of this Johnston, lady, get vaccinated," he shouted, before attempting to stop another passerby. "I don't mean to interrupt, sir, but have you been vaccinated?" he was saying as Oshaya departed from his con.

She laughed to herself as she made her way toward Minute Maid Park, and that's when she saw him. He wore a fitting, gray, turtleneck sweater, a pair of tattered blue jeans in which she noticed hugged his sculpted backside, and the gray pair of New Balance shoes he wore completed his relaxed attire. Oshaya studied him curiously as he used an artist's pencil to exile the images from his mental and bring them to life upon the canvas.

She admired how his long dreads twisted into an intricate gridlock of oiled snakes at the back of his head, and he'd tied them into a bun, usually reserved for women, but on him, the look seemed powerful. The soft wind carried the fragrance of his Jean Paul cologne, which caused Oshaya's mouth to water. Though she didn't want to disturb him, her curiosity was a navigational system that led her closer. And as if he'd sensed her, the man's drawing hand paused. When he glanced over his shoulder, it was as if the act set off an alarm, and only then did she get the first warning ... *Grrrrrr!* Picasso's guttural growl was vicious. Oshaya's eyes cut to the massive pit bull, and she took a step back at the sight of his jaws pulled back over his sharp teeth. The dog was already crouched to pounce when the man acknowledged her.

"Who are you? What do you want?"

"I-I'm sorry. I was just walking by and saw you drawing- umpainting, and—" She stammered before taking another step backwards. The tenseness seeped from Mirage's posture at the sound of her feminine voice.

"At ease, Picasso, down boy!" he demanded, and as if the dog was a programmed robot, he slouched to his stomach, tongue lolling out of his mouth as he studied her. Mirage's hand began to move again, the sound of lead dancing across the canvas becoming the melody that fed his creativity. Oshaya was cautious but taking the man's vibe as an indication of his acceptance, she took timid steps closer. Her eyes bounced from man to dog, dog to man.

WOOF! Picasso's loud bark caused her to jump in alarm. "He's harmless by nature, only a killer by demand. You're good," Mirage spoke over his shoulder. With one last glance at the beast, Oshaya finally fixed her pretty eyes on the canvas and what she saw, reached down into her lungs and stole her breath away.

"Lord, Jesus." The words slipped from between her lips in an astonished whisper. The canvas was covered in shades of grays and black. The image depicting a woman seemingly falling from heaven, through clouds, and the contradiction of the fall was found in the beautiful details of her facial features. Rather than the terrified face of a fearful woman, the woman Mirage had created in the picture was smiling big as she fell from dangerous heights. At the bottom of the canvas, he'd drawn turbulent, dark waters.

"I call it, *The Fallen*," Mirage revealed.

"Why, I mean, I see why, but where is she falling from? Heaven?" Oshaya asked, as she leaned in to get a closer look. That's when she noticed the girl hugged a small sun, a dark moon, and sharp star to her body as gravity pulled her down.

"Love, she's falling from love," Mirage spoke without a pause in shading his creation, "Though I've never seen it, your reaction tells me it's deep."

"*Love?* I don't understand ... *love?*"

"Have you ever been in love before, ma?"

"Yes."

"How did it feel when you were falling into it? Love?"

Oshaya paused to think and that's where she found understanding. *Like I was flying! Love is always beautiful in the beginning,* she thought. Mirage took her silence as confirmation.

"What's your name?"

"Why?"

"What's your name?" he repeated, with a tinge of finality in his tone.

"O-Oshaya."

"I'm Mirage. Oshaya, let me ask you something." He paused to face her and that's when she registered the dark lensed, Versace glasses that hid his eyes from her. She nodded to let him know it was cool to speak his speak. "You ever wonder why the terminology *falling* is reserved for something negative, *except* when it comes to love?" His question brought a look of confusion to her face.

"I don't follow, what do you mean?" she inquired, as her eyes trailed to the strange drawing.

"Like, when a man meets a woman others view as loose, they say he *fell* for her seductions. Or when a woman gives into a man's charms, people say she *fell* for his game. When one trips, they say he or she *fell* on their ass, yet how does *love* change the negative connotation?" he asked, as he pointed to the canvas. "Why do people relate the feeling of love to the feeling of *falling*? Why not rising? Why can't I *rise* in love? Feel me? It's the *speed* of falling or rising that causes that butterfly feeling, ma. Love is like this woman right here… the beginning is an adventure, the middle is a trek, and just when you've allowed love to carry you too far away to turn back"—he paused. And just as her eyes drifted to him questionably, Mirage slammed a closed fist into his palm— *"Bam!"* he exclaimed. She jumped. He smirked. Oshaya frowned.

"You realize that rising in love was a more passionate feeling than falling. You realize that *falling* always gives you butterflies, no matter if you're falling in love, out of love, or merely just falling on your ass. *That's* why, huh?"

Oshaya didn't understand the question. "Why? What do you mean, *that's* why?"

"Exactly what I said, Oshaya. That's why *you* find yourself exploring downtown Houston on Christmas day, alone. You realize that no matter how you *fall*, it's a *downward* spiral." He pointed at the woman in his creation. "Maybe you should try *rising* in all that you do, at least then you can determine if the fall is worth it."

"Fuck you!" The words escaped her lips before she could trap them.

WOOF! WOOF! Picasso barked. Mirage smirked." Merry Christmas, love," he whispered as she turned and stalked off.

Renta

CHAPTER 4
The Plug's Mother

Baby daddy, look man, I'm woman enough to admit that I was wrong at visit, but my feelings were hurt. Like, damn, pa, what you want a bitch to do? You got 65 years, Gambino, and I'm out here doin' the same amount of time with you, but if you can't trust me to hold it down, to rep you correctly, then, like, what are we doin'? I received this bullshit-ass letter you sent, soooo ... I don't get it. Like, since I missed a few days writin' you, I'ma hoe now? Lol! Boy, stop!

Gambino, I ain't fucked a nigga since you've been gone. I'm not the dick-pressed type, so miss me. See, it's your insecurities that got you in there mind-fuckin' yourself ... but let me tell you a secret, daddy, if yo' high-yella ass would've spent more time at home with your gal and child, you wouldn't be laid up in that bunk, worried about another dude gettin' yo' pussy. Look, this gonna sound fucked up, 'specially comin' from me, but it's real! Gambino, if I'm gonna fuck another nigga, I'm gonna fuck him, period! If I choose to ride wit' you, I'm gonna ride wit' you. There's nothin' you or nobody else can say or do to stop that, so why waste your time stressin' over shit like that. I'm all in wit' you nigga, I'm showing you that!

It's hard out here, Baby Daddy! This Covid mess got everything crazy and these White folks are "literally" killin' our people. Execution style! Gambino, I don't have a million-dollar job. I do hair! And I'm takin' care of our seed, alone! So miss me with all the, "tear my asses," "fake bitches", and the, "you not sweatin' me's!" You know I love you, boy, but when shit ain't goin' your way, or if shit ain't moving fast enough for you, you panic! Baby Daddy, you been gone almost four years and I ain't left yo' ass yet!

Sit down, bae! Please? Stop comin' at me with all this little boy shit. You wayy too bossed up for that! I'm the one holdin yo' no-good ass down out here! Not yo' dope fiend-ass mammy! Not these bullshit-ass niggas! Not ya lil brother! Me, Baby Daddy! Me! I'm that bitch who doin' life with you! So stop clockin' my pussy lips and try not to drop the soap, nigga!

KMSL! JK, Baby, I love you...

For the fourth time, Gambino read the letter from Monay. Even when his mental hated the thoughts of another man playing daddy to his seed, even though he despised the position he'd placed himself in, and though it made him sick to his stomach to envision another man running dick in Monay, his heart was tender for lady. He folded the JPay letter and placed it beneath his mattress before lying down. Big Country was on the top bunk, snoring so loud it vibrated off the walls. If Gambino's head wouldn't have been so cluttered, the sight of the big man's leg and arm hanging over the edge of the small bunk would've pissed him off, but shit was ugly in his world. *Damn! I'm missin' commissary! Lil bro out there wildin' and can't nobody find that fuck boy Cat Eyes! I want this nigga's head;* he'd been thinking when a shadow paused above him.

"Gambino, look out, fam." Tay's voice was raspy. "What's the B-I, my guy? I know you ain't laid up in this mu'fucka stressin'." He chuckled as Gambino sat up in bed. The smell of weed smoke and faint baby shampoo told the tale of how he had spent his Christmas. Gambino glanced back at the clock—*2:30 a.m.* His vision returned to his ace before drifting to the broom he held.

"Naw, Naw, just thinking my dude. Merry Christmas though, family."

"Nigga, fuck Christmas." Tay's response got a laugh out of Gambino as he slid out of the bed. He had grown accustomed to the black hearts of men who the cold bricks had robbed of sensitivity, and he knew the holidays were hardest on the ones who wouldn't't see the city lights for a while.

"Santa Claus ain't did shit to you, Dude. What you doin' out after rack-up anyway? Thought you were second shift SSI?"

Every convict was assigned a job when he got to a unit, and SSI was the title for inmates who were assigned to keep the unit clean— *janitors.*

Tay rested his broom against the third floor railing. "You know how crazy shit is, bruh? Christmas is a day celebrated for the birth of Jesus, *but* the day's mascot is Santa Claus." He chuckled as he leaned against Gambino's cell door.

"So, what's wrong wit' that, bro? Santa Claus inspires the children. He gives—"

"A lie, dawg. Santa Claus has *nothin'* to do with Christmas!" Gambino smirked. Though it was dark in his cell, the lights hanging from the roof above the tier illuminated part of his face.

He studied the man standing before him. He and Tay had been locked in since they'd met, and quiet as kept, many men, the old as well as the young, looked up to Tay because of the way he gave it up. The man *loved* choppin' game, and from the way he glanced at him, Gambino knew dude was about to feed his brain.

"What you talmbout, Tay? I know you not 'bout to hate on Santa Claus."

"Hate! Never that, playboy, *but* I am gonna wake yo' sleepin' ass up." Tay glanced toward the front of the run before his droopy, big eyes trailed to Big Country's sleeping form. He frowned at the man's calloused feet, but after the man's loud snoring assured him he was as unconscious as a man in a coma, he reached down inside his pants and pulled a tightly wrapped package from beneath his nuts. Though the act was strange to many, to the prisoners who knew the significance, it was as normal as breathing. Gambino watched Tay reach through the bars and toss the package onto his bunk before speaking. "Bruh, you ever heard of a cat named Thomas Nast?"

Gambino thought for a second before nodding his head *no*. "Naw Naw, who is he?"

"Dude was a white man from Germany who moved to America back in the 1800's. He started working for a major newspaper in New York, called *Harper's Weekly,* during the Civil War. Dude is a cartoonist who created the democratic donkey, the republican elephant, and even that hoe-ass cartoon image of Uncle Sam!" Tay spat, as if the name of Uncle Sam left a vile taste in his mouth.

Gambino shrugged indifferently. "Fuck that gotta do with Santa Claus, bruh bruh?"

43

"In 1862, *Thomas Nast* created Santa Claus. The soldiers of the Union were going through it, and it wasn't guaranteed they'd win the war. Infection was killing them more than their enemies' bullets were, and they were far from home. So ole Nast created Santa Claus wearing a suit with the same pattern as the American flag. The picture he drew depicted Santa Claus passing out gifts to uplift soldiers of the Union." Tay chuckled at the look of suspicion on Gambino's face.

"More cleaning and less talking, inmate! What are you doing down there anyway?" the officer called out, as he made his way up the stairs. The expression on Tay's face was alert, as his eyes widened and fell to the package he'd just handed Gambino.

"Be careful and keep your game face on, playboy. I gotta dip. Merry Christmas and all that good shit, huh," he spoke quickly, before grabbing his broom and heading toward the CO. "I was just talkin' to my homeboy. I was just tellin' him 'bout the man who made Santa Claus." He gave half-truths.

"Oh yeah, and who was that?"

"You ever heard of a guy named Thomas Nast?"

Gambino laughed as Tay led the man back down the stairs. Eyes falling to the package in his hand, Gambino slightly bounced his hand, attempting to gauge what it was by it's weight. Curiosity got the better of him and he began peeling the tape from around the package, until the thick layers of a cellophane began to tear. As soon as the first layer was off, the edge of a hard plastic that caught his eye caused Gambino's heart to pound in his chest, and impatiently, he hurriedly tore through the rest of the thin plastic wrap. A smile eased onto his face when an ounce of exotic ganja fell into his lap. But not even the potent aroma of that good could steal his vision away from the gray and silver Galaxy touch screen he held. *That boy Tay stay in some shit, mane, on God!* he thought, as he noticed the small kite tapped to the screen. He peeled it off and unfolded it …

What's ovastood ain't gotta be explained, playboy. I'm checkin' in to let you know I already activated yo' shit and set you up under a 45 dollar a month plan, so all you gotta do is power this hoe on and do you. I know

the holidays can be hard, especially for niggas like us who got it out the mud our whole lives, but shid, nobody said it would be easy. They say Christmas is Jesus' birthday, so I don't know why mu'fuckas give each other gifts on another person's celebration. Shit crazy! Lol! Merry Real Nigga Day, bruh!
P.S. Don't be trickin' all your time on them hoes who wasn't writin' when you was on ya knuckles! Suckas do that!

Gambino chuckled before balling the piece of paper up, and aimed his shot toward the toilet bowl. *Thunk!* It bounced off the steel and tumbled to the floor. He shook his head with a smirk on his face. *That's why I never played sports,* he thought, before powering the phone on. As soon as the screen glowed to life, a crooked smile graced his lips.

"Let's see why the fuck the streets ain't got no love," he whispered, as Big Country's snores grew bolder.

***

The city of Houston had quickly become a tourist attraction for celebrities. The city's culture was lit, and attracted people from all over the world, especially successful crooks. The sun had fallen asleep for the day and the moon presided over the city as if it were an overprotective goddess. Katy, Texas is a suburb just outside the city where the more prestigious Houstonians finds refuge.

That night, situated on ten acres of manicured land, Hector Tapia's mini mansion was the meeting spot. A fleet of exotic cars were parked side by side in his circular driveway, and as Dunte eased his slab up to the hired valet, he low-key felt inferior. The Lamborghini Huracán, Aston Martin Roadster, and especially the Rolls-Royce Wraith, belittled his candy painted Buick and caused him to despise the Super Poke type rims on the car he was sitting crooked within.

"Damn, bro, this the life we dream of," Tyke, the man in the passenger's seat whispered in awe. Dunte's eyes drifted to him, taking note of how his only friend outside of his brother, Gambino,

45

stared wide-eyed, lusting on the riches of a kingpin's life style. Neither man had ever reached the zenith of his hustle, but Hector Tapia had taken a liking to the young killer and he'd decided to introduce Dunte to the next level.

"We're on our way, fam, tonight is the night that's gonna secure our bag. You crawled through the mud wit' me since we were lil niggas runnin' 'round aimin' cap guns at people, Tyke, now you gonna ball wit' me," Dunte vowed, before extending his fist for a pound.

"You know how I'm rockin', brodie— from the cradle to the grave." Tyke dapped him up with the profession and Dunte nodded his agreement. He knew his mans was a shooter by nature and loyal to the bone marrow, and that's why he'd brought him along. A knock at the driver's side window caused Dunte to jump in surprise while going for the fire on his waist, but the smile the Hispanic valet gave him eased his clutch on the handle of the GLOCK 27.

"Scary ass," Tyke chastised in between laughter, but he too was low-key clutching his own weapon in anticipation of that gangsta business.

***

12:30 a.m. Christmas Night...

♪ *I wanna lick you up/ let me lick you down/ turn around, baby, let me lick you all around/ let me be ... ohhh let me be, yo' candy licka, girl.* ♪ Marvin Cease's *Candy Licker* played loud from someone's sound system as several couples danced to the old school jam.

"A'iiiight now!" someone shouted drunkenly. The tinge of good ganja smoke floated in the air, and intermingled with the delicious aroma of barbecue pits.

The mood was festive and though it was only his second day of freedom, Pierre was looking good. Leaning against his brother's black-on-black Range Rover, he knew his fit was thumbs-up material. The white Gucci V-neck T-shirt matched the soft gray Levi's he'd worn, and though many had worn the standard cowboy boots for the event, Pierre wasn't on the wave. The cool gray Jordan's complimented his fit and brought out the light-gray bandanna tied sideways on his head. His demeanor was as cool as a breeze, but his head felt as if it would burst from all he was seeing.

Huntsville, Texas, was a small country town known for being populated with most of the state's prison systems, and it was also the place they executed death row inmates. Yet, just beyond all those bob wired fences, hoods like *The Swamp, TCO, and 1200 Block* were alive. *Trail rides* were common to most East Texans, but they were also a thing the cities of Northern Houston, Crockett, Trinity, and Conroe enjoyed.

That night, Carla's trail ride in Huntsville was where Pierre found himself in awe. He'd always assumed trail rides were some backwoods shit that playas couldn't't two-step to, but he was sadly mistaken. Though horses were rode by some, the event was a fashion show for all. People had brought out their slabs, motorcycles, and foreigns to showcase. Older women in skin-tight jeans and skimpy shorts showed they still had it, while the younger thots tried their damnedest to prove youth was a beautiful thing.

As Pierre watched a group of sistas strut by in little to no clothes and cowboy boots, he couldn't't help but stare. *Mane, these country hoes ready ready!* His thoughts were lustful as he feasted his vision on a stallion of a woman in a sheer, purple one-piece and a pair of cowboy boots not meant to be worn with the outfit. "Damn, lady thick," he mumbled.

"Huh? What you say, bruh?" his brother asked, from where he sat with another cat, on the bumper of the truck.

"Naw, I'm sayin', fam ... when females get so bold! Bro, on mama's life, I swear before I got jammed they wasn't dressin' like this! Look at all this ass!" Pierre was blown.

"Nigga, you been gone too long! These hoes turnt out here, ass out, and ready!" His brother and the other man laughed before dapping each other up. Pierre nodded before holding up a finger and going on the prowl. His bro elbowed the dude beside him in jest. "Look at my lil bro, tryin' to be all playa and shit." They laughed as they watched Pierre approaching the group of women.

"Say, hold up, lil mama, damn," someone shouted over the music. The brotha was presentable in designer, and his jewels were water as he beat Pierre to the target. He reached out and gently took the hand of the lady of his fascination. She turned with her nose scrunched up, ready to spazz, but paused when she took in his drip. Her four friends stopped with her and observed the scene. Dude licked his lips at the yella skinned diva as she slipped her hand from his. Her long, curly hair was pulled back into a tight ponytail that fell to the middle of her back, and her backside was juicy.

As they vibed, Pierre had paused to watch, and a strange expression had eased onto his face as he studied lady. The dude she'd caught a vibe with had slipped his arm around her waist, pulling her closer. He whispered in her ear, and just as Pierre was about to chalk up his loss, the strangest thing transpired; he caught a good look at her facial— *I know her from somewhere ...* The thought was powerful. Though the night was absolute, the many bonfires people had set to illuminate their surroundings only fed his surety. *Lady look too familiar!* So, he tried it. He made his way over and spoke his peace.

"Look, I don't mean no harm, and it's my bad for interrupting your vibe, playboy, but I think—"

"Pierre? Is that you, boy? When you get out?" one of the group members bopped.

"I don't know when he got out, or who he is, but he's so disrespectful. I know he sees her talking to someone," another of the group got verbal, but dude the stallion was talking to paid Pierre no nevermind. Though the lady had fixated Pierre in her gaze, the other man was determined to win.

"Girl, that's Pierre, he been locked up for a long time, that's JuJu 'nem cousin."

"What unit he was on? Ouuu, I shole hope he don't know my baby daddy!"

"He's cute cute, gurrrl!" the group of women all spoke at once. Pierre's lips had firmed into a straight line, and his eyes fell to slits as his mind ricocheted him back— back behind the walls of that unforgiving prison...

"Yeah, this my BM, Bro. I love the woman, but she don't know how to love a real nigga," Gambino confessed, as he handed Pierre the pictures of his peoples. Pierre had to fight not to lust— the girl was bad! He quickly handed the pictures back and the action didn't escape Gambino's notice. He chuckled. *"I ain't trippin', family, you can look at lil one."* He opened doors that should've stayed bolted closed to a man of the same circle, and Pierre wasn't feeling none of that.

"Naw, bruh, you "should" be trippin' tho! Yo' potnas should never look at yo' gal with lust in his eyes. That ain't how it go!"

"Piierre, Monay is baby, but the bitch wildin' out there and lyin', tellin' me she ain't. I ain't a lame, nigga. I know how hoes get when their nigga out of pocket."

"Every bitch ain't the same, brodie, you been listenin' to Tay's crazy ass too much!"

"Excuse me, hey, dude, can you hear me?" The sound of her voice carried him back to the present and Pierre snapped back to find Monay snapping her fingers in front of his face. "Damn, you okay?" She gave him *the stank face.* The brotha who had been shooting his shot was walking away, programing something in his phone, and at that moment, something evil eased into Pierre's spirit.

He gritted his teeth— "Mane, see, it's bitches like you who got the game fucked up. Look at you"— he spat while looking her up and down. "Thot shit don't suit you, ma."

"Uhuhh, nigga, you done lost yo' everlasting mind."

"Jail done made dude crazy! Cray Cray!" Monay's girls wasn't feeling his vibe, but Monay was stunned silent for a moment. Then, recognition dawned on her. *Shit! This dude who used to go to visit with Gambino! Damn! Damn! I'm never gonna hear the end of this,* she thought, before trying it.

"Umm, I don't know you, and you need to back up before my dude sees you over here harassing me and—"

"Bitch, yo' *dude* is locked up stressin' 'bout yo' triflin' ass!" Pierre spat back, impulsively taking her by the arm. Attempting to lead her toward his car, his intent came from a solid perspective, but

Monay wasn't feeling the physical. She jerked away from him aggressively.

"Get yo' hands off me! You don't know me like that!" She spazzed, causing unwanted attention. Pierre glanced around at the curious onlookers before shaking his head at the stares he received. Though some couples danced, and others low-key searched for a place to do the nasty, he knew one of the men out there was bound to play super-save-a-thot for a hoe *who wasn't theirs's.*

"See, mane, this what I'm sayin'… a bitch ain't shit. Instead of just being one hundred with your man, you *dry* writin' and lyin' to his face like he some kinda lame. That nigga a real one and it's bitches like you that turn good brothas sour."

"Nigga, you don't even know me to be out here judging me, so fuck you." Monay spazzed. Pierre chuckled while shaking his head in pity.

"You right—I don't know you, but from my view, it ain't too much to find out. You just another punk bitch with an a'ight body, pretty face, and no class."

"Girl, fuck him! Jailbird-ass dude!" One of Monay's girls was ready to get it poppin'.

Pierre laughed before pointing at the group of girls. "*This* part of your problem right here!" He nodded. "You can't do better when you surrounding yourself with people who can't elevate you. *A nothin'-ass bitch* can't inspire you to be nothin' more than that— *a nothin'-ass bitch.*"

His decision was made as he stepped forward and reached for her for the second time, but as soon as he did, all hell broke loose! *Wap!* The first slap stung the side of his head, and before he could confront whoever the hell had just put their hands on him, all five women became a whirlwind of nails, slaps, and kicks.

"You got us fucked up!"

"Keep- yo-hands- to- yo'- self!"

"Bitch!" They became derogatory as Pierre attempted to block their onslaught. *What the hell I done got myself into?* he thought, as his bandanna was snatched from his head.

"Bitch, wait til' Gambino find out 'bout this here," he growled, before attempting to make a quick escape.

***

The table was almost as long, but surely as wide, as a car. On either side were seven chairs situated side by side to accommodate the guests, and at the head of the king's setting, Hector Tapia sat with an accomplished smile on his face. At the other end, his brother, Bito, sat, silently studying the two Black men Hector had spoken so highly of. As he sipped brandy from his glass, Bito seethed.

He hated newcomers and felt his older brother was becoming reckless. Dunte and Tyke sat to the right of Hector, at the head of the table, and on numerous occasions throughout the night, Dunte had caught Bito's disapproving eyes on him. He hated that he and Tyke had shown up dripping in Gucci with a pair of crisp Jordan 11's on their feet, but their street apparel paled in class to the suit-and-tie attire the other twelve men had worn.

Dunte's vision fell to the feast before him and it blew his brains out—*figuratively speaking!* There was enough food to feed a hundred men, not to mention, each dish was exotic and inspired by cultures from distant lands. Closest to him was a decorated, silver platter with an entire stuffed and roasted omnivore, and the pig was highly seasoned with a green apple stuffed in its mouth. He almost laughed but held his composure. *This shit wild wild, bruh— from the slums to eatin' with the plug,* he thought.

"So, Dooonte," Bito began.

"*Dunte*, my name is pronounced *Don-tay*," Dunte corrected, already knowing he wasn't feeling dude's vibe.

"Sí, Don-te, my apologies. Así que,"— Bito smiled big, but the gesture didn't reach his eyes. Clapping his hands together, he nodded—"so, tú and ju amigos think you're ready for de next level, sí?" His accent revealed that his chosen tongue to speak in was Español. For some strange reason, Dunte had the urge to spit in the man's face, but instead, he lifted his glass of coconut rum to his lips and took a deep swallow.

"We *been* ready for this shit. Ghetto dreams, we did it all to get here, dawg," Tyke answered for him. All eyes drifted to him, dark eyes revealing spite—dislike.

Each Hispanic man was a member of the Gulf Cartel, killers, and most weren't as accepting as Hector was of Black men in their business.

"A dream can quickly become a nightmare if it's de wrong man dreaming, yes?" Bito retorted, followed by the dangerous snickers of a few men at the table.

"Fuck that's 'pose to mean, Ese, you think something'"— The sound of Hector clearing his throat cut Dunte's gangsterisms off. The older man's eyes bored into his younger brother's.

"Bito, you will respect my guests." He spoke casually, but the threat was in his gaze, and though Bito's glare was just as fierce, he grudgingly nodded toward his elder brother before slipping from his seat. Bito reached down for his drink before downing it in one gulp. Slamming the glass back down onto the table, he nodded at the men, save for the two street thugs.

"Gentlemen, good evening, but I've suddenly become ill." His tone was mocking. Hector called to him in Spanish, but to no avail; instead, the man made his exit without looking back.

The tension was as thick as a bar of gold, but Hector smiled in spite of. His dark eyes traveled to the two empty seats to his left, and as if conjured from the depths of his mind, the sweet song of girlish giggling diverted all eyes to the entrance where Bito had just made his exit.

?qué opinas¿" a beautiful Hispanic woman asked a younger Latin girl her thoughts of the dress she wore.

"Me gustó mucho." The younger lady expressed her appreciation of the dress.

As they entered the dining room, the men around the table stood to their feet, nodding toward the pair as if they were royalty. Dunte and Tyke were the only two who stayed seated, naïve to the customs of respect in the culture. The younger woman was no more than nineteen years of age and the older lady no older than mid-forties. As they took their seats, Dunte couldn't take his eyes off the younger woman who took the seat closest to Hector—she captivated him with her beauty.

"Madre? Hija?" *Mother, Daughter,* Hector acknowledged the two women before waving his hand toward Dunte and Tyke. "This is the man, Dunte, I've told you of, and his close friend, Tyke." He brought a fist to his mouth and cleared his throat at the mention of the name. He knew his mother would frown upon such a name for *a man.* "Dunte, um, *Tyke,* mi mama and daughter, Christina." He made the formalities.

Dunte found it strange that he'd give his daughter's name but not his mother's but chalked it up to some strange Mexican thing.

"Dunte, are you Mexican?" Hector's mother's voice was soft, with a heavy accent. It was clear that *Tyke* was of African descent due to his chocolate skin, but due to Dunte's French and Afro American mixed Heritage, he was always mistaken for Latin. Dunte's vision shifted to hers and he became swallowed within a gaze that made him almost gasp from it's intensity.

"Naw"— he shook his head—"I'm French and Black."

"Tú madre is Creole and tú padre is Negro. Tú hermano's name es Gambino who es serving sixty-five years on the Estelle unit for murder. Tú mother is a drug addict who stays on Buck Street in the Fifth Ward section of the city and you jus killed a man for selling drugs to her." The woman's insight into his day-to-day caused a light sheen of sweat to break out across the bridge of Dunte's nose.

At that moment, Bito and another man entered the room. Bito made his way behind Tyke, and the other man, behind Dunte. Dunte glanced back, suspicion etching into his expression.

He placed both hands on the edge of the table and began to slowly rise from his seat; however, the feel of iron suddenly poking him in the back made him pause.

"Mane, what the fu—" He began as his eyes shot to Hector Tapia.

The man merely smiled before reaching over and refilling Dunte's glass with more coconut rum. At that moment, the man's mother rose from her seat, smiling at Tyke before nodding for Dunte to follow her.

"Come!" She demanded before excusing herself from the table. Tyke tried to rise from his seat but the feel of the steel digging in his back froze him as well. He silently cursed himself for not being on point.

"No tú, tú siéntate," Bito hissed through clenched teeth. Dunte glanced at him, again wishing he hadn't relinquished his burner when they'd been searched at the door— *"You don't enter a friend's home with your weapons, Dunte, it's an affront to one's character and shows a lack of trust..."* He remembered Hector's *con*. When his eyes drifted to the man, Hector merely smirked with an indifferent shrug as he leaned forward, and used a large fork and a sharp butcher's knife to slice through the roasted pig.

"It's jus business, my friend, and in this business tú mas have los cojones, *balls*, *nuts*, Dunte. Follow mi madre, we'll keep tú amigo company, ey." He smiled while piling slices of pork onto his plate.

"So this how you gonna do the game, huh, Hector? I thought your people stood on a code of honor, you"—

Bam! Hector slammed a fist against the polished, wooden table. "Don't speak to me about foking honor, Dunte"— his voice held a tinge of threat—"your people know nada about honor! Now vamos! Go!" he repeated, and nodded in the direction his mother had made her exit.

Dunte's vision took him in before pushing away from the table and glaring at the Mexican man that stood behind him. The man's eyes were pools of blackness as he aimed a nickel plated .357 at him.

"Come..." A feminine command beckoned the attention of each lion in the room. Dunte and Christina Tapia's eyes did the tango before she turned on her heels and followed her grandmother. He lost control of his vision as his eyes fell to the sway of her small hips— the subtle curve of her delicate ass.

"Off limits, Dunte! I'll castrate you and feed your balls to wild dogs," Hector growled.

"Man, fuck all that! Why these boys got their tools aimed at us? Dunte, what kinda shit this is!" Tyke raged, but Dunte merely glanced back at him before his focus drifted to Hector, who was stuffing his face with meat.

"Be easy, Tyke, let's see what the plug's *mother* talmbout," he whispered, before heading into the unknown.

"Fuck!" Tyke swore, before slapping the plate of food, Hector had just placed before him, off the table, .

Splisssh!— it shattered and food flew everywhere. Hector paused; his fork held a thick piece of pork skewered onto it, halfway to his mouth. He and the young black man's eyes locked, wolf-to-wolf, as the remaining men slipped from their seats. Two of the men exited the room with haste as the remaining men glared at the only non-Mexican in the room.

Hector Tapia nodded some sort of inner acknowledgement before dropping his fork with the meat still impaled on the end of it. Though there was no grease on his fingers, he retrieved the hand-kerchief from the table and made a show of cleaning his fingers before using it to dab at the corners of his mouth. At that moment, the two henchmen returned with a metal drum that was usually reserved to transport crude oil. They sat it down beside the table with care before one of the other men ran over with a crow bar and wedged the forked edge into the crease of the drum and the top that held it sealed.

!Cuidado¡"" Hector warned them to be careful as his eyes slid to Tyke. The top of the barrel popped off and a sizzling sound ensued from within as if there was something cooking inside. "What chu tink, Tyke, ey? Have you ever heard of sulfuric acid? Plenty of sulfur dioxide!" He smiled while sliding from his seat.

Tyke's eyes took in the barrel before briefly touching each man surrounding him. *I wonder if Dunte's already dead. Are these fuck boys tryna scare us to see how we handle pressure, or is shit 'bout to get funky? Damn! Fuck I give up my banga!* His thoughts were a maze, but his expression was neutral as he leaned forward, and rather than going for his glass, opted to take the bottle of rum by its neck. Tyke locked eyes with Hector before smirking and tilting the bottle to his lips, swallowing deep, frowning from the burn in his chest.

"Arrrugh!" he growled, before slamming the bottle down onto the table. Wiping his mouth with the back of his hand, he nodded toward the drum of acid. "Yeah, I heard of the shit, and it's usually used to make fertilizers, paints, detergents, and even explosives, but"— he paused with a crooked grin on his face and fixated his sight on Hector— "the bad guys use it to make shit *disappear!*"

CHAPTER 5
To Cap the Night Off

The headlights of the jet-black Hellcat illuminated the apartment unit as Pierre pulled into the parking spot in front of Monay's building. He muted the music, and for a moment, they sat in silence. He was still heated about the many scratches and welts he'd incurred from the altercation with her and her girls.

Monay sat pouting, with her bottom lip poked out and her arms crossed over her chest as she contemplated initiating round two. "Are you gonna unlock the door or what, dude?" she spat with attitude. The childproof locks disengaged without his verbal. "What-the-fuck-ever," Monay sassed, as she pushed her door open, allowing a cold gust of wind to invade the car. She paused with one foot out, purse in hand, and a suspicious look in her eyes. "You not gonna tell Gambino about this, right?" she semi plead. Pierre smirked before nodding his agreement, but Monay wasn't satisfied. "Look, you could talk *plenty* back at the trail ride, so you can talk now," she huffed.

"Naw, I'm not gonna pull Gambino's coattail to how you out here disrespectin' yoself, shid, my dude got enough stress as it is. No need to be up in that hoe-ass cell wastin' his time givin' energy to the thoughts of a bitch like you."

"A bitch like me, huh?" Monay laughed bitterly before pulling her leg back in and closing the door. Pierre glanced at her curiously, her features aglow from the neons of the car's screens and amenities. "He must'a gave you a wonderful impression of me since you got such a high opinion," she spoke with sarcasm.

Pierre eye'd her before exhaling a strong whoosh of breath and slouching back into the soft leather of the seat; he was dog tired. He closed his eyes and tried to tame his annoyance.

"You know the problem with niggas that's locked up, dude?"

"*Pierre.*"

"What?"

"My name ain't *dude*, it's *Pierre.*"

Renta

"Cool, *Pii-eerre.*" She let the name drag off of her tongue in that girlish way. "As I was saying, the problem with dudes in jail is they don't know how to control their minds. See, I wasn't doin' nothin' wrong tonight, but if Gambino heard about it, his mind would automatically go apeshit. Like, y'all get caged up and want *everybody* y'all love to be locked up, too." She huffed. Pierre glanced at her to see if she was serious.

"You bullshitting, right?"

"Does it look like I'm bullshittin'?"

Pierre chuckled. "Men who locked up has nothin' but time to think, and yeah, we can be a bit insecure, but it's *some* shit that has nothin' to do with insecurity. Like tonight, you out *barely* clothed, wit' a whole man's arm around your waist like you not gonna write *your* man an alibi for the *just-in-case.*"

"*That shit back there was innocent.*"

"*Innocent?*"

"Yes, *innocent.*"

"Fuck is another man gropin' you *innocent*? Shit crazy out here, a bitch comes out her house damned near naked, panties and bra exposed, pussy *purposely* on display, and y'all call it feminine expression, sex appeal, but when a nigga looks too hard, or comments, it's called rape? He's wrong? Or the "Me Too" movement gets involved?"

"It was innocent." Monay was adamant.

"Innocent means *not* guilty."

"I'm *not* guilty."

"Not guilty because you trickin' yoself into believin' how you rockin' is innocent? Or innocent because you made a deal with the only one who can reveal your guilt, to keep the secret that you're not so innocent?"

Monay studied him, looking at him as if he had two heads before pushing her door open again. "Thanks for the ride, and I'll make sure to let Gambino know how good a friend you are." She rolled her eyes before slipping from the car. Pierre had to fight not to look at all that ass she carried; the cat suit hugged her flesh like an extra skin.

58

"Monay," he called out.

"What?" She turned around to find him extending a small roll of money to her. "Fuck?"

"It ain't much, but—"

"Dude, I don't need yo money, the fuck? What you on?"

"It's not for *you*, mane, it's for my goddaughter, Khloe."

"Your goddaughter? Humph ... I don't know where you got—"

"Man, just take the damn money, damn! It's Christmas and my man's out of pocket. He'd do the same for me." Pierre's patience was running thin. Monay studied him for a second before accepting the gift.

"Thank you. I'll make sure she knows her *godfather* got her something."

"Let me ask you somethin', fam."

"I ain't your *fam*, and hurry up, it's colllld," she whined, while hugging herself and shifting from foot to foot.

"When Gambino was home, did you love him?"

"I still love him."

"When he was free, did you go out and flirt and shit?"

"Mannnn..."

"Answer the question, ma."

"Nah, I was too busy being wifey."

"Maybe you *still* need to be wifey, and *still* not do the shit you wouldn't do if he was home. Leave fake shit to fake bitches, baby-girl," he offered.

"Dude, what- ever!" She rolled her eyes once more before slamming the car door and running up the stairs to her apartment. Pierre shook his head in thought before unmuting the music and allowing Moneybagg Yo's *Got Time Today* to knock throughout the whip.

***

"Dunte," the woman called over her shoulder, when he found himself standing in a long hallway with ancient portraits lining its walls. The gunman still aimed the .357 at his back, though he'd

59

eased up and allowed some space between them. Christina made her way beside the other woman and both women gazed up at a portrait depicting the Mexican War, the 1848 war that ended with Texas and California breaking free. "Your country, your state has strange customs, yes? Did you know that after Texas defeated Santa Anna, it was denied its admission as a state by *antislavery* forces of Congress? Did you know that after your people stole our land, Texas formed an independent republic from 1836 until 1844 when it became a part of the United States in 1845?"

Dunte shrugged indifferently—" What that got to do wit' why you and yo people treatin' me and my potna like we the enemy, lady? I don't even know *you*. I came here for Hector, and—"

"Who works for *me*. *My* son works for *me*." Her profession rendered him speechless. "As I was saying, Texas was, and still is, a proslavery state, but it was admitted to the Union, a faction that was fighting to end the demonic behavior of their ivory-skinned brethren. Strange! Just as you and your people's customs, Dunte, you—"

"Fuck that 'pose to mean, *my people?* You mean *Black* people?"

"Yas, *Black* people, Dunte. Black people have a culture that looks down on snitching, but your people doesn't have any honor. Blacks talk to policía."

"So does *your* people! Mexicans! The cartels have more rats than anything, and though y'all scream all this weak shit 'bout Blacks havin' no honor, y'all have now adopted *our* culture! A Black culture! Y'all use our lingo, your people are from *the same* ghettos *my people* from! Yet, snitchin' ain't got *no culture,* it's just the cowardice of every man and woman who too pussy to take their own medicine. Blacks snitch, Whites snitch, Mexican's snitch and—"

"We kill them!" the woman spat, with fire in her eyes as she turned to face him, and Christina did the same. Yet, rather than contempt, her gaze was pregnant with curiosity.

"Mane, look, it ain't *that* much killin' in the world, but look"— Dunte waved them off—"I ain't got time for riddles and I surely don't give two fucks 'bout Texas history. I'm from the bloody nickel, fuck the rest. So, look"— he paused, glancing from woman to woman before turning to face the gunman—"if y'all brought me out here to whack me, fuck you waitin' for? I don't give a fuck 'bout death, what's the business homie, you scared to use that bitch, or what?" he gritted with a nod toward the pistol. The older woman's soft laughter tickled his ear and it surprised him how silently she'd snuck upon him. "Say"— he began, but the shrill screams that ensued cut him off.

"Ahhhrrrrr! Helllp Me! *Please!*" The plea sent chills down Dunte's spine— *Tyke!* His mind registered. He spun to face the two women as the distant growl of what sounded like a chainsaw drifted down the hall. Though the older woman's expression was neutral, Christina's smile was bright as she extended a small digital device to him. For a second, he wondered where the hell it came from, but when Tyke's tortured scream's bounced off the walls again, Dunte's mental began to connect the dots. His vision danced with Christina's, but it was the older woman who spoke.

"I like you, Dunte, and so does my son, and—" she paused as a curious expression eased onto her face as her eyes drifted to her granddaughter—"apparently, so does my nieta." She smiled as Christina's eyes dropped to the floor in embarrassment. "But, tú amigo?" The woman shook her head in disgust. "Not so much. Listen, my friend, listen and see what scares me of your people," she offered with a nod toward the recorder in her granddaughter's hand. Dunte's curiosity was piqued. He almost snatched the device from the lady and at the same time, his best friend's screams became a mantra that fucked with his composure. Glancing down at the device, Dunte hurriedly pressed play—

This is Agent Givens and"—there was a pause—*"State your name for the record."*

"Mannnn..."

"This is just for my notes."

"My name is Murry Williams."

"What do the streets know you by?"

"*Listen, homie, I'm not 'bout to give you my entire life story, this wasn't part of the deal!*"

"*No, you listen, motherfucker! You can either play nice or take your chances with these ten ounces of blow we found on you. I'm sure you'll look real cute in an all-white two piece, serving a fifty year sentence in one of our hotel de la prisons, but I'm offerin' you a get-out-of-jail free card! You only get one! Now, what the hell do the streets know you by!*"

"*Tyke, mane, they know me by Tyke.*"

"*That's better, Tyke, I mean, Mr. Williams. That's much better. Now, we found ten ounces of cocaine in your possession, where'd you get it?*"

There was a brief pause before Tyke exhaled. "*I got it from my homie, Juvenile.*"

"*And Juvenile is Joseph Wilson? Brown-skinned African American with freckles?*"

"*Yeah.*"

"*Will you be able to testify to this in a court of law if*"—

A lone tear fell from Dunte's right eye as he pressed his thumb down on the stop button with force. He'd come out the mud with Tyke, loved him as if he were his flesh and blood. And at that moment, he knew his brother from the womb of another mother wouldn't't be leaving that place alive.

"So, chu say you're ready for the life, right?" Christina's voice was as soft as a woman's skin who had bathed in milk her entire life.

Dunte's spirit and mind were torn into jagged pieces. When love was real, a man still loved no matter how wrong the one they loved were, because love was rare in the streets, and when that love became tainted, it could rip a nigga's soul loose. Dunte's eyes slowly lifted to meet hers before he nodded his confirmation. Christina returned the nod, but hers was due to understanding. She made her way over to him until they stood a foot apart.

"Riviera," she called to the gunman, before extending her hand, palm up. The man placed the .357 in her small hand before stepping to the side. "Chu have to show us a token of faith, Dunte, it's the only way," she whispered, before placing the big gun in his hand. As soon as his fingers wrapped around the handle, Dunte felt that animal come to life. He contemplated doing *her* first … *Damn, Tyke, my nigga… you sold yo' soul, dawg!* His mental was his sound board as his eyes lifted from the cold steel and returned to the woman.

"You place a gun in my hand after all this?"

"Yas, chu a smart man, Señor Dunte, me tink so." Her accent turned him on even in that moment.

"What y'all want *me* to do, lady? What makes me so smart to you?" he asked. Christina stepped forward, and to his surprise, cupped his face in her delicate hands and kissed his forehead.

"Chu smart enough to know that if chu don't kill him, me will kill tú, sí?"

Renta

CHAPTER 6
American Dreamin'

Three weeks later ...

Herman Park was a known park located in downtown Houston, and just one of many that Houstonians went to picnic or merely enjoy a leisure day. And on this day, as Oshaya relaxed on a bench, the breeze gentle, and the sun reigning supreme in the heavens, she thanked God for the day. She'd frequented the area for years and was fond of the vibe. Most times, she merely sat on a bench and *people watched* people doing the things people do when they felt other people weren't watching.

The view of the large hospital, the sounds of the trains at the nearby train station, and merely the view of the towering sky scrapers that made up downtown Houston, all gave her a deeper appreciation of the city that used to be the capital of Texas. *Yet,* nothing had her attention more than the man who stood a mere four feet away, shirtless, and drawing his life away beneath a cluster of three aged maple trees.

Mirage's back was to her as he sketched to life a masterpiece from the breezeways of his mind. Oshaya's vision found pleasure dancing back and forth between the still life he was capturing upon the canvas, and the ripple of his back muscles with the slightest of movement. It didn't hurt that his long dreadlocks cascaded down the defined back. It amazed her to see that somehow, each lock of the Rastafarian-inspired hairstyle knew not to obscure his vision as he worked. It shocked her at first, when she'd stumbled upon him there, but taking it as fate, Oshaya had merely taken a seat and became lost within his vibe. She was in awe of each dance of his pencil as it immortalized beauty, captured within a beautiful imprisonment.

The picture he'd manifested was that of a beautiful sista with a head filled with *sistalocks.* The woman lie on her back, legs spread eagle, skin seeming to glow. Her head was thrust back as she smiled up at the sun, but the most profound essence of the picture was the gift she was depicted giving birth to. Mirage had painted a black-and-white world—a picture of *earth*, seemingly exploding from the woman's femininity. It was a risqué, yet, beautiful connotation of a black woman's womb.

"What do you call it?" Oshaya asked.

"Don't you have a life, lady?"

"You don't own this park, dude. I have just as much right as you to be here."

"All I'm sayin' is, a sista should always have somewhere to be. A job, tendin' to her seeds, creating her legacy…"

"Oh, and a brotha is supposed to spend all his time in a park, drawing, painting, or whatever this is you do?" She sucked her teeth with a roll of her eyes. "Don't worry about where *this* sista is supposed to be. Why you all up in my business anyway?" she snapped, still not accustomed to his crass responses and lack of sensitivity. Mirage chuckled. Oshaya rose from her seat, feelings turbulent, rejected.

Picasso barked from his position down by the man's side, and Oshaya rolled her eyes at the beast. As if he understood her *non*verbal—*WooF! WooF!* He barked again before lying down, resting his big head on his front paws, and studying her curiously.

"So"— Mirage spoke over his shoulder without slowing the stroke of his pencil— "*this* is your reaction when a brotha is trying to get to know who you are *beyond* the name?"

"Get to *know* me?" She sucked her teeth with another roll of her pretty eyes. "Feels like you're badgering me, like-like my presence is unwanted."

"Maybe it's just that you're so used to the ways of little boys, when a real man gives you real conversation, it becomes *too* real for you? *Maybe,* if I run some good game on you and add a little flare to fancy words, you won't be so offended?" The gospel was still the gospel whether it was spoken form deceptive lips or quoted from the New Testament. Mirage paused before turning to face her, the lenses of his Versace glasses were tinted from direct sunlight, and at that moment, a few dreads swung free, dangling over the left lens. "Maybe you've been around so many uncultured men that when a

66

brotha who was bred by a culture of Black Kings steps to you correct, his words are so foreign it seems offensive?"

"*I'm* a cultured woman who demands respect from the uncultured."

"There's a difference between culture and a cult."

"Excuse me?"

"Culture is the traditions, beliefs, and customs of *a tribe*— a lifestyle agreed upon by a generation of people. A cult is what Lil Wayne created with this young generation. A cult is something *one* individual creates and is followed by many, even though it may be built off of bullshit."

"Well, I know nothin' about cults, occults, or any of that mess White people do, and I don't understand the reference to Lil Wayne."

Oshaya studied him peculiarly. Mirage smiled and just before he responded, a young Black brotha wearing a hoodie and a pair of sagging, skinny jeans was walking by, but paused when he saw the art. Black man looked no older than nineteen, and as he pulled his ear buds out of his ear, his eyes bounced back and forth from the masterpiece to the couple.

"This shit is lit. Who drew it?" His question received a comical response. He adjusted his backpack at the same time the two spoke.

"He did." Oshaya pointed at Mirage.

"She did." Mirage pointed at Oshaya. The young man laughed with a wide-eyed gaze as he studied them. Studying them curiously before his vision fell to Picasso who had rose to his paws and watched him intently, Black man shook his head in amusement before glancing back at the beautiful creation.

"Black woman giving birth to civilization," he spoke in reverence. "You know they say Black people were the first people on earth?" he asked, trapped in the detail of the art. Mirage nodded. The music playing from brothaman's phone was Jigga Man's "American Dreamin'," a track from his *American Gangster Album*.

"Louis Leakey used a series of fossil discoveries in Tanzania to argue convincingly that humans evolved in Africa," Mirage whispered as his eyes drifted to his creation.

Renta

"Who is Louis Leakey?" Oshaya was curious.

"The Leakey family was a group of British and Kenyan scientists who studied fossils and shit. They believed civilization began right there in the Motherland," the young brother answered, before putting one of his ear buds back in his ear …

♪*Seems as our plans to get a grant/ Then go off to college didn't pan or even out/ we need it now/ we need a town/ we need a place to pitch, we need a mound/ for now, I'm just a lazy boy/ Big dreaming in my La-z-boy / In the clouds of smoke, Been playin this Marvin/ Mama forgive me, should've been thinkin bout Harvard/ But that's too far away, niggas starving* ♪ Jay-Z's lyrics emitted from them.

"Yeah, *but*"—Mirage began, before beginning to gather the little bit of supplies he'd brought. "Scientists have found ancient remains in Australia that are said to be the oldest ever discovered, *and* they're saying the man's structure is that of a Black man. Matter of fact, just Google the word *Australoid*, and it'll tell you everything you need to know. Get up on it, Black brotha."

"Interesting," Black man mumbled, with a thoughtful expression.

Mirage chuckled. "You attend the university?"

"Yeah, Clear Lake, but look"—the young brotha began before glancing around suspiciously. When his vision recaptured them, he nodded toward his backpack— y'all smoke?"

"*Smoke?*" Mirage lifted a brow.

"Yeah, like, smoke ganja? I have Maui Wowie and Pineapple Express."

Oshaya frowned—" You got a license to sell Mary and Jane? You know what"— she paused and held up a palm to stop him from answering— "don't answer that! You know what? It matters not if you got a license or not, in Gregg Abbot's State, they'll find you guilty in a court of law. I don't do illegal." She waved him off. Mirage shook his head at her before smiling at Black man.

"Tuition should be illegal." Youngin' huffed.

68

"Uncle Sam hittin' them pockets, huh." Mirage chuckled before reaching down into his pocket. "Give me a half of Express."

"Uncle Sam *and* Aunt Utility Bills." Black man turned his backpack around, unzipped it, and rummaged until he found what he was looking for. Vice was exchanged for currency, before the young brotha thanked them as if they'd just exchanged gifts at Christmas time then he made his way toward the train station.

Oshaya's eyes found Mirage in a questioning gaze." Didn't know you smoked."

"There's a lot you don't know about me."

"Smoking is illegal in Greg Abbot's State."

"This ain't that sucka's state, it belonged to Coahuiltecan, Jumano, Tonkawa, Caddo, and Karankawa people before Americans debo'd it," Mirage jeweled, while giving her a suspicious eye. "You a cop or something?"

Oshaya laughed— "If I were, your ass would be cold busted. But no, I'm just a sista who's trying not to visit one of Gregg Abbot's plantation jails"—

"Freeze!" I said, "Freeze, son of a bitch!" The demand was filled with malice, and when their eyes shot in the direction it had come from, they were shocked to find the young brotha from earlier, running full speed toward them. The look on his face was panic-stricken, an expression that rocked Oshaya's foundation when she noticed who his pursuers were. Two White officers were in hot pursuit and neither looked too happy about it. She quickly pulled her phone from her purse, logged onto Facebook, and hurriedly went live. "Please Lord, don't let these people kill this kid." She prayed, and at the same time, the devil smiled from the other side of the park, which happened to be the direction the college brotha with the backpack full of Maui Wowie and Pineapple Express was heading—two squad cars skidded to a halt and HPD jumped out and quickly unholstered their weapons before taking aim.

"Freeze! Don't come any closer, son, just stop right there!" an out-of-shape Black officer shouted. With a defeated expression on his face, the young brotha who didn't have a license to sell Mary and Jane in Gregg Abbot's prejudice ass state slowed his flee to get free. Even from twenty feet away, Oshaya could hear the disappointment in his voice when he spoke.

"Damn! Damn, man," he spat, before stomping his foot in frustration.

"Put your hands up *slowly*, young man," the Black officer demanded. Mirage shook his head before spitting on the ground in spite; he hated police.

"This man is unarmed and is not a threat, Facebook, so there's no reason for the extras," Oshaya told Facebook. At the same time, the young brotha's voice filled the air.

"A'ight! A'ight, I'm puttin' my hands up. All I got is a little smoke. I don't have any weapons, and," he began, while lifting his hands in the air.

"He's got a gun!"

"Drop the weapon, motherfucker!" The two cops who'd initiated the pursuit shouted.

As Oshaya watched the scene unfold, it was as if things were playing out in slow motion. The voices became muffled in her mind— almost distant as her heart pounded against her rib. It pounded so powerfully, she could hear it in her ears as she stared in horror at the college brother attempting to turn around and face his accusers. Vaguely, she noted the iPhone in his hands that Jay-Z's "American Dreamin'" had just played from, the same phone the corrupt officers *purposely* mistook for a gun. She recognized the fear and the shock in the young man's eyes, as he waved the phone to show that the only trigger it had was the call icon.

Boca! Boca! Boca! Boca!

Boom! Boom! Both officers fired simultaneously. Mirage stiffened beside her at the sound of the gunshots.

"No! NOOOOO! Th-they just shot him!" Oshaya screamed, and forgot she was recording *live* footage. Her hands flew to her mouth in shock. She was so lost within the moment of hysteria, Mirage reached out and pulled her to him, and though they were practically strangers, she sought solace in his arms and buried her face in his chest because she couldn't understand the *why?* She cried because her husband had fallen out of love with her. Oshaya cried because crying wouldn't change shit; yet crying was the only way she could prevent her tears from drowning her internally. So—she cried.

***

"Un-unnn, heifer, if a nikka's dick is too small for me to grip with both hands, jack him off, *and* suck the head at the same time, it's *toooooo* small! We might not make it or he gonna have to be a expert at lickin' the cootie cat," Sissy's admission was met with a chorus of sentiments.

"Girl, he may just need a pump! An enhancement pill or something," Carla added with a giggle, before giving a sideways glance at the child in Sissy's chair.

"Don't they got some kinda surgery for small dicks? Uh-uh, girl, and God should be ashamed of himself for cursin' that man like that," Monay declared, with a bitter shake of the head.

"Hallelujah!" JuJu lifted his hands in the air in praise.

"Uh-uh, God ain't got nothin' to do with a man's penis bein' small 'cause He's not *that* cruel. That shit is genetics … *his papi*, uncles, and grandaddy need a killin' for givin' him that curse!" Juicy laughed.

Andrea Styles was packed as usual, and as usual, the gossip, grown woman talk, and smell of hair being processed ran wild. The woman in JuJu's seat giggled, but Juicy glanced over at the little girl Sissy had in her chair—"A child is present y'all, so be respectful."

" I got you, Juicy, but for real, y'all know what be crazy to me?" Mika, the girl in JuJu's chair, offered.

"What's that, Mika?" Sissy asked, as she parted the girl's hair. The zigzag pattern she was styling was *cute cute,* and as the child's mother sat in the waiting area looking at something on her phone, she shook her head in amusement at the raunchy back and forth between the ladies. Occasionally, she glanced at her seven year old to see how she reacted to grown-woman talk. The curious glances the child was giving everyone who spoke was evidence that the young mind may not have understood the depth, but surely it understood the implications of the ladies.

"Why men always want a bihhh to be as freak nasty as a porn star? Want us to bust it open, put our legs all behind our head, and swallow their—"

"Wait, gurrrl!" Juicy's outburst caused the women in the room to rear back in surprise. She made her way over to where the child sat in Sissy's chair before covering the girl's ears and giving Mika *the eye.* "There is a baby in here, y'all hussies watch your mouths."

"Juicy, my daughter done heard worse, she's okay." The girl's mother opened doors which Juicy felt should stay closed to a child. *That's why these little girls out here pregnant at fourteen and fifteen. Babies having babies 'cause they're being raised by grown folks who had babies when they were only babies ..* she thought, with a sad shake of her head. "Gurl, I rather she hear it *here* while I'm present, and from y'all rather than out in the streets where fast little girls can only *show* her just how fast she can be," the girl's mother rationalized. Juicy was hesitant, but relented when Sissy gave her a questioning stare. She rolled her eyes before removing her hands and kneeling down until she was eye level with the girl. The child smiled at her.

"Don't listen to these women, baby, they're bad women. You grow up to be a good girl and—"

"I know what dick is Auntie Juicy." The little girl's confession froze Juicy. Sissy's hand flew to her mouth in shock, and the girl's mother frowned.

"Jericka!" she demanded, as all eyes shot to her. JuJu burst into laughter.

"Uh-uhh, hussy, you should be more careful around your child. Don't be tryin' to act like the model mother now. Umm-umm, honey!" He laughed, before placing his manicured hands on his hips.

"Ask her, Juicy!" He shouted. Juicy twisted her lips and shook her head at her friend as if to say: *Boy, you's a mess!* Turning her attention back to the child, she almost burst into laughter at the

72

frightened expression on her face. The child glanced from Juicy to her mother, silently asking for permission.

"You're not gonna get into trouble, baby, I promise," she vowed, with a challenging look back at the girl's mother. The woman rolled her eyes. "Tell Auntie Juicy what the *D word* means." Juicy's eyes was soft when she returned them to the girl.

"My mama's boyfriend always say, 'suck my di'"—

"Girl!" Sissy, Carla, and the girl's mother shouted in union. Juicy shook her head once again as she made her way back to her chair.

"Shame." She sucked her teeth.

"Juicy, don't." The child's mother gave her the hand with a roll of her eyes. JuJu laughed.

"What were you saying, Mika?" Sissy attempted to get the conversation back on track and get their minds off of the woman's parenting. Carla smacked her lips, JuJu umphed, and the child's mother gave them the finger. As JuJu began cutting her split ends, Mika spoke with her hands.

" I was just sayin', Sissy, men always want a bitch to be porn star freaky, but when you show them you can be nastier than Pinky *and* Beauty Dior, they get all insecure and shit."

"Biiiiitch, you ain't never lied!" Sissy fed the vibe—*unfit parenting forgotten.* "Then, when you making that booty pop, they wanna know *who* taught you how to do the nasty!" She laughed before doing a little jig. The three women with their heads beneath the hairdryers nodded their heads at the same time. Uumhmm!" They agreed.

"What kills me is after a man sees that you know *how* to make him cum, all of a sudden he wants to know *how many* other brothas done had the kitty cat," Juicy added. "How many niggas you done fucked? Do I know any of 'em?" she mimicked in a mock masculine voice.

"Umhmm," Sissy agreed.

"Don't forget about this though," Carla puffed her chest out and deepened her voice. "Was it good? Is his bigger than mine!"

The women laughed. "Does he do it better than me?" Juicy was too through as the high-fives and laughter filled the room.

"Gurl, what if you told your man *yes*? The last nikka works that thang better than you!" Sissy laughed hard with the question.

"Bihh, OJ Simpson won't have nothin' on the man you say those words to, and if he goes to trial and tells the judge why he killed your ass, the judge gonna sympathize with his ass and say, if the glove don't fit"— Juicy left the rest hanging in the air and on cue, most of the older women recited the phrase OJ Simpson used in his 1994 murder trial for killing his ex-wife.

"You gotta acquittttt!" they sang in unison. The room exploded in laughter, but as always— *JuJu*.

"What about when they go to hintin' at that *backdoor* lovin' *Let me just stick the head in,*" he mimicked in his *man's* voice.

"Boyyyyy!" The three women with their heads beneath the hair-dryers protested in union, their heads twisting in his direction so fast the action appeared inhuman.

"Girl, please"— he gave them the hand— "Y'all know *exactly* what the hell I'm talkin' about." He laughed.

"Carla, what ever happened to ole dude you were so gone be-hind, what was his name?" An overweight, light skinned sista probed as she waited for her turn at the rinser. All eyes drifted to Carla. It was a known fact that Lil D, a 44 Acres Homes hustla was taking care of her needs and a lot of women were low-key jealous. Carla rolled her eyes and continued to rinse her client's mane.

"Who, Lil D? Girrrrl, *Palease!*" JuJu snickered, knowing he was on his Messy Bessy vibe. "Ms. *Me so horny* had to cut all ties with Mr. Tall, light skin and *small!*" His comments brought shocked expressions before explosions of laughter. Sissy laughed so hard, she doubled over and Carla glared at JuJu.

"Ain't nobody told you to volunteer my business, hussy! It's not my fault I assumed all tall men with big feet came with big meat." She giggled and the laughter was contagious.

"Bihh, *what!* Don't tell me, Carla, *all* that *mannnnn*, and girrrrl…" Monay shook her head in shame.

"Six foot four, I'd think he could *at least* hang mid-thigh." Juicy had a look of disgust on her face.

"Bihhh, please, six-four, and wearing a size fifteen shoe! Hell naw, that thang thang should swang to his knees!" Sissy snaked her neck.

"With some girth!" JuJu declared, as his hands raised in a *hallelujah* motion.

"*Gotta* have some fat to that muscle," Juicy seconded.

"Well"—Carla paused with a thoughtful expression. "*Maybe,* maybe when the doctor circumcised him, he accidentally nipped *a little too much.*" She burst into laughter.

"Uh-uhhh, biiiiitch, you so mean!" Sissy exploded.

"A man should come with a sticky note! Like, when he tryin' to holla and give a woman his number, we should be able to read the size of his dick, how many baby mamas he got, *and* if he still stays with his mama, on that sticky note," Juicy counted off with her fingers.

***

Oshaya sat hugging herself as she rocked back and forth on the couch. Vaguely, and just beyond the shock, she wondered how she wound up there? On the sofa, in a practical stranger's home? Yet, after what she'd just experienced, *anything* and *anywhere* was better than being alone and trapped with the thoughts of the cold blooded murder she'd just witnessed. So, she sat. Sat and rocked on a practical stranger's sofa as the practical stranger stood a mere few feet away.

Mirage stood with his back to her as he splashed a collage of different colored paints across the canvas— a passionate scar of red, soft strokes of green, and angry splashes of blacks collided against its surface. A song by Maxwell played softly as he worked, and as Oshaya allowed her eyes to explore her surroundings, she was sucked into the messy beauty. Complete, as well as incomplete, works of art rested some of everywhere around the room, and the

75

more her vision feasted, the more she grew to appreciate the man's talents. A finished piece which rested against a far wall depicted the silhouette of a shapely Black woman trapped in still life, in a beautiful, yet, sensual dance. Another one depicted a Black brotha, eyes dripping tears as he bit down on the barrel of a pistol. The ugliness of the creation's beauty was found within the bullet that was shown exploding from the back of the man's head... Upon its exit, what should have been blood and brain matter, had been created into rose petals falling from a blossoming rose—*BAM!*

The sound of things clattering disturbed Oshaya's appreciation as she jumped in surprise. Her eyes shot in Mirage's direction and found him gritting his teeth in frustration as he stared down at the mess of pens, pencils, and other art supplies he'd knocked over.

"Damn, man," he cursed himself, before dropping to clean the mess.

"You okay?" she asked.

"Yeah, I'm cool, just movin' too fast," he responded, after standing back to his feet with the bundle of supplies in his hands. Oshaya frowned slightly when she watched him miss the opening of the can the supplies went in; *twice!* That's when the strangest thing dawned on her and her mind took her back to the first time she'd encountered him in the park...

Why, I mean, I see why, but where is she falling from? Heaven?" she'd asked when she'd set eyes on the drawing he'd created, of the girl falling as she hugged the sun, moon, and stars to her bosom.

"Love, she's falling from love," Mirage had responded. "Though I've never seen it, your reaction tells me it's deep." It was with those last words playing within her mind that realization stole her breath. Oshaya blinked as her eyes focused and she stumbled back to the present with her mouth slightly ajar. She slid from her seat, never taking her eyes away from him, as she made her way over to the dreadlock artist. Once there was only a breath of air between them, she studied him.

"Why do you always wear glasses?" she whispered. Reaching up, she pushed his dreads away from his face before going for his glasses.

Grrrrrurr! Picasso's growl was menacing as Mirage caught her hand and held it in a firm grip. Oshaya's eyes were searching—heart pounding in her chest as time stood still.

"What are you doing?" He had suddenly turned cold.

"I-I just ..." Her words trailed off as her vision fell to the dog whose face had become vicious, teeth bared. *I have to know— have to,* she thought. "This is a seeing eye dog. I just thought you needed help seeing?" Her statement was more of a question. Mirage seemed to be studying her as if she were a science project. "Can I have my hand back. I'd like that very much." She gave him a funny look with the request.

"Take them off." Mirage seemed to have come to some sort of resolution.

"The fuck? No!"

"I meant the glasses." His clarification turned her skin a brighter tint red from the embarrassment; she had assumed he'd meant her clothes. Oshaya giggled. Mirage didn't crack a smile. Composing herself, she reached up and slowly pulled the designer frames from his face, and when her eyes captured his, she found a distant Bermuda Triangle that threatened to swallow her. Oshaya inhaled deeply, *speechless!* Mirage's eyes were demonic, yet beautiful. They were *entirely* black! He'd had the whites of his eyes as well as his pupils tattooed onyx black.

"Don't worry, mama, I'm not some sort of monster. I just had my eyes surgically tatted because they were scarred. A light bulb blew up in my face when I was younger and it damaged the cornea and iris parts of both eyes. I got so tired of people asking me what happened that in an act of rebellion, I flew to Europe and had both eyes dyed *completely* black."

"Oh my God, I mean, can you see?"

"No. I see *the outline* of people, places, and things occasionally, otherwise, I'm as blind as a bat."

"Bu-but"—Oshaya waved her hands in a sweeping gesture toward the many paintings— "how?"

"*How* what? How do I create?"

"How do you *see*?"

"With my mind."

"So, you can't see *me* right now?"

"Yeah."

"I thought you couldn't see?" Oshaya's face became a mask of suspicion. Mirage stepped closer, and his black eyes were seemingly frozen, like dark glaciers.

"I can see *your heart*, queen, I can see the shit you put up with at home in the name of a love that don't know how to love you back. I might can't see your black eyes or busted lips, but *physical* abuse mostly just hurts for a moment, *mental* abuse can last a life time. The shit I *can't* see about you or life has lost its hold on me, and the things I've *learned* to see is what others don't like"— he paused to run a hand down the side of her face. Oshaya flinched beneath the touch. "What you deserve you're not receiving, but you smile as if receiving what you don't deserve is worth receiving," he whispered. The shift of her perfume told him Oshaya's body had moved. Picasso barked, and when Mirage heard his front door click open, he smirked. Oshaya paused in the threshold without looking back. Mirage chuckled.

"You love pain. You don't recognize it, just like every other woman who believes love is pain. He won't change."

"You don't know me."

"*You* don't know you, Oshaya."

"You can't see, don't see, but you act as if you see it all."

"A mirror sees, Queen."

"A mirror *reflects*, King."

"Yes, a mirror shows you your reflection, but in order for you to see your reflection, your reflection must see you back."

Oshaya gave a bitter laugh at his words as her eyes watered. "The things I've been through in life have all made me avoid my reflection."

"An internal mirror won't allow you to—"

78

"Then maybe I should break the mirror," she snorted, before wiping her eyes.

*♪I'm not gone cry, no/ it's not the time/ 'cause you're not worth my tears/ I know there are no guarantees/ in love you take your chances... ♪*Mary J. Blige's lyrics played within her mental.

"Oshaya a mirror shows you your reflection, if you shatter the mirror, it only becomes *multiple* mirrors. A million jagged pieces, Love. And you can pick up *any* of those jagged pieces, and just a piece of that broken mirror will still show your reflection." Mirage offered truth.

Oshaya responded with a fading fragrance of her perfume before the door clicked shut. She was heading home … to ignore her reflection in the mirror.

Renta

CHAPTER 7
How it Starts Out

Mo3's, "No Love", single rumbled in the trunk of the candy painted Buick as Mya navigated through the city streets. It was like New Year's Day, and the city of Screwston Texas had turnt up, masks off, for the occasion. Dunte had fallen asleep in the passenger seat, and when Mya glanced at her man, it was all she could do to not laugh. He had a trail of drool drying in the corner of his mouth, and she found it almost amazing that no matter how deep he slept, the Styrofoam cup filled with oil, *codeine*, never so much as tilted, let alone spilled any of its contents. A black pistol rested in his lap and for the umpteenth time, she wondered what had happened to him within the past few weeks. She couldn't quite put her finger on it, but she knew it had to be something sinister. Not only did Dunte seem to move with more caution, *suspicion*, but at times, he mumbled things in his sleep— words of death and betrayal. Sometimes, her man *cried* in his sleep, and that was something he'd never done before.

She glanced up at the rearview mirror and smiled at the long line of candy-green coated slabs that snaked behind the car. In Houston, most of the neighborhoods had a thing called slab lines, where the entire hood had a car highly glossed with the same colored paint, something like a car club. A few different hoods had a red line. Tidwell and South Park were just a few. Trinity Gardens was trophy gold, but that day, boys had brought their toys out because Governor Greg Abbott's sucka-ass had lifted the lockdown on the state.

MLK Boulevard was lit lit and as Mya led the procession of Liberty Road's green line, it was a fashion show. There were trunks popped and neon lights glowed brightly from their lids. On the underbelly of each popped trunk, boys had mirrors and neon enhanced words built into the metal. This trend was slab official, and each trunk was lit with catchy phrases like *Free LeLe, Stayed down to come up, Triple Beam Dreams, Actin' bad for that bag,* and so many others. She pulled the car into a big field just off MLK and watched as the many green-coated slabs followed suit, parking their cars side by side like roller skates. At that moment, she noticed Dunte's phone glowing on his hip. She muted the music and shook his leg— "Baby, bae, wake up," she called to him while trying to sneak peeks at the phone's screen. *This bet not be one of his little hoes, I'm not for the fuckery today. I swear,* she thought, and just as the thought passed, the boogeyman appeared. With speed of a striking snake, Dunte snatched the tool from his lap, and in the same fluid motion, aimed it at her right eye.

"Dunte!"

"Why, my nigga, why?" he spat, with a wild look to his glare.

"Baby, don't!" Mya cried in shock at the animalistic madness in his eyes. Her hands shot up in a surrendering gesture. "It's *me*, bae, you were dreaming!" She reasoned as she watched the animal in his eyes retreat back inside him.

Dunte looked shocked as his eyes focused, and took in the horrified expression on his lady's face as he aimed the life snatcher at her. *Damn,* the word traveled throughout his mental like a loud bang in an empty building. He shook his head as he lowered the tool, fucked up he'd almost outted her.

"Shit crazy, baby, damn. My fault. I—"

"Nigga, you almost shot me," Mya cut him off, before pushing her door open. "You need to get your life together, dude, before you do something you'll regret." She spoke over her shoulder as she slipped form the driver seat. "Don't wait on me, I'll catch a ride with my cousin."

"Mya, I—"

"Don't," she said, simultaneously raising her hand and rolling her eyes.

Dunte watched her strut off before lifting the cup up to his lips and allowing the cold syrup to slosh down his throat. Still gripping the tool, he slouched back into the soft leather seat and rested his head against the headrest, but peace was short lived. His phone began to vibrate on his hip, and though he wasn't in the mood to talk, he didn't wanna miss the call he'd been waiting for. Slipping the phone off his hip, he gazed down at the screen. *Unknown.* Usually, he wouldn't answer numbers he didn't know, but since he didn't know the number the plug would be calling from, he answered. "Yeah, yeah?"

"Damn, brodie, why you got me blowin' up ya jack!" Dunte's face instantly balled up, and he was on the verge of spazzing until the voice registered in his mental.

"Big Bro? Gambino!"

"What's the bidness, Flesh and Blood, yeah, it's me, but damn, ole Lego block, Sponge Bob Square Pants head shaped ass boy, why you ain't been answerin' the phone? I been at you ever since I got your math from mama," Gambino checked in. Confusion blanketed Dunte's face. *Fuck out of here!* he thought, as he pulled the phone from his ear and swiped the phone icon on his screen. His call log showed six missed calls from an unknown number. Putting the phone back to his ear, he exhaled a long whoosh of breath.

"My fault, Big Bruh, I been out here livin' crooked and ain't even check my phone."

"Yeah, word travels fast, especially on the prison wire. Hearing you out there steppin' on *everythang!* You and ya mans, Tyke. What's up with that boy anyway?"

The mention of his childhood friend's name cracked Dunte's heart. Lifting the cup to his lips, he took a deep swallow of the medicine as he stared through the windshield. The morphine in the drink caused his eyelids to droop as he watched Mya standing with four other scantily dressed *thots* who bopped for a cock and would give up the ass for a little bit of cash. They leaned against someone's slab, laughing loud, and standing as if they were bowlegged, or pigeon-toed; *whichever pose would get them chosen.*

The bass vibrated from the car they stood by, and Mya became the life of the party when Da Baby and Megan Thee Stallions, *Cry Baby,* came on. She began to twerk as she looked back at it, catching the attention of many of the hustlas who parlayed in the closest proximity. Dunte gritted, barely taming the urge to jump out and embarrass lady, but— *playas never sweat these hoes!*

"Mane, big bruh, Tyke tripped the fuck out, famo. Sad story, my "G", but family is no longer amongst the breathin'," he whispered, almost as if he detested the confirmation.

"Fuck? What you mean brodie ain't amongst the breathin'? Tyke gone, as in DOA?" Gambino sounded shocked. Hurt. He'd had a hand in breeding both Dunte and Tyke and considered the latter man just as much flesh and blood as his actual flesh and blood. Dunte chuckled bitterly.

"Yeah, nigga, he dead! Closed curtains! Over wit', Gambino." His words had come out harsher than intended as his grip on the banga tightened.

"Dunte—"

"Sup, Bro?"

"Bruh—"

"Dead, he had to go," Dunte whispered, as a salty tear dripped from his right eye. It ran down his cheek and as soon as it dripped off his chin, Dunte's mind twisted backwards and forced him to re-live the night of treason—*the night he was given the blackest flower he'd ever seen.*

***

The older woman, Christina and Dunte returned to the dining room to find the once-beautiful setting converted into a blood bath. The long dinner table, still adorned with platters, plates, and spreads of exotic foods, were now splotched with splashes of dark blood. The stuffed pig was bathed in the crimson liquid, and as Dunte's eyes trailed from the roasted swine, his vision found a crooked scene that almost made him reconsider his decision.

Tyke was tied to one of the many chairs; his shirt shredded and stained with blood. Where his stomach and chest shone through the destroyed material, Dunte could see where the hedger had cut through the man's flesh. Trails of blood dripped down the Tyke's upper body.

YNNNNN! Vrooom—YNNNN! Hector reeved the small chain-saw-like hedger and his smile was similar to that of the Joker on the movie Batman. "Ahh, Dunte, me amigo, when I heard of the rat, no me gusto` nada, no, at all, amigo," he told Dunte when he'd heard of the rat— he didn't like it at all. Dunte had to force himself to hold the contents of his stomach as he watched thick squirts of blood splash across the man's face. YNNNN! He ran the hedger across Tyke's left shoulder, cutting down to the bone.

"Goddddd! Ohhhh, Godd! Please, pleaase, Dunte, help me!" he cried in agony.

Dunte could feel all eyes on him and the moment was surreal. Though his heart bled in his chest, he knew his friend's blood 'had' to stain his own fingers. His vision clouded as his hand tightened on the rubber grip of the big .357. When his eyes met with Hector's, and then the older woman's, he knew he had to get a grip on his emotions and step to the business.

The hedger quieted, and with blood splashed all over his Italian suit, Hector Tapia nodded his understanding before taking a step backwards. Dunte's cold eyes found his longtime friend, the man he'd shot his first man with, and he shook his head in disappointment. Tyke was drifting in and out of consciousness, and when his eyes drifted back open, he tried to focus. His vision fell to the heat in Dunte's hand, and when they lifted to his dude, he cracked a weak smile. "Th-they had me by th-the nuts, fam, I-I—"

"Shoulda took yo' licks!" Dunte finished for him. And with a step forward, he leveled the banga and squeezed—

Boom! Boom! Boom! Boom! The explosions were monsterous as the slugs rocked Tyke to sleep, and as soon as his soul had betrayed his body, Dunte fucked the world up. He swung the tool until it was fixed on Hector— "Nigga, you invite me here to kill my friend! You wanna kill 'me', mu'fucka, huh!" He shouted like a madman; spittle flying out with his words. "Let's do it!" The grimace on his face never wavered as the sounds of the many weapons being cocked echoed throughout the room. Hector's men were strapped up, but even the devil has a reflection. Dunte was 'bout it— Fuck it! he thought as his finger twitched.

"Dunte, you may want to see this." Christina's tone carried a tinge of caution. Dunte's trigger finger stilled, but he never took his eyes off his target. Christina stepped beside him and extended a phone toward him— "Pride is a dangerous ting, sí," she whispered. As curiosity got the best of him, Dunte's eye's flickered to the phone's screen.

"Dunte? Heyyyy, baby, I was wondering when I'd hear from you. Thank you for this little vacation, baby, mama needed it." Ms. June's smile was big on the FaceTime. Dunte's gun hand lowered as a frown graced his face. He snatched the phone from lady; checkmated!

"Fuck? Mama? Where you at!" He was shocked as his eyes watered. He noticed the Mexican man who sat beside his queen and without being told, he overstood the threat.

"Baby, Javier here has had me runnin' all day! I been shoppin', had a day at the spa, and let me tell ya', Dunte, yo' mama ain't eva been to nobody's spa! Them people sho knows how to get the knots out the bones and thangs. Javier told me he yo' friend and you sent him to give me this special day, thank you, but"— Her rambling trailed as she registered the look on her son's face. *"Dunte, what's wrong, boy?"*

"Mama?"

"Yes, baby?"

"Where are you?"

"We just now pullin' up to the house, baby, but Dunte Terrell, Wha"— she was saying before she glanced over at the man sitting beside her. A worried expression could be seen on her face, and just as her shocked eyes grew wide, the screen went black.

"Mama? Mama?" Dunte shouted as his hands became a blur of danger. Tossing the phone, he snatched Christina to him and placed the still-warm barrel to her temple—*"Fuck y'all on, y'all playin' with my family? Okay, lets—"*

"I like you, Dunte, tienes mucho corazón, sí, pero tu problema eres tú no not how to control tú emotions. Mi friend only took tú mother out to enjoy herself and this"— Hector's mother waved a flippant hand at the hold he had on her granddaughter— *"this how you repay us?"*

She'd stepped around him and into his line of vision, and as soon as their eyes connected, he frowned at the shadows dancing within the woman's beautiful iris's. It was at that moment that he realized she wasn't merely just the Kingpin's mother. Dunte was intimate with the soulless depth in the lady's gaze and recognized

86

the gaze of a cold-blooded murderer. The woman smiled before nodding her confirmation of his brief assessment. "Release my nieta, por favor, she's too beautiful to be held in such a dangerous embrace, sí?" Her statement lingered questionably.

"I agree with mi madre, Dunte, and I no appreciate tú putting tú hands on mi hija," Hector growled, before yanking the string on the chainsaw-like machine. Vroooom! YNNNN! It came to life and its sharp teeth rotated in a vicious game of ring around-the-rosy as he lifted it high above his head.

Dunte's mental was a mad house as he released his captive. As soon as she was free, Christina spun on him with fire and brimstone burning within her glare, and as quick as a leopard, she slapped spit from his mouth.

"Don't ever touch me!" she spat, her English rugged.

Dunte wanted to splatter her noodles all over her grand-mother's pretty dress, but the sound of Hector Tapia bringing the rotating blade down on Tyke's left shoulder quieted the urge. The sound of the sharp teeth cutting through flesh and bone was sicken-ing, and the haze of blood that peppered the air seemed to float be-fore staining Hector's face in a fine mist.

At that moment, three henchmen rushed Dunte unexpectedly; one quickly disarmed him as the other two held his arms tightly by his sides.

"Watch, Dunte, watch so ju know the consequences of betrayal! Watch to see what happens to rats!" Hector raged like a psychopath as Tyke's left arm separated from his body and slid to the floor. When the other arm, his head, and piece by piece, the rest of the man's limbs were cut free, Dunte vomited. Bito rushed over and forced his head up, forcing him to watch his people be dismem-bered.

"Enough!" The demand was feminine but firm. All eyes shot to the woman with the strange-colored eyes as she made her way over to where Tyke's limbs lay in a macabre pile. She bent at the knee before reaching down to pick up an arm by the wrist. "From this night forward, I will make you a vedy rich man, Dunte, but"—she paused and slowly dipped the arm into the barrel of acid. It sizzled *as the liquid digested the cold flesh—* "always be an honorable *man, si?" She nodded before making her way over to him. "Release him!" she demanded. And as soon as the command was heeded, Dunte leaned over and allowed his stomach to empty itself.*

After he composed himself, he ran the back of his hand across his mouth. His eyes were vacant but he registered the woman's extended hand. His eyes fell to it and he noticed her manicured fingers drenched in blood. "In my country, I'm known as La Rosa Peligrosa, the Dangerous Rose, but, here"—she waved a dismissive hand around the room— "here, in this country, where my people aren't welcome, and your people will never live de American dream, I am jos Rosa. Rosa of the Gulf Cartel, Dunte ... you ever heard of de Cartel?" she asked with a smile. "Verdy nasty, dangerous people, si?"

"Dunte, look out, bruh, you don't hear me, fam?" Gambino's voice snatched him back into the present.

"Damn, huh? Yeah, I hear you, Big Bro, I was just thinkin'."

"Thinkin'? Nigga, you was *sleepin'!* You was havin' a nightmare or some shit."

"Mannn, fam, you trippin', what you talkin' about?"

"Dunte, I swear, family, you was talm'bout legs and arms gettin' cut off, and some shit 'bout Tyke, and you kept sayin' some weirdo shit 'bout a Rose and the cartel." Gambino laughed. "Whatever you gettin' lifted off of, I need some, that's that high tech!"

Dunte chuckled bitterly before bringing the cup to his lips and taking a deep swallow. "If only you knew, big bro, if only you knew," he whispered.

"What? I couldn't hear you, my guy, what you just say?"

"Naw, I was just wonderin' how you callin' me, I didn't hear that operator askin' if I wanted to accept the call," Dunte questioned.

"This a jag I got from the black market. It's my shit so you can bang my line whenever. Lock my math in."

"Jag? Fuck is a jag?"

"A jag is a code for *phone* down here, lil bruh, but fuck all that, who whacked Tyke, we gotta see 'bout them boys, ASAP!" Gambino growled. "And, I need you to get up here this weekend."

"I'll be there, big bro, on Fifth Ward. I been meanin' to make that trip, but the devil been havin' a hold on me, my "G"."

"I ovastand the ills of life, family, and I don't hold it against you, Flesh and Blood, I just got some shit to run by you. Say, you didn't hear what I said tho?"

"Naw, what you say?"

"Nigga, who the streets say did it to Tyke, I *know* you hurtin', fam, that was like ya twin. That boy was family. The streets ain't talkin' or what?" Gambino's chest hurt with just the mention of the loss.

Dunte's gaze fell to the tool in his lap before he raised it for a closer inspection. After taking another sip from the half-empty cup, he tapped his temple with the barrel of the burner.

"You wouldn't believe me if I told you, my nigga."

***

Frowning, Monay huffed as she pulled herself away from her smart TV. She was tuned into her girl, Regina King, doing her thing in the episode of *Black Monday,* but someone was laying on their car horn like they'd lost their mind, and it seemed that whomever it was, was parked right outside her second-floor apartment. Making her way to the window, she had to reach back and pull the tight fabric of her boy shorts, that had crawled up between her cheeks. She peeked through the blinds and smirked when she saw who it was. Pierre had been sliding through, dropping off money for Khloe and he'd also give her some to put on Gambino's books, but she had a hunch, there was more to his visits than merely being a solid dude.

"Who is it, Mama?" Khloe ran into the living room with her tablet in her hands.

"That's none of your business, little girl, now go back to your room and play. That room better be clean too, Khloe Denise Ridge, or I'm takin' your phone, and that tablet, Monay threatened.

The little girl smacked her lips with a roll of her eyes. "Mama, I already cleaned my room, dang!"

"What I tell yo' ass about—" Monay hissed with a threatening step in the child's direction, but Pierre leaning on his car horn, coupled with Khloe turning and running to her room, gave her pause. *This little girl is gettin' too grown,* she thought as she turned for the door. Slipping her feet into the pink sandals she kept in the small foyer, lady made her way out into the sunshine.

The day was humid, and the smell of BBQ wafted through the air. It had been just the other day that rebels stormed the capital, and though the state had opened back up, the days of the sixties, seventies, and eighties had been resurrected. Police brutality ran rampant across America as if Eugene *Bull* Conner had made president, and though the sun stood proud in the sky, Monay got chills every time she stepped outside her home.

She made her way down the steps, and as if she could feel his eyes on her, she put an extra sway to her hips. Pierre was eyeing her from the inside of the sleek machine and the AC was throwing snowballs as Moneybagg Yo's, "Streets", knocked low from the trunk. He was slouched in the passenger seat and a high-yella beauty sat behind the wheel sizing the approaching woman up. Pierre noted the way Monay's nipples pushed against the fabric of her baby tee … the way the skintight, white boy shorts stretched against the bow of her hips and caused the bulge of her lower lips to protrude. He observed how *poetry* could become motion as her thick thighs seduced him. He had to *check* himself for the lust as he glanced over at Ms. New Booty in the driver's seat.

"Damn, dude, close yo' mouth 'cause you droolin'." She rolled her eyes with the words. Pierre chuckled. He'd met LuLu on *the Gram*— she was a perfect picture of gorgeous even though he knew a picture only captured what the *poser* wanted the lens to see. They'd been rocking for a few weeks, and he could tell that after running some good dick in her, dick did to lady what only some good dick could do to a woman who placed her feelings inside her vagina.

Not knowing he'd arrived with company, Monay made her way to the driver's side and stood with her hands on her hips. *She real sassy-like,* Pierre thought. LuLu sucked her teeth at the woman attempting to stand as if she were pigeon toed, but cut her eyes at Pierre when his jack vibrated.

"You gon' let the window down or nah?" Pierre was curious as he glanced up from the screen of his phone.

"Who is she?"

"Bitch, let the window down and stop twenty-one questionin' me," he growled, and again, she sucked her teeth.

When the window rolled down, Monay took a step back in surprise.

"Ain't nobody gonna do nothin' to yo' scary ass," LuLu spat with a contemptuous giggle.

"Bitch, I'm not bothered, *but* if you want smoke, I can *happily* oblige. Matter fact—" Monay began, before slipping her feet out of her sandals.

Pierre leaned toward the driver's side window so she could see him. "Monay, chill out, ma, you gotta excuse lady, you know how disrespectful *little* girls are these days." He gave LuLu a disgusted look. Monay frowned in confusion, she hadn't seen him in the passenger's seat and had assumed LuLu was one of his *thots* who had shown up to try and get stupid. She sucked her teeth at the girl before slipping her feet back into her footwear and making her way to passenger's side. Pierre let the window down with a smirk on his dark face.

"I don't see nothin' funny, dude. You may need to choose the type of girls you deal with from a different side of town; one who has just a *little* bit of class." Monay used her fingers to show how little she meant.

"Hoe, why you shootin' slugs, we can handle this like"—LuLu pushed the door open before she could finish her sentence.

"Sit yo' ass down somewhere," Pierre growled, while reaching over and yanking her back into the seat. LuLu pushed his hand away.

"Get off me, nigga, you *should* be holdin' *that* bitch back!" she spat. Seeing that she'd slammed the door and wasn't in a rush to feel his wrath, he turned his attention back to Monay. She stood akimbo— hands on her hips and elbows turned outward as she glared at him.

"It would be nice if you called before you came. They do have this invention called cellphones. You heard of them, right?" She lifted her brow as she began to bounce her right leg. Pierre chuckled before extending a small knot of money to her. Every two weeks he'd drop a band off— five hundred for Gambino's commissary account and five hundred for Khloe. Neither saw a dime of the loot and she knew he suspected it.

"Duty calls, mama, a real nigga's job ain't ever done. Plus, I don't have ya number."

"Well, next time, sideline your little *company*. Matter of fact"— she paused before reaching into his lap and retrieving his phone. Her fingers danced across the screen before she returned the device— "there, now you have my math." She was being messy; knowing the other woman would catch her drift. Monay smirked before turning and heading back toward her apartment; her ass cheeks jiggled as she purposely added some extra slut to the sway of her butt.

"You like what you see, so why not gone in there and fuck your man's gal?" LuLu shook her head in disgust. Lust was blind, and though love, loyalty, and lust all began with the letter *L*, *lust* had the power to add another word that began with the same letter— *lies!* And when those four *L* words had an orgy, the climax cried out a word that also *ended* with an *L— betrayal!*

"Bitch, watch your mouth, that's sis. Her dude's my brother," he gritted, before busying himself with his phone. LuLu tossed the shift into reverse before laughing.

"Yeah, that's how it always starts out," she whispered.

CHAPTER 8
Estelle High Security

Next Day ...

Estelle High Security was an extended section of the unit, but a totally different building from the main prison population. It housed the more unruly inmates who prison officials considered bad, really bad, or untamed. The building was divided into two different levels of security— closed custody and administrative segregation.

Closed custody meant that two inmates, a lot of times, men who didn't get along, were locked in a small box considered a cell, and the two men had to shit, eat, and attempt not to lose their marbles around each other for *twenty-two* hours a day. Outside of the two hours of rec they were allowed, there was no other reprieve from the madness of prison. Admin seg., on the other hand, was the bottom of the bottom. It was a form of punishment reminiscent of Hitler's 1933 concentration camps, minus the gas chambers and crematoriums. An inmate was held captive within Pandora's box for *twenty-three* hours out of the twenty-four that constituted a full day. Alone! Trapped with their own demons! Rats run freely, terrorizing shit, and roaches are fearless, but the saddest reality about the mind-melting conditions are the men trapped within them.

Most of the men had long-ago lost their mentals to the four concrete walls. Many resulted to talking to themselves merely to give themselves some form of company, some cut on themselves craving some form of attention, and others? Others merely drown reality by seeking an escape through psych meds. Zoloft, Tegretol, Thorazine, and Haldol, are all used for recreation and escapism. Even after admin segregation was deemed inhumane around the year of 2016, the state of Texas gives two fucks, and continues the mind-altering process. Their loophole being, rather than "call" it seg, why not just merely change the name. So, now, rather than referring to it as administrative seg., the name is *SHU— Special Housing Unit.* Same process, same form of mental corrosion, but in different name.

As Tay made his way down the highly polished hallway, silently praying he never found himself locked on the other side of one of those doors, it dawned on him what the building put him in the mind of— *an asylum!* He shook his head at the thought as he wondered where Papa was.

Papa had worked in high security for years and had a lot of pull in the area. He'd used it to get Tay an SSI Job out there and there was sure to be some shit with those two in the same place at the same time.

"Lamar?" a feminine voice called from down the hall. And as soon as he glanced up at the speaker, he knew he was in trouble. The sight of the caramel skinned lady rocked his playerism, causing his dick to harden, and he had to sweet talk his mental into not venturing toward the fantasy of sexually slaying her. The C.O lady was *ready ready.*

"Stay playa ... fam, you had bad bitches yo' entire life, nigga!" He gave himself a pep talk while he and lady's eyes danced in curiosity as he made his way to where she stood. With long silky hair that braided back into two devil-horned plats, queen's beauty was natural, but it wasn't until they were face to face that he noticed the scar that ran across the bridge of her nose. He wondered how she'd incurred it, but even more, he wondered how a scar only added to her allure. *Damn!* he thought, after noticing the Marilyn Monroe mole just above her top lip.

"Uhh, are you okay?" She snapped him out of his appraisement.

"Huh? Oh, yeah, yeah, I was just thinkin'. My fault, mama."

"Kennedy."

"What?"

"My name is *Officer Kennedy*, not *mama*, and you're Lamar?" She referred to him by his last name. Tay nodded his confirmation.

"Okay, cool, come on." CO Kennedy turned and headed toward a small office. The way that ass moved in her uniform pants demanded Tay's attention and he fed the demand. Her skin looked soft, as if it would melt in his hands, and her natural thickness made him wonder if she'd gotten it from her mama. He followed her, never taking his eyes from her backside.

"Today we have to prepare about six"—she began before glancing up to find him in lust—"um, excuse me?" she snapped. The expression on her face evidence enough that she was irate. Tay's vision lifted, giving her a false innocence, but CO Kennedy was all business. "My mouth is on my face."

"What? What you mean? Where you want me to look, fam?"

"Not at my ass!" The lady rolled her eyes. "Look, there's a lot to be done around here and if you're not grown enough to control yourself, or *at least* be more discreet with your disrespect, then you can leave," she snapped.

Tay's face melted from his flirtatious smirk into a mask of seriousness. He glanced down at the floor in thought before reclaiming her with serious eyes. *"Disrespect!* Look, ma—"

"Kennedy—"

"A'ght, yeah, all that shit, but dig this, Ms. Lady, *disrespect* would be me callin' you out your name, touchin' you without your consent, or round this mu'fucka on some lame ass shit. Me *appreciatin'* you shouldn't be considered disrespectful."

"It is *here*, where my job requires it to be!" CO Kennedy wasn't hearing none of it. She turned toward the scarred desk which was cluttered with plastic containers, filled with bippy and rows of small coned cups.

"Listen, we have a lot to do. We have to prepare six hundred of these small cups with bippy, as well as make sure each of the six hundred and forty inmates in this building has rolls of toilet paper and soap," she informed him, before using one of the small cups to scoop up a small amount of the cleaning powder, to demonstrate how things were supposed to go. She glanced back at him to ensure he understood and Tay nodded, but his mental was far beyond bippy and small cups. *Lady ready, this gon' be my wife one day,* he thought, as their vision became one. "You ready to work?" she asked with a cordial smile.

"Shid, if that's what it takes."

"Excuse me?" CO Kennedy frowned in confusion, not catching his loaded response.

Tay chuckled with a shake of his head. "Naw, I was just thinking out loud."

***

"I'm tellin' you, homeboy, the dictionary was created by racists who want mu'fuckas to think Black people are whack, ignorant, and negative, and Google ain't shit but a digital one." Gambino gave a devious chuckle. He and Big Country were lost in one of their famous debates, and the Caucasian man couldn't do nothing but shake his head in amusement. Disbelief.

"Now tell me, brothaman, how the hell you conjure up that belief? *The dictionary* is racist now! Get the hell outta here, G." He laughed hard while slapping his big hands against his thigh.

Gambino's response was to get his dictionary and open it to the *A* section. He pointed down at his chosen word to fight his point.

"That *belief* is *facts*, White man, look here"—his finger poised above the words: *African American English* (AAE). "What, Black people speak a different language than everybody else in this fucked up country? It says here that it's an *informal* vernacular."

"Mannnn," Big Country protested.

"Hold up! Just vibe with a Black man real quick." Gambino held up a calming hand. "Just below that bullshit is *African American vernacular English!* It says that it's a *nonstandard* form of English, *but* the fucked up, *unspoken* point is that their using forms of language to try and recreate the outside slave versus the house nigga effect."

"Dude," Big Country began, with an expression of disbelief. He couldn't understand how Black people still harbored ill feelings for a wrong, that in his mind, had been corrected almost two centenaries ago. Big Country made his way to the small desk in their cell and began to make himself a cup of coffee. "Gambino, your people *doesn't* speak *correct* English, homeboy, no pun intended, *and* I think you're being a little extreme with the slave analogy, don't you think?"

"Fuck no! See, you thinkin' like the typical *pale* man, Big Country. This dictionary is speaking of two different classes of

Black people, bruh. The average African American speaks improper English, but it says here that *African American vernacular English* is the *nonstandard* English spoken by *the working class* nigga, *the house* nigga who tries to kiss the pale man's ass!" Gambino spat, punctuating his point with jabs of his finger against the paper.

"Crazy part is, they're sayin' even after a black person gets a job and begins paying their dues to Uncle Sam's Kernal Sanders lookin' ass, even after my people learn to speak your people's version of proper English, it's still nonstandard! Meaning *uneducated*." He was on a roll as he licked his fingers and began flipping the pages of the American Heritage Dictionary. "These dick suckas even gave Afro American's our own lingo!" he spat disgustedly. Gambino jabbed his finger down at the word he was indicating— *Black English!* "Why they don't have *White English?* Why *everything* with *Black* in front of it has a negative connotation, period? *Black art* means witchcraft! Black face, Black ball, Black everything is negative in this mu'fucka!"

"Gambino, *English* is a White man's language, brotherman."

"At least it *was*, that is, until the Dutch arrived in Jamestown Virginia in 1619 with the twenty and odd"— Gambino declared, but paused with a thoughtful expression on his face— "even though Africans came to this rotten mu'fucka a hundred years before the Mayflower touched Plymouth Rock! But you know what I'm sayin'," he said, as an afterthought.

"Huh! What the hell are you talkin' about, Black man?" Big Country asked with a confused expression, as he took a big gulp of *cold* coffee. "What the hell does the Dutch have to do with anything?" He wanted to know.

Gambino chuckled before snapping his dictionary closed with force. "The Dutch brought the first slaves to North America in 1619 even though the Chattel Slavery Act wasn't legalized until 1650. My point is, *English* didn't even derive in England, it was created by Germans, the same crazy mu'fuckas Hitler led to torture and kill six million Jews. When the Dutch, which are Germans, brought the first slaves here, English was no longer a White man's language,

White man. It became the language our slave masters bestowed onto my people— *African American English!"*

***

"Ms. Kennedy," Tay disturbed the silence. He and her sat around the small desk, halfway done with their task, and buried within their own thoughts.

"Yes?" CO Kennedy glanced up at him.

"You believe in love?"

"Wha-what?" The question caught lady off guard.

"Love ... do you believe in it?" Tay's eyes seemed to be searching for entry into her mind. As Kennedy wondered if the conversation was appropriate, her mental couldn't help but open to the thoughts of her current relationship with a semi-pro basketball player. She loved him, but knew she deserved better.

"Yeah, I believe in love. Love is real, Lamar, but not everyone knows how to give it. Why you ask that? Don't *you* believe in it?"

"Fuck no!" He chuckled, but as C.O Kennedy studied him, she sensed a loneliness that ran deep inside. She frowned.

"Why? I mean, just because love didn't work with one woman, doesn't mean it won't with the next."

"Man, love is a fable, just something people created to rationalize what they can't explain. Love is a fool's game, and believin' in that shit has left people empty inside."

"Maybe you were just loved by the wrong woman."

"I've *never* felt love or been loved. The only love I ever saw wit' my own two eyes was the same shit that made people cry. A woman tells her dude she loves him, but turns around and crosses him. A dude says he loves a woman, but breaks her heart on some bullshit. Naw, mama, everything *I* know about love is crooked."

"Love is none of that stuff. Love is pure, love doesn't hurt people, people hurt people. There's a big difference between loving the *feeling* someone is giving you, versus loving the actual person. That feeling they're giving you can change, but if you love the actual person, you don't love based off of feeling, but more so, worth.

What's that person worth to you in spite of a season. You know what I'm sayin'?" she asked, before filling another cup with the cleaning supplies.

Tay studied her as if he'd find the fountain of eternal life somewhere in her features.

"What does loyalty mean to you?" He wanted her perspectives, but even more, he *needed* what any other street nigga craved when life had become so dark, it was hard to find their own hearts. He needed something, *someone,* to believe in ... even if it was only for the weekend, and C.O Kennedy seemed like the perfect candidate.

"Loyalty is deep. *Everybody talks* it, but when the well runs dry, thirst will lead them in search of new streams. A lot of times, people confuse loyalty with foolishness and expect you to be the *fool* in their fool*ishness.* There's an old saying my grandmother use to use. She'd say, *'Gal, yuh can't be faithful to somethin' you don have faith in. Everybody wants loyalty, but everybody don wanna be loyal,"* she mimicked in her grandmother's Tobagonian creole dialect. C.O Kennedy smiled a sad smile as she remembered her late G-lady— the woman had been her world.

"To me, loyalty merely means to the end, Ms. Lady, *till death,*" Tay whispered passionately, as he scooped bippy into the last cup.

"Well, we're finished with—"

"Teach me." He cut her off. Confusion etched into her features.

"*Teach you?*" she repeated. Studying him as she wiped her hands on a towel, C.O Kennedy felt a strange feeling she knew was forbidden under the circumstances— *attraction!*

"Yeah, you say love is real, that maybe I was just loved by the wrong bitch—"

"Woman—"

"Women and bitches become synonyms depending on the situation. Either or, I don't believe you. I don't believe in love nor your *magical* ass description of it." Tay smirked as she tossed the towel onto the desk and began to separate the soap, razors, and toilet paper which had to be passed out to each inmate in that building.

"I honestly don't care what *you* believe, but—"

"*That's* why I never believed in shit; you say I had a fucked up example, but when I *ask* for proof, you do just like every other bitch did, you—"

"But"— she sliced through his rant. They studied one another. Her, him. Him, her. Watching each other. In a place where establishing a relationship was a sin. In a place where dreams weren't meant to come true.

"But, I- I'll teach you." C.O Kennedy surprised even herself. She was raised to never judge a person for their past, so she carried that same perspective into those walls. Though she'd been warned of the slick tongues and manipulative convo of seasoned convicts, and though she'd vowed to never cross that thin line that separated convict from officer— attraction was a monster that slept beneath millions of beds. Though she'd found many of those men attractive, as did every other woman who found themselves working for an United States prison system, lady had upheld her oath to the board of prisons. Until *that* moment; as strangers within that strange place, allowed chemistry to create history. Tay extended his hand, pinkie finger jutting forward.

"Pinkie promise?" he challenged.

C.O Kennedy tried to keep a straight face, but the vision of the five foot eleven, chocolate skinned brotha, with all those tattoos extending his pinkie, stole her laughter. She laughed hard. Tay didn't crack a smile. Holding up a palm while placing the other to his chest as if it were a struggle to tame her laughter, C.O Kennedy composed herself.

"Okay, okay, I'm sorry, Lamar. That just caught me off guard."

Tay merely studied her, pinkie still extended. "Promise?" he repeated.

Studying him, lady realized the man was as serious as police brutality, and though she felt elementary as she lifted her hand and intertwined her pinky finger with his, as soon as their flesh connected, C.O Kennedy knew she'd keep the promise. The promise of teaching the man how to love, even though along with that same love, pain was a next door neighbor that often showed up to welcome a mu'fucka to the neighborhood.

CHAPTER 9
A Crooked Night

6 Hours Later

"I'm a wicked man from a wicked land, middle of nowhere like a scarecrow in a corn field/ know how that storm feels/ spent so many cold nights beneath the streetlights I forgot how being warm feels/
Being Black, wearing a hat got George killed/ so I scratched from the bottom to find my way to the surface/ My house – I keep the grass cut, I'm terrified of the serpents/ I see the world through Stevie Wonder's eyes, Piano dreams, pushin' more keys than I can purchase/ I ride my own wave, inhalin' moon rock while I'm surfin'/
Crooked pigs killed Mike Brown, beat the charges and ain't even need an alibi/ havin' hair like Bruce Lee Roy will get a nigga whacked— no dragon fly/ narcotics got my block on fire, so hot it'll make a dragon cry/
In the kitchen wipin' magic, the type of shit that made the carpet on Aladin fly/ lost my brother to the streets, at times I can feel the hurt comin'/ sidelined my ex bitch, no turf runnin'/
You niggas followers, waitin' on the next wave like the surf comin'/ got me lookin' at niggas crooked, Feds tryin' to book me, fam, I'm hard up/ fuck the preacher gon' tell me to keep prayin' if he ain't ever experienced hard luck/
That's why my shootas stay ready, ready to murda somethin'/ pull up wit' them tools like they 'bout to work on somethin'/ hit a nigga with that pole, have his ass shakin' like he twerk or somethin'/ federales watch my line like they heard I got that work or somethin', but I'm watchin' niggas flexin' on the gram like the reaper ain't on the lurk or somethin'/ B-I- P to Mo3, his situation shoulda learned you somethin'.

Gambino's pen paused in its glide across the paper. He read over the lyrics he'd just laid down before his eyes drifted to the

101

alarm clock on the table of his cell— *2:30 a.m.* He'd given his phone to J-Bo, his next door neighbor, so the youngin' could get in touch with the world, and just that brief four hours of not having the device seemed as if he'd *just* gotten locked back up.

"Gambino, you up, bruh?" J-Bo's voice was low, and the sadness in his voice caused Gambino to frown as he slid from the edge of his bunk. *Bruh just off out that world, and soundin' like he wanna cry!* He chuckled at the thought... Gambino smirked; knowing behind those concrete walls, a cellphone wasn't only one's gateway to the reprieve they needed from the cell, but the simple accessibility was like a drug to a mu'fucka who had never gotten the chance to vibe with social media.

"Yeah, yeah, I'm up, family, what's the business?" he asked, after making his way to the bars. J-Bo reached out and handed him the phone.

"'Preciate you, fam."

"No doubt, you know you my mans and nem, but fuck you soundin' like you lost your best friend for?"

"I have—"

"Huh?" Gambino was lost in the sauce as silence became dominant. Big Country's snores were deep as usual, but for some odd reason, a strange feeling eased into the atmosphere.

"G, have you ever felt"— J-Bo's tone was soft as he paused, searching for the proper word to describe his thoughts. "Tired?" The word slipped from his lips in a tone that carried a finality that caused Gambino to glance at the wall that separated their cells; as if he could see through it and set his vision on the troubled youngster.

"Yeah, I've felt tired and wanted to say fuck it a lot of times, but—"

"Naw, big bruh, I'm talkin' like, *tired tired*, ready to end it *all!*"

Frowning, Gambino gazed up and out the barred window, which was ten feet away from their cells, and showed a view of the silent rec yard. The crescent moon was high and the stars bright, but from the view on his side of the gate, the vision only made him wonder what he'd be doing if he were free.

He rubbed his hand over his silky waves, homesick and wondering what Monay was doing at that late hour. He still hadn't called her on the illicit cell phone even though he'd slid through her Facebook and Gram pages to see what she'd been up to and, even as the thoughts of his rogue baby's mother drifted through his mental, the thoughts of C.O Givens made a pit stop, and he yearned to tempt fate. He wanted to get at lady— *should I?* The thought plagued him for the millionth time. He'd slid through her social medias as well, and seeing the woman outside her uniform made him thirst for her like a mirage in the middle of the Sahara Desert.

Gambino glanced down at the phone before returning his attention to the man-child in the next cell.

"Though that's a weak man's conclusion, I'm sure every mu'fucka who's locked in one of these cages has felt that shit, lil bruh. When a man loses his freedom, he forfeits his kingdom if he wasn't the type of king who was more king in his heart than he was in title. Prison has a way of making us find peace in lies, family. No man wants to know that his woman, the one who holds his heart, has traded him in for the physical aspects of companionship. A nigga doesn't want to face off with the truth of another mu'fucka havin' to raise his seed because he's out of place! A lot of us wasn't shit in the world, bruh, but come to prison and make it seem like we were bossed up out there. What type of man"—he paused to push the power button on the flat device, and when the screen came to life, he saw that J-Bo was still logged into his Facebook account. He frowned at the picture of a woman being embraced by a dark-skinned brother, and beneath the pic was a caption that read: *Kayla Benson*. The name registered and it made him sick to his stomach. Kayla was J-Bo's gal, the woman he'd raved about since he'd been on that unit. Gambino could only shake his head as he gazed upon what had stolen his boy's usually goofy spirit.

"What type of dude wants to know that sometimes, love is only love when love is physical? Nobody gives a damn 'bout a nigga who can't provide, my "G". When layin' up in this concrete for *years*, mu'fuckas gone *have* to lie to themselves and convince self that it's gonna be a'ight. If not, your mind gon' snap! If any person can lay up in this bitch and find sanity in not seeing home for *years* ... in losin' it all, in not being able to *show* their worth, *that's* a mu'fucka who should want to end it all! So *I* lie to me about how shit will turn out, 'cause truth is"— Gambino paused and shrugged as if J-Bo could see him— "we don't know how shit will spin while lost behind this concrete. Every animal has a predator that feeds on them, and the system has swallowed us whole!" he spat, as the phone vibrated in his hand. The number fifteen showed in the message box on Facebook, and as he scrolled down and tapped the message icon, all he could do was shake his head in disgust as he began to read:

> *J-Bo*: *Kayla? Damn, get at me. I ain't heard from you in months. What's up with this nigga in the pic with you? Come on, mane!*
> **Kayla Benson**: *Who dis?*
> *J-Bo*: *Kayla quit playin'!*
> **Kayla Benson**: *Look, I ain't got time to play, who dis in my gal's inbox?*

J-Bo: *Yo' gal! Say Kayla, if this you, this shit ain't funny! You just gon' fuck over the kid like this? Damn, I gave you everythang, what—ain't got no love for me no more?*

Kayla Benson: *Oh! This must be her ex-nigga, dude in the pen? Look, Kayla has moved on, bro. She's pregnant with my child and she's happy.*

You had your shot, playa, now let her be happy.

A picture was posted with the word *love*. It was clear that the woman was prego, and though he didn't know her, Gambino's heart developed a deep hatred for her. He thought to himself ... *punk bitch, mane!*

J-Bo: *Where's Kayla, fam, let "her" tell me.*

Gambino stared at the phone as if it had offended him. He couldn't understand *why* after people had learned the truth of broken love, why'd they want to hear it from the betrayer?

Kayla Benson: J-Bo?
J-Bo: Man, WTF is Kayla!
Kayla Benson: Jamorion Kieth Boston, this is Kayla ... Look, I'm sorry you had to find out this way. You'll always have a place in my heart, but I've moved on. Please respect that.
J-Bo: Bitch, I held you down when I was out there! Come on Kay Kay, don't do it like this.

There was a brief pause before she answered.

Kayla Benson: Bye, Jamorian. Please take care of yourself.
J-Bo: Kayla?

J-Bo: Kayla!

Gambino hated snake shit, but seeing his boy sweat a nothin' ass female truly fried his fuse. The convo had ended at 1 a.m., but the last message that had just came in read:

Lose this number, playa, me and my gal 'bout to get us some sleep. You try the same in there wit' Big Bubba!

"I'm tired, G, I think I'm gonna end it," J-Bo whispered from the next cell at the same time that a text message caused the phone to vibrate. Gambino logged out of Facebook and touched his finger to the Message icon before smiling: *You up?* He read the text, and at the same time an attachment appeared. The picture emerged and instantly made his nature rise.

Rayshell was a tender Gambino use to pipe when he was free, and though she'd left him for dead after the judge had banged his gavel, he hadn't expected anything different. So, when he'd found

105

her on Snapchat, he knew if anything, lady would be an essential piece on his chess board, or if nothing else, the bitch was good for a quick nut. As he studied the clit pic, he unconsciously reached down and squeezed his dick head— the picture depicted Rayshell lying with her back against blood-red sheets, legs splayed open wider than an Eagle's wings when it soared. Gambino's vision feasted between her butter pecan thighs, where she used two fingers to part her clam and show her pearl.

"You feel me though, big bro?" J-Bo's voice caused him to glance up from the screen.

"Huh? What you say, fam?" Gambino had forgotten all about the convo. J-Bo exhaled with a long whoosh of breath.

"Ain't nothin', bro bro. Do yo' thang, and I'll holla at you later," he whispered. And though Gambino detected something strange in the man's tone, the anticipation of the cybersex he knew Rayshell was seducing him into had stolen his interest. Facebook Messenger, Tango, Skype, and every other Facetime app was a man behind the walls next best thing to being at home.

That night, as Gambino logged into his Tango account, preparing to fuck Rayshell down, he could've never guessed how much that nut would cost.

***

"Girl, what! You didn't know? Gambino been all over the Book and the Gram posting pics! He fine too, girl! He know he dead wrong for havin' that phone and not callin' to check on you and his child. Word on the street is, that girl Jimeace from Trinity Garden had been going up there to see him, I'm tellin' you, Monay, you need to just leave his dog ass alone! Monay? Nay, you hear me, girl?" her friend girl put that key in her back.

"Yeah, yeah girl, I hear you. I'm lookin' at his Facebook now! Says the nigga was just active twenty minutes ago." Monay hissed into the phone, truly hurt that the father of her child had gotten his hands on a phone and didn't have the decency to check on her. Even if it was more for the benefit of their child. Though she used this as an excuse to act on her impulse, a snake never needed a reason to bite— it was first nature. So, when her phone alerted her that she'd received a text, Monay checked her inbox:

P: Sup, ma, just checkin to see if you and my Goddaughter straight, I know it's late, so fuk wit' me when you wake up.

Pierre's text brought a sneaky smirk to her face.

"I'm tryna tell you, Monay. Monay, you hear me, girl?" Fay was saying as Monay's fingers glided over the screen in a quick succession.

"Yeah, I hear you, I hear you, sis, hold up though," she spoke irritably, as she texted:

M: I'm up… it is late, but what you doin?

The brief pause made her giggle. She knew Pierre was so used to her stand-offish ways, her response had knocked him off his pivot. Monay could only imagine his facial expression as he stared at the screen of his phone.

"Girl, whats so funny?" Fay was ever nosey.

"Hold up, bihh, damn!"

"Girl, I'll just call you back when you not so busy!"

"Bye!" Monay spoke nonchalantly and laughed when *call ended* flashed across the screen.

Just left the club. Bout to get somethin' to eat. Pierre's text finally came.

M: Why you ain't tell me yo man's had a phone?

P: Who?

M: Gambino!

P: Didn't know

M: ;(

P: Whats the mad face for?

Pierre questioned the emoji. Monay's response was a line of emoji's. The angry face, the middle finger, a pair of praying hands, and finally…. the crying face.

P: Cant be that bad... Pierre's response came through. Monay next:

M: Why niggas always on the slick shit?

P: The man may just got the phone, and all men ain't gotta be slick.

M: Slick.

P: LMFAO! Are you serious?

M: SMH

P: KMSL! Monay?

M: What?

P: What's up? You good? I really wasn't talmbout shit, fam.

M; I'm...Not...Your...Fam!

P: LOL! You... "Are"... Family! His text caused her to exhale a deep breath before …

M: Come through... She texted. There was a brief pause before his response.

P: Come through??? That don't sound right!

M: I want to show you something... it's important. Monay awaited his response.

"What the hell am I doing? Really, Monay?" she whispered to herself, but … if she didn't know exactly what she was doing, she had better figure it out 'cause Pierre's next text came in the form of his own emoji— 👍 *(the thumbs up emoji).*

***

Hour later...

"Three row, chow time! Get up, be fully dressed when you step out of your cells, chow time, three row!" the female officer shouted, as she made her way down the dim tier. "Doors," she shouted to the correctional officer in the control picket.

Gambino had hid his phone so the authorities wouldn't find it if they came to search his cell.

"Can't believe you're going to chow, baller. You usually sleep in," Big Country spoke from behind him.

Gambino chuckled as the door rolled open. "Gotta meet someone in the chow hall. You know I ain't goin' for the pancakes; I'll never eat another soup or flap jack as long as I live if I get out this bitch," he spoke over his shoulder, before stepping out of the cell. At the same time the C.O made it to the back of the run, and the moment was surreal as their eyes connected. Beneath the dim lights, time slowed down as C.O Briggs gave him a seductive smile. Gambino smirked with a playa's nod, and simultaneously, their eyes were drawn to a shadow that moved lazily in the doorway of J-Bo's cell.

"Ahhh!" C.O Briggs' scream was so loud, it echoed down the tier.

"What the—" Big Country's words trailed off in shock.

"Damn, fam!" Gambino spat, his heart instantly turning black in his chest as his mind carried him back an hour prior in time ...

"G, have you ever felt tired?" J-Bo had asked.

Tears drowned Gambino's vision as he came back to the present and his and J-Bo's eyes connected. Though J-Bo had a slight smirk on his face, Gambino shook his head in shame, guilt staining his facial features. He barely registered when Briggs grabbed her radio.

"Initiate ICS, Flash, Flash, Flash, G1 pod, three row! I repeat, G1 pod, three row! I have a ... God!" She broke down into tears, unable to complete the sentence.

Gambino stepped to the cell. "It don't matter, ma," he whispered, as he gazed up at the smirk on J-Bo's face, "my nigga, fuck you do?" he asked the younger man. J-Bo merely stared at him with that same dull smirk on his face. No words. Gambino spat on the floor as if there was a bad taste in his mouth before gently pushing the young man to the side and stepping into the cell. That's where he found J-Bo's celly, a young Caucasian man, huddled in the corner of the cell, hugging his knees to his chest as he whimpered. When Gambino entered the cell, the dude lifted his head and stared up at him.

"I-I tried to stop him, bu-but he-he—" he tried as he cried, but what he'd just witnessed had rocked his foundation.

Gambino's vision trailed from him and captured the knotted sheet J-Bo swang from. The man had made a noose out of his bed sheet and tied it to the top locker.

"Rest, lil bruh, get you some rest," Gambino whispered bitterly, as he remembered Kayla Benson. Prison was a cold place with no love, that housed men and women who needed love, but found love in the wrong people. "Big Country, come help me get fam down." His voice was rugged as he grasped J-Bo's cooling legs to stop the man's swaying body from swinging back and forth like a child in a swing at the park.

***

When the door opened, Pierre's lips parted in a surprised *O*. Monay stood in a tee shirt that she'd stretched to mid-thigh. "Sayyyyy, mane, kinda shit you on?" he spat, giving her a suspicious glare.

"Boy, boo! Ain't nobody worried 'bout you. Come in, you lettin' my air out." She rolled her eyes before stepping to the side to let him in. Pierre hesitated, eyes impulsively falling to her small bare feet, before slowly taking in her legs and her thick thighs. And at that point, knowing if he crossed that threshold, that would be a sin in the city.

"Pierre," Monay called to him.

His eyes lifted to hers. "Monay?"

"Why are you actin' brand new?"

"Why you say come through in the middle of the night, Monay?"

She sighed dramatically. "Why you lettin' yo' boy play me like I'm stupid?" she whispered ... seduction gone ... pretense evaporating ... The woman in her was swimming to the surface. Pierre saw the water cloud her gaze and he inhaled deeply and exhaled a long sigh before rubbing a hand over his southside fade in exasperation.

"Look, Ms. Lady, fam ain't playin' you. See, you on auto with accusin' him 'cause you know *you* out here bad. You don't know *why* homie ain't got at you, shid, he ain't even got at *me* yet. *You gotta* give a nigga a chance to do right by you in order to know if he'll do you some wrong. But if you countin' fam out before he can prove his worth to you, you'll never know what type of man you got." He gave it to her *like a man.* Then, Pierre sinned in the city. He crossed the threshold.

***

Oshaya rolled over in bed and allowed her eyes to crack open. It took her a second to gather her bearings, but as her vision settled on the clock beside her bed, a funny feeling took over her spirit. She rolled over and reached for Nigil, but not only was he not there, but as she ran her palm over the place he usually slept, the coolness told her he'd been absent for a while. For a second, she lie there and listened. *Silence.*

Curiously, she slipped from the bed, stretching in the process. The clock read *3:50 a.m.* "This man always trying to raid my kitchen in the middle of the night." She giggled before slipping her robe on and making her way to the kitchen. The house was dark as she made her way through the hallway, but Oshaya knew her way through her domain as if it had been the birth canal from which she'd been birthed. When she made it to the kitchen, she frowned as she glanced around suspiciously. The area was as spotless as she'd left it.

"Ummmm …" An erotic moan made her pause as her eyes slowly drifted to the door that led to the garage. The soft moans and deep grunts were barely audible, but as her eyes became slits, Oshaya knew that might well be the night she'd commit murder. She silently made her way to the counter where her steak knives were, and pulled the biggest one from the wooden knife holder. It gleamed in the darkness, and as if on auto-pilot, the sharp blade poised above her head, the lady made her way to kill her husband.

***

There was a thick fog of weed smoke that hovered above their heads as they sat laughing on the couch.

♪ *You should come through, tonight/ I'm chillin' on the west side, boo/ call my girlfriend and tell yo' best friend he can slide too/ on the low on the location, I don't want 'em to see me gettin' faded* ♪ H.E.R and Chris Brown's latest hit played low as they caught a vibe.

Pierre tilted the bottle of peach Cîroc to his lips and took a quick sip. Monay held the blunt, examining it as if it were the world's eighth wonder.

"I never knew weed could be this *gooooood,*" she sang before giving into a fit of giggles. Eyes low, and tight like a chink, Pierre glanced at her with the side eye. Seeing how turnt she was had him place his playa to the side as he laughed hard at her goofiness.

"Like, I feel soooooo, umm … wait"—she paused with an expression of confusion on her face before glancing at him with a goofy look— "I don't even know what I was just sayin', mannnn," she slurred before they both burst into laughter.

"Here"—she began before extending the blunt to him— "blow me a shot gun."

"*A shot gun*? Like, a charge?" Pierre needed clarification.

"Yeah, dude, a charge! A blast, shotgun, whatever you wanna call it?" She rolled her eyes dramatically as if he'd asked the lamest question. He studied her for a brief moment. *Fuck it,* he concluded, as he placed the lit end of the Backwoods in his mouth and watched as Monay leaned over and seductively placed her full lips on the other end. He blew, she inhaled. Her eyes became wet as the exotic smoke invaded her lungs. They watched each other from opposite ends of the blunt until Monay's lungs couldn't take anymore. Smoke exited her mouth and nose as she fell forward, coughing and chocking on cannabis smoke. Her hands flew to her chest, and her heart felt like it would burst at any moment. Pierre was beside himself in laughter as he reached over and patted her back.

"You good, mama? You know you can't play wit' this widow like that," he schooled handing her the bottle of liquor. "Here, wash that shit down wit' this," he offered.

Monay was beyond being cute; she just wanted to ease the attack on her lungs. She took the bottle to the head. "Ummmgh," she cried from the hot trail, as it ran down her throat. Wiping her mouth with the back of her hand, she slammed the bottle down on the coffee table like a man in a bar filled with biker thugs.

Pierre laughed uncontrollably at her antics which led Monay's mischievous eyes to focus on him. The liquor was wreaking havoc on her system, and as she gave him a seductive smirk, she slid off the couch and made her way over to the smart TV to accessed YouTube. When she found what she was looking for, she began to sway her hips. Making her way to the middle of the room with her backside facing him, she began to make that ass clap to the City Girls "Twerkulator". ♪*It's time for the twerkulator, I'ma shake what mama gave me...* ♪

Pierre watched, his mental declared war against his first nature. *...this lady on some otha shit, it's time to mash out before some goofy shit happens,* the real nigga in him fought against his high. Still, as he brought the blunt back to his lips and sucked the spirit from it, the snake in him reared its ugly head ... *but, damn, this*

113

bitch thick, he thought, as he reached down and gripped his hardening, lower self. He exhaled a thick cloud of smoke and frowned.

♪ *One time for my freak bitches, after hours no sleep bitches* ♪ Yung Miami fed the fire as Pierre shook his head to clear it of the tricks the liquor was playing on his mind. *I know I'm trippin',* he thought as Monay put her hands on her knees and began to do exactly what the song suggested. She twerked and showed that work as if she were attempting to give Yung Miami a run for her money. Pierre sat transfixed as her ass cheeks gave him a vulgar round of applause, and as he admired the show, the answer to what he'd been wondering all that night was answered. The shirt she wore rose to reveal a pair of *bare* ass cheeks, and the more her backside vibrated, the more his view opened doors to *fuck shit!*

A lot of people were *naturally* serpentine, but hid it behind false loyalty that only needed a reason to become betrayal. At that moment, both Monay and Pierre were exploring what they already wanted to do out the gate, but merely didn't know how the other would react. Yet, liquor and good smoke had given reason for treason, and as his vision fell a little lower to where her trimmed oasis sat, there was no turning back.

"Bring yo' fine ass here, Monay," he growled, lust riding the tone of his voice. Monay wound her hips a few more times before following the demand. She made her way to the couch and stood before him.

"What?" she purred before seductively biting down on her bottom lip. Cocking her leg out to the left and placing her hand on her hip, she became a sexy *adulteress.* Her eyes lowered to slits as Pierre signed their betrayal in stone. He reached down into his Champion joggers, and freed his strength. His dick stood tall as he began to stroke it. Pausing, he slid his sweats completely down.

"'Sup, what can you do wit' this mu'fucka?" He smirked as Monay ran her tongue over her top lip. All pretenses were finito. She pulled the tee over her head and struck a sexy pose before allowing the garment to fall to the floor.

Lady's body was a masterpiece, and as she fell to her knees before him, Pierre was ready to skeet even before she wrapped her slender fingers around his shaft and planted a wet kiss against his dick—*Muah!* Precum oozed from his slit as Monay glanced up into his vision, and for a second, an expression of uncertainty emerged. "Should we stop before things go too far? I mean, this-this ain't how it g—"

"Mane, that nigga can't do nothin' wit' this pussy. He won't be home for a long time, ma, so let's just enjoy us. Besides"—he added, before reaching down and guiding her head down toward his lap— "we done came too far. He'll never know." His encouragement was enough.

Monay's eyes never left his as she lowered her head and wrapped her lips around the head of his dick.

"Ahhhh, fuuuck!" Pierre growled through clenched teeth, as she began to suck the precum out of him.

Monay stroked his gun as she bathed his barrel with her tongue— sloppy spit. Her other hand molested his nuts as she prepared to commit an erotic suicide by making him shoot her in the mouth. Switching techniques, she popped him out of her mouth. She bowed her head lower and sucked his balls into her warm mouth, and her hand tightened around his snake; firmly as she began to rapidly pump him.

"You gon- nu-nut-in my- outh?" Her words were incomprehensible as she sucked, licked, and pleasured his family jewels.

"Hmmmm? You— *muah!* Gonna—*muah!* Nut— *ummm-muah!* In my mouth?" She punctuated her question with kisses and licks before running her tongue from his sack then up the long vein that ran along the bottom of his dick, and finally, wrapping her lips back around his inches. Bobbing her head up and down, Monay drove him to a wild place and like an animal, Pierre grabbed a fistful of her long hair and pushed her face down on him. She gagged and her saliva leaked from the sides of her mouth. "Ummmm," she cried. And as she glared up at him, she showed him why Gambino was so gone over her. She relaxed her throat and swallowed his nine inches like a boss bitch, her eyes saying: '*look, nigga, no hands!*'

***

"Shit! Shit! Daaaaummn!" The feminine cries escaped from the garage as she eased the door open as silently as possible. Oshaya's eyes instantly watered as her vision beheld treason. Nigil had Patrese bent over the tailgate of his truck, stroking her from the back as if fucking her best friend was a privilege rather than a sin.

"Yeah! Yeah, you- little- freak! Rrrrugh," he growled. And just as his nut was escaping his body, Oshaya plunged the sharp blade into his back. "FUUUUCK!" He cried out in surprise, pleasure betrayed as pain surged through him. Oshaya was lost in her blood lust and plunged the blade into him three more times before it got stuck in his shoulder blade. "Arrrrugh, you fuckin' bitch!" he cried, as he slipped from inside Patrese and spun to find his wife covered in his blood.

"Wha-t, nooo, don't stop, I'm 'bout to"—Patrese was oblivious to the crime of passion taking place until she glanced back in time to see Nigil attempt to lunge for Oshaya, but fell to his knees, in pain.

"Oh, my God, Shay, he- he- he raped me!" she cried as she hurriedly gathered her clothes and held them up to cover her private areas.

Nigil reached up and yanked the blade out of his flesh. A long squirt of blood shot out in its wake, and he stared in shock at the knife. When his vision lifted to find his wide-eyed wife, he flung the blade to the ground—

"Y-you st-stabbed me, you bitch!" he spat in shock.

"I hate you, muthafucker! I hope you die," she raged.

"Yeah, after I beat yo' ass," he swore, before attempting to climb back to his feet. But as soon as he did, blood loss pulled him back down, in pain. Patrese had used the distraction to make her way around the truck and was *almost* making her exit when Oshaya spun and grabbed a handful of her hair.

"Uhuhhh, Bitch, where you think you're going!" She demanded before trying to yank her bundles free.

***

116

"Piiieeerrrre!" Monay cried in ecstasy. He had her bent over the couch, gripping the arm of the furniture for dear life as he knelt behind her with his face buried in the crack of her ass. He held her cheeks open as he slowly ran his tongue around the rim of her exit wound; his free hand creating magic on her clit as he ate the groceries, and the stimulation was driving Monay mad.

"Je-s-us! E-eat this a-a-assssssssss, daddy, plea-se- don't stooooop!" She cried at the same time he began finger fucking her backdoor. He'd heard that women could cum from their rectum and he stared transfixed as her hole secreted a whitish release.

"Oooweeeee, I'm 'bout t-t-to- cummmm!" Monay cry- moaned as the man replaced his finger with his tongue. The passion was alien to her, and as her clit throbbed beneath Pierre's touch, Heaven descended from her love box.

"You- mutha- FucK-KK-KA!" she cried, as she exploded and buried her face in the arm of the couch. She bit down on it with a growl as Pierre used his tongue to clean her from clit to asshole.

Renta

CHAPTER 10
Caught Naked

7 a.m. the Next Morning

Do I ever cross your mind/ anytime? Do you ever wake up reaching out for me/ Do I ever cross your mind/ I miss youuuu... Though Bryan McKnight's lyrics couldn't truly be heard as Mirage blew his soul through the saxophone, the melody of the song couldn't be mistaken. Picasso sat beside the stool he sat on, and as Mirage brought the piece to an end, his eyes cracked open to a beautiful vision. From seventeen stories up, he gazed out at how the Heavens lit up the skyline of Downtown, Houston, and the floor-to-ceiling windows of the condominium were the only barrier between him and the seventeen stories of open air.

"Well, Mr. Mirage, will there be anything else you need? Dinner is on the table and"—Marisol, his Mexican housekeeper began, but paused when the intercom buzzed by the door. She made her way over and tapped the button— "Yes?"

"Sorry to bother, Marisol, but can you ask Mr. Jackson if he knows a woman named Oshaya? Please give him my apologies. I know how he hates interruptions, but the woman is quite persistent," the receptionist for the building informed.

Marisol glanced over at her boss; he hadn't so much as moved a muscle since he'd rested his sax across his lap. Picasso lifted his massive head and barked at him, and only then did the man's devilish eyes desert the view of the city and fall to his best friend. The pit bull tilted its head with a curious gaze in his blue eyes, before turning and gazing out at the sun lit skyline as if he didn't give a damn.

"Let her up," Mirage invited. His visionless eyes returned to what he could only imagine. The *sight* of his city! Yet, no matter what his eyes couldn't see, his mental was a beautiful canvas where he'd painted pictures of Oshaya running away with his heart. He'd been lonely for far too long, and ever since they'd met, he had fantasized of introducing her to the beauty of the blind. Blind lust ...

119

blind love, and blind desire— where one doesn't see flaws, scars, the past, or limitations—where all one could see is what they can *feel!*

***

Dunte knocked a little harder on the apartment door, and just when he was saying, "fuck it," and about to walk away, the door opened. "Hey, Uncle's baby!" He smiled genuinely.

"Uncle Dunte!" Khloe shouted gleefully, before jumping into his arms. Dunte carried her into the apartment and kicked the door closed behind him. "We're going to see my daddy? I wanna show him my report card! Him said he buy me a new bike! I got my daddy a newwwww picture I colored too! Him like alllll my pictures and-and—"

"Khloe, chill, girl, damn!" Dunte laughed at his niece's excitement. Instinctively, his eyes took in the living room, and he frowned at the disarray before him. The smart TV was on some sort of cartoon, and he knew Monay was gonna have a fit when she saw the Fruit Loops cereal her daughter had spilled all over the couch, but it was the slight tinge of weed smoke that lingered on the air that fried his fuse. There was also a half empty bottle of peach Cîroc that someone had forgotten to put the top back on, and that alone had Dunte's temp on the rise. *What if my niece would've accidentally drunk this shit, mane? Monay's slippin',* he thought, as he lowered his niece to the ground and placed the top onto the bottle.

"Where ya mama at, K-ma?" He addressed her by the nick name he'd given her. Khloe's eyes grew as large as an owl's.

"Mama in her room wit' Uncle P! I think Uncle P hurt her 'cause she was screamin' last night, but-but when I knock on her door, she yelled at me and told me to go to my room!" She poked out her lip in a cute little pout, and if Dunte's eyes hadn't lifted and focused on the door of Monay's room, he may have found it funny.

"Khloe, clean this mess up and get ready to go. I'm takin' you to Grandma's house," he instructed, but didn't wait to see if she'd heard him. He was too busy freeing the burner off his waist.

***

"Is he dead?" Mirage asked, and even as Oshaya sat on the man's couch with blood smeared across the material of her silk robe, she couldn't detect an iota of judgement in his tone. Before she could answer him, Marisol entered the room with clean clothes. "Here, um, you go, señora, clean robe for you. I'll try and clean yours, but blood is—"

"Burn it, Marisol." Mirage made the decision. Two pairs of eyes drifted to him before Marisol nodded slightly.

"I will do dis on my way home, yes?"

"That's cool, love, just be careful."

"Sí, Señor, sí," the housekeeper agreed, before nodding at Oshaya and excusing herself.

"You gonna answer my question or just sit there as if blood isn't all over your hands and clothes?"

"You have a *housekeeper?*" Oshaya asked, though the question was rhetorical.

Mirage frowned in frustration as she sat rocking, with her arms wrapped tightly around her chest. He didn't give a damn about the discussion of Marisol, but just as he was about to let her know just that, Marisol reentered the room. She motioned toward the bathroom before nodding at her robe.

"I ran you a hot bath if it's okay with Mester Jackson?" Her vision drifted to Mirage for acceptance. He nodded his confirmation.

"Right this way, Ms." Marisol waved toward the hallway leading to the restroom. "I need you robe, sí." The Hispanic woman's accent was strong, and at that moment, it seemed as if Oshaya suddenly snapped out of a state of shock. Her eyes grew wide in embarrassment as they slowly drifted down to her attire. She'd been in such a rush to leave the house; she'd discarded the idea of changing clothes.

"Oh my God," she cried out, and her cheeks turned rosy in shame. Mirage chuckled, knowing that the shock of her possible kill had worn off and she was now seeing how she'd left her house and entered the abode of a man she barely knew. Little did he know, the beautiful woman before him had been shitted on by life all her life, and being naked before strangers was nothing new to her.

"I have to leave." Oshaya stood in a hurry, but paused, gazing around uncertainly.

"You may want to take a bath and get rid of all the"—Mirage's words trailed off as he waved toward her state of dress—"the *evidence*." He chuckled once more when she cringed from his choice of words. "Follow Marisol. She won't bite," he offered, before turning his black orbs back to his view of the crooked city he called home.

***

Dunte had the pistol clutched tight as he eased the bedroom door open. The lights were off but the sunlight pouring in from the cracked drapes was the *guidance* he needed to spot his prey. Monay slept on her stomach, arm stretched across where her lover's chest would be, but the other side of the bed was empty. Dunte's eyes were slits as he studied the scene. The smell of sex rode the air, and when his eyes fell to the pile of discarded clothes at the head of the bed, he knew shit was about to get crazy—even before the door to the bathroom opened.

Pierre stepped out ass-naked, dick and balls swinging freely, as if he paid the rent in that mu'fucka. Half asleep, he didn't notice Dunte until the barely audible sound of the safety being clicked off alerted him to the demon that had slipped into the room. His eyes snapped up and instinctively, he made for the pile of clothes.

"Don't die over no pussy, pimpin' … that shit been gettin' boys whacked since Jesus nem days," Dunte hissed, just as Pierre knelt to, no doubt, go for a weapon. The kiss of the steel planted against his cranium caused him to freeze and give in to his fate— *caught slippin' with his pants down!*

"Fuck!" he spat, as he stood and put his hands up. "Damn, my nigga, the bitch told me she ain't have a man, I—"

122

"Mane, shut yo' goofy ass up!"Dunte cut him off before kneeling, tool still focused on his target as he reached down into the pile of clothes. When his fingers wrapped around the rubber grip of the .45 Pierre had been going for, he smirked knowingly. "This pretty bitch ain't doin' you no good buried under all these clothes, playboy." He chuckled as he erected himself and faced off with his prey. Nodding down toward the pile of clothes, he gave the man a reason to breath a bit easier." Get dressed, fam, somebody loves you."

"You ain't gonna plug me if I—"

"Get dressed, scary-ass dude," Dunte cut him off with a growl.

"Wha-whats goin' on, Pierre, why are you"—Monay's eyes cracked open in confusion. Her groggy voice trailed off when her vision zoomed in and settled on her brother-in-law. Her hands flew to her mouth in shock, and a small whimper escaped from between her fingers. She knew Dunte's story held chapters of death, and though he was cordial with her, his heart was upside down, *no love for her.*

"Dunte- I- I can explain. Me and Pierre were—"

"Fuckin'!" he cut her off, without taking his vision from Pierre as he dressed. He placed the extra burner in his pocket with a smirk.

"No, we just-we just had a little too much to drink and—

"And you *accidentally* fell on his dick," he completed for her. "Bitch, you don't owe *me* no explanation 'cause *I* saw the snake in you out the gate," he spat. Pierre had finished getting dressed and seemed unsure of what to do, but Monay had, had enough.

"Fuck?" she asked with a frown. Though she knew he wasn't Team Monay, it was the first time his feelings had become verbal, and it caused her to disregard death. "You know what"—she hissed, as she scrambled out of the bed, titties and ass jiggling everywhere as she stomped over to him– "nigga, you ain't my daddy or my mu'fuckin man! You walk up in this mu'fucka pullin' ya lil gun out on people, makin' threats and shit, but *I* ain't scared of you! You just—

Before she could complete her rant, Dunte had lost his self-control. He snatched Monay up by the throat and chipped her tooth when he shoved the barrel of the pistol into her mouth.

"Bitch, I'll blow yo' mothafuckin' noodles out the back of all these bundles in ya head!" Spittle flew from his mouth with the growl. Though he was seeing red, he didn't miss Pierre's movement. Flinging Monay toward the bed, he swung the business end of his toaster toward the other man, and his teeth clenched so tight, his jaw muscles were prominent. Dunte was ready to cook the man's breakfast until he realized that he wasn't attempting to play super save-a-thot but was merely trying to make his exit.

Pierre froze in his tracks and threw his hands up in the air as if he were a praise dancer for a mega church.

"Whoaaa, hold on, bruh, I'm just tryin' to—"

"Fuck outta here, clown!" Dunte cut him off, before waving the tool toward the door. Pierre wasted no time making his escape, and at that moment, Dunte had to fight to control the laughter that threatened to overtake him. His eyes fell to the crisp pair of Jordan 9s that rested beside the bed, and he knew that in his haste to cheat death, Pierre had left barefooted.

Monay's soft cries brought his attention back to her as she sprung to her feet with tears running down her face as she stepped in his mug. She glared at him for a moment's time before a strange expression formed on her face. She took a step back, now studying him. Dunte's suspicious gaze was demonic as he contemplated clapping his brother's BM. Though a light trail of blood leaked from the corner of her mouth due to the impact of the gun he'd crammed between her dick suckers, she had the nerve to give him a seductive smirk. She slowly began to rub her small hands down her succulent breasts in an enticing, snaking trail.

"Ohhh, I see," she purred, giving him the *come-get-this-pussy* expression, before running the tip of her tongue over her top lip seductively. *"You* mad *you* wasn't the one gettin' the—

"Bitch"— Dunte gritted before closing the distance between them. His hand reclaimed her throat with evil within his intent. "How 'bout I jam this burna up that funky mu'fucka, huh?" he spat through gritted teeth, as he nodded toward her essence. "I guarantee it'll give you the hardest explosion you ever experienced." He chuckled with the words. "I wouldn't fuck you with Eazy-E's dick, and if you *ever* come at a real nigga like this again, my brother and niece will have to forgive me 'cause I'ma push yo' lace fronts so far back, you'll give George Jefferson a run for his money!" he raged, as he squeezed her throat.

Monay scratched at his hands as he jammed the barrel into her left eye.

"Uncle, Dunte, I ready. Mama?" Khloe's voice was the woman's saving grace as Dunte smirked before releasing her. He spun to face his niece, but not before hiding the tool behind his back.

"You ready? Cool, go to the livin' room and wait for your uncle, I'll be there in a minute, me and your—"

"Mama? Why are you crying?" Khloe cut him off, as she studied Monay's face with an innocent curiosity. Monay glared at the back of Dunte's head before plastering a fictitious smile on her face. Wiping her face with her palms, she rolled her eyes as she passed him and made her way over to her child.

"Mama not crying, baby, there was something in my eyes." She soothed her. "Where are you goin' without givin' mama some of your kisses?" she asked, while pushing the girl's loose braids away from her face.

"Uncle Dunte say we goin' to get ice cream and-and we gonna go to granny's house, and then we gonna get Tyler and go to the park and, and then—"

"And then you gonna stop lyin', lil girl." Dunte chuckled, before tucking the burna beneath his shirt and making his way toward his exit. "You don't wanna grow up to be a lyin' slut like your mama."

"Mama—" Khloe called with a confused expression on her face. "What is a slut?"

"Watch your mouth, Khloe, that's a bad word. Little girls shouldn't talk like that."

"Mama?"

"What, Khloe?"

"Why are you naked?" Khloe asked, eyes studying the woman who had given birth to her. A surprised expression fell over

Monay's face as her vision fell to her bare breasts then to her bare lower self.

"A slut, Khloe, *that's* what a slut does," Dunte spoke from the hallway.

"Mamaaaa, Uncle Dunte said a bad word!" Khloe tattled as if her uncle would get an old-fashioned ass whoopin'.

"I was about to take a bath, baby, but give mama kisses before you go," Monay lied, before pulling her baby in for a hug. She glared at Dunte from over the child's shoulder, and if her eyes could talk, maybe he would've known the future would descend upon him with an evil smile.

***

After she had showered and slipped into the robe, Oshaya's mind ran wild. *What am I doing here?* she thought, before turning to the gigantic mirror. It had fogged from the steam of her hot cleansing, and as she ran her hand across its surface to clear it, the most prominent plague of her mental was: *did I kill him? Is my husband dead?* Staring at her reflection, she lifted her hands to study them, they shook as if she had Parkinson's Disease. Her vision blurred from the salty water baptizing her eyes, and before she could tame it, a pained cry slipped from between her lips, and she clamped a hand over her mouth to muffle the sound of her pain. The power of a broken heart melted her to her knees where Oshaya rocked back and forth, body wrecked with sobs.

"Is everything okay?" Mirage called, from the other side of the door. And for some reason, the question only served to make her cry harder. He must've gotten the hint because the sound of retreating footsteps danced with the sound of her cries. Oshaya cried her cry, a woman scorned— set aflame by the ones who should've never ignited her. It took a second to get it together, but everything in life depended on time. She climbed to her feet and faced off with her reflection, and with her eyes red, face wet, and heart in pieces, lady knew that all demons had to be faced.

"Get it together, Oshaya, crying ain't helping shit," she whispered, and at the same time, a smoothed melody drifted from the living room. She frowned slightly. *Is that a Saxophone?* she wondered, as she registered the piece being played. Twisting the knob on the sink, the woman scooped water into her hands before splashing it against her face. The melody to Tink's "Somebody" played so perfectly that she began to sing the words ...

"Somebody real, is hard to find/ somebody worth, all your time/ somebody who, will tell you the truth/ someone who, loves you for youuuu/ someone who knows, all of your flaws and/ doesn't impose, try to control them/ doesn't deceive, let's you be free, gives you a chance to believe," she sang. After drying her face, she turned for the door—she was going home to get some answers.

Renta

CHAPTER 11
Love and Flowers

The next morning ...

The visitation room was filled with the chatter of visitors and their captive loved ones. Dunte sat at a back table, waiting for Gambino to be brought out, as he waited, he was enjoying the session of eye fucking he was having with a beautiful Latina woman who sat waiting at the table beside him. He could tell from her smoldering gaze that she wanted his Africa to invade her Mexico, and with a quick glance around, lady surveyed her surroundings before reclaiming him within her dark gaze.

With a seductive gaze, she nodded toward the visitors' restrooms. On the ordinary, Dunte wouldn't have wasted a second's thought on rendezvousing with lady, bending her over that toilet and making her sing like Jennifer Lopez, but time was a thief. He nodded behind her with a mischievous smile and señorita glanced over her shoulder with a look of confusion on her face.

"Hey, baby, what's up?" A tall Hispanic dude made his way to her table. Lady plastered a false smile on her face as she slipped from her seat and gave the convict a nice, tight hug.

"Heyyy, papi, it's soooo good to see you, but you kept me waiting!" Dunte could hear her deception. He shook his head in amusement before his vision caught his approaching brother.

Gambino was fresh fresh, and if Dunte didn't know any better, he would've sworn prison was doing the man some good.

"'Sup family, why you smilin' like the Joker on Batman?" he asked, before taking his seat. Dunte chuckled before opening the bottled Sprite he'd purchased from the vending machine.

"You fuck wit' Vato over there?" He nodded toward the smiling couple where the Eva Mendez look alike was now portraying the perfect wife. Gambino glanced over before returning his gaze to his brother.

"Naw, that's Insane, he ratted on my dude Tay, the eses just waiting for the perfect time to dust him." Gambino's eyes lowered in suspicion. "Why? Wud up?"

"Naw, his bitch was just out of pocket, but it don't even matter now, I'm gon' get that pussy. You say he foul, shid, homie don't deserve no respect." Dunte was nonchalant as he took a sip from his drink.

Gambino shrugged indifferently before allowing his gaze to drift around the visiting room." Where's mama and Khloe? I thought you were bringing..." His words trailed off when Dunte nodded toward the vending machines. Khloe and his moms were getting snacks. He smiled at his favorite girls before returning his attention to Dunte.

"Dig, I got some shit I need to holla at you 'bout before they come over here," he began, before glancing around to ensure no one was listening. "Look, word on the streets is you just jumped a major plug wit' the Mexicans?" He jumped off the cliff and studied his flesh and blood inquisitively. Dunte studied him with a shocked expression on his face.

"Huh? What! I- I mean, sayyyy, brodie, how the fuck"—He was truly fucked up mentally. He couldn't understand how his business had reached his bro's ears when he hadn't whispered a peep to *anyone*. Gambino chuckled before lifting a calming palm.

"Chill, my guy, your secrets are still a secret, but behind the wall, you can't imagine the things we find out. Niggas in prison probably knew where Osama Bin Ladin was before Obama did." They shared a chuckle as Gambino leaned closer to him.

"The cartel is *everywhere*, Dunte, even in here. They pulled up on me on some, *because of you*, type shit." He nodded at Dunte. "Fuck all that, look"— Gambino paused to glance toward his mother and daughter who were making their way toward them. Talking faster, he spoke his peace—

"Bruh, I got a potna named Pierre in that free world and he been fuckin' with me heavy. He just got home from doing a bid, fam, and you know how shit is when a nigga tryin' and tryin' but can't make shit jump. Look, I need you to put him on *for me*, Dunte, he's a good dude and—"

"Daddyyyyy!" Khloe's gleeful scream sliced through his spiel. "Heyyyy, daddy's baby!" Gambino gave her a big smile before slipping from his seat and scooping her into his arms. She giggled as he spun her around.

"Boy, put that girl down; she's too big for all that," his mother admonished with a smile. When she offered him her cheek, Gambino leaned and planted a juicy kiss on it-

"Uh uh, Grandma, my daddy said I never get too big for him!" Khloe giggled as Gambino began showering her face with stolen kisses. He sat her next to him as he took his seat. His eyes were appraising as he studied his mother. Though she'd attempted to clean herself up, he recognized the monkey that rode her back, and her stolen beauty cut Gambino deep. She saw the look in his eyes and dropped her head in shame.

"I'm gonna get help," she whispered. Gambino wanted to believe in her; in her words, but he was grown enough to understand that if a person would lie to themselves, lying to him would be as natural as breathing. He merely nodded as Ms. June took her seat.

"Say, bruh, I got at the lawyer 'bout two weeks ago and dude sayin' he can get your feet back on the black top, but the boy sayin' it's gonna run us a few more coins," Dunte changed the subject.

Gambino glanced at him curiously. "How much?"

"Twenty more bands," Dunte confirmed with an indifferent shrug. "Ain't shit, I'll run that sack up soon and—"

"You need to keep yo' lil ass out them streets, Dunte Terrell, I done told ya hard headed ass! Ain't nothin' in them cold streets but a bunch of no love and a lot more no love," Ms. June griped. Both men's vision found her as she glared at her youngest son. They respected their queen inspite of her flaws, and when her beautiful eyes captured Gambino, they were accusative. "G, why do you encourage him to follow in your footsteps, baby, *you* already know the outcome. This is your younger brother, I taught y'all better than this, didn't I?" The question was more *self*-reflective than it was directed at them, but they both felt it.

Renta

"Yeah, Ma, you did good, but we're—"

"Save it!" Ms. June cut Gambino off. Water floated within her gaze as she glanced from him, to Dunte, and back. "Negro, I been runnin' these streets for the past forty years, there's no excuse, Gambino Mortay Ridge! No excuse to love something so deep, something that's stabbed you in the back, lied to you, and abandoned you over and over again," she spat, jabbing a finger against the table for emphasis. "These streets hate you, and y'all just keep on givin' them more and more of yourselves like some love sick, pussy whipped stalker. What its gon' take, huh? Can't either of you mu'fuckas see this shit is killin' a bitch? First, these streets took ya daddy, then you— my eldest boy." Ms. June used her palms to ruffly wipe the tears away before sliding from her seat. She glared down at her boys.

"Now these stankin' mu'fuckas threatenin' to steal my baby boy. Look at you, Gambino, Look-at-you!" Her words were harsher than the winds of an Alaskan winter. Ms. June finger combed her dry hair, feeling self-conscious. "Just as handsome as you wanna be. A handsome, breathing, *corpse!* Look at what your precious streets has done to you, boy... to *meeeee!*" She cried. Low. Deep. The Hispanic woman Dunte had the brief prelude with, glanced up at her curiously.

"Daddy, what's wrong with Memaw? Why she cry?" Khloe's big eyes grew wide in alarm as she paused from eating the bag of chips she had.

"She's okay, baby," Gambino calmed her as his vision claimed his queen. Her words cut deeper than the bullet that stole MLK's dream. "Mama, I—"

"Gonna get yo' brother killed, *that's* what you gonna do, and when that day comes, you may as well consider me just as dead as he'll be to you." Ms. June interrupted before a small whimper escaped her. And after she raced toward the exit, Gambino knew the doves didn't need to cry for him, 'cause no man, let alone, him, could find it easy to digest that kind of pill. His eyes misted as he glanced over at his younger brother. Dunte's eyes touched

132

everything but the pain in his family's eyes, and that's when the smallest girl in the room dropped the biggest bomb.

"Daddy, are you crying because mama was naked when Uncle P hurt her?" Khloe asked innocently. Gambino's vision held Dunte with a suspicious glare before falling to the child beside him. He knew *Uncle P* was Pierre, but, *naked? Uncle P hurt her?* His mental attempted to conjure a different reason than treason, but as his eyes fell to his seed, he knew she was too innocent to just make up something so vile. Gambino frowned, confused.

"Khloe?" he asked. The child took a break from her snack and glanced up at her father like she was in trouble. "Was your mama and Uncle P in her room?" he asked. Gambino's tone was murderous, and the smile on his face was the only pretense he had for his daughter's sake.

"Mannn, you trippin'! Don't bring that little girl into y'all's—"

"Nigga, I'm talkin' to my child," Gambino cut him off as they eye wrestled; killer versus killer. Teacher versus student, and it was at that moment that it hit Gambino like a Mike Tyson punch.

"You know," the words slipped from between his lips with an air of disbelief. Dunte's gaze never wavered.

"Look—"

"Tell me, nigga! Fuck all the other shit!" Spittle flew from between Gambino's clenched teeth. Dunte knew his brother better than anyone else, and that was the main reason he hadn't pulled his coat to the fuck shit out the gate. He rubbed a hand over his long, silky braids with a long exhale of breath.

"Look, bruh, yeah … I caught the lady doin' her with some random nigga, *but* damn, G, what you expect, fam? You *knew* what kinda bitch you had *before* you put a baby in her. You can't control that pussy from the—"

Bam! Gambino slammed his fist against the table as his eyes burned. "I held that nigga down in here when his scary ass was lookin' like food to these wolves," he spat vehemently.

Dunte was lost. "Who? Fuck you talmbout, bro?"

"Him talkin' about Uncle P, Uncle Dunte, duh!" Khloe didn't know how to stay out of grown folks' business. Dunte's mouth fell open in shock.

"*You* know the boy, bruh?" he asked, trigger finger tingling. Gambino's vision fell to his daughter as she licked the chip seasoning from her fingers.

"Yeah, I *thought* I did, bruh. On God, I thought I did." He shook his head with pain running as deep as a bottomless pit.

Dunte dropped his head. He felt his brother's pain. If he would've known Pierre was that much of a snake, he would've stretched him *and* Monay when he had them down bad.

"Daddy, Uncle Dunte said mama is a slut, but my mama-my mama said slut is a baaaaad word!"

"Watch your mouth, Khloe, you're too young to use that word.

"But, Daddy, Uncle—"

"Khloe!" Gambino gave her a no-nonsense expression, and though he'd been on lock most of her life, she knew her father. Khloe's eyes watered as she dropped her head, feelings hurt. Usually, Gambino's heart would melt since he was a sucker when it came to his gorgeous little girl, but at that moment, it was as if Medusa had gazed at his heart and turned it to stone. The pain gave him the look of a wounded animal, and it fucked with Dunte's gangsta. He slid from his seat, knowing the visit was over.

"Don't sweat it, bro bro, I'll buy 'em both some flowers," he vowed. Gambino nodded.

"Make sure they know I sent my love," he acknowledged before slipping from his own seat and locking hands with his brother. When they embraced, he spoke close to his ear.

"Closed caskets," he whispered, knowing that the love and flowers Dunte would give would no doubt rest on top of Monay's and Pierre's graves.

CHAPTER 12

He hadn't been back in his cell five minutes before digging his phone out of the stash spot. Powering it on with the intent of getting straight to the business, Gambino's mental caused him to clutch the phone so tightly, he had to toss it on his bunk to prevent from snapping it in half. He paced the floor with hands gripping the sides of his head as if he had a massive headache. Shit was ugly! Tears of fire bled into his eyes as he pictured Pierre pipin' his BM, and before he could control it, he punched the wall as hard as he could.

"Fuck!" he spat, as he felt the bones crack in his hand. The pain was instant, but not powerful enough to overpower the power of the betrayal. As he retrieved the phone, Gambino was thankful his celly wasn't there to see how wounded he was. He scrolled until he found the number he'd programmed then he touched a finger to it. It rang three times before it was answered.

"Yeah-yeah," Pierre answered, sounding as if he was smoking something.

"You's a bitch-ass nigga, bruh!" Gambino's growl was rugged.

"Fuck? Who this playin' on my—"

"Nigga, I trus-I trusted you!" Gambino had to fight through the crack of his heart. The silence was thick as Pierre registered the voice, and at that exact moment, Gambino swallowed his pain and allowed that *G* shit to take the wheel.

"Gambino?"

"You know what, bruh? I'm out of line for even callin' you. See, it's bitch niggas like you who got the game fucked up, nigga, you pussy! *I* was the nigga holdin' it down for yo' scary ass when the wolves wanted your head! It was *me* who gave yo' punk ass the game, and you go out there and fuck *my* bitch, Pierre? Out of all the hoes out there you could'a fucked? Huh, nigga!" he spat, clutching the phone tightly to his ear.

"Mannn, G," Pierre began, before exhaling a long breath of air. He knew it was only a matter of time. When Monay told him who Dunte was, it had fucked his head up. To top it off, it had been fuckin' with his conscience ever since he and lady had violated the code, but no matter how hard he tried to stay away, the pussy had a hold of him. "Bruh, I know this shit is fucked up and neither one of us wanted this shit to happen. It, shid, it just happened, dawg, and—"

"And it cost you your life."

"What? Nigga, don't be on my jack threatenin' me! I let you get away with that shit a minute ago, but—"

"Nigga, suck my dick! You 'bout to die, but before you do, let me tell you somethin' … it's not even 'bout the bitch, it's bout bein' a real nigga! You didn't have to be on no slimy shit just to fuck that hoe, *you* could'a told me you was feelin' her and it wouldn't be shit, but naw, you turned snake and let the streets tell me. For that, you—"

"You know what nigga, fuck you! You always thought you was lit, anyway! Yeah, I fucked the hoe, and guess what, bitch nigga?" Pierre had shedded his skin. "I'ma fuck the hoe again too! Might even put a baby in the bitch, I mean, fuck *you* gone do with the pussy, you rottin' in that cell." He laughed hard. Gambino laughed with him before ending the call— he had another call to make.

***

"Monay, your phone blowin' up, girl!" JuJu held up Monay's phone she'd left on the counter in the salon. She'd stepped out for a cigarette break and had totally forgotten the device.

"Thank you, girl." She took the phone from him and frowned at the *936* area code.

"Hello?" she answered, before exhaling a long stream of nicotine laced smoke.

"Let me ask you somethin'."

"Heyyyy, baby daddy. What the fuck? Why it take you so long to call me?" she shouted gleefully, totally forgetting her anger toward him for not hitting her when he first got the phone. Gambino's silence caused her to frown. "Bino, I know you hear me."

"Out of every other nigga you could'a fucked, *why* one of *my* niggas, Monay? That shit rocked me, fam." The rugged rawness in

136

his tone shook her foundation. *What he talkin' about? This nigga!* She rolled her eyes, chalking it up to one of his *usual* tirades.

"Boy, I ain't got time for your crazy ass mind. What you doin'? I miss you, bae," she coo'd, rolling her eyes at JuJu who was all up in her mix.

"Yo' boy Pierre just let me know the bizz and"— Gambino paused to chuckle— "and he'll die first, but you ... you the type of serpent that deserves to die slow ... real slow. See, I always told you when a bitch's pussy begins to purr louder than her self-control, she becomes the most dangerous reptile 'cause she don't know how poisonous she is. It's cool though. It ain't even your fault. I'm learnin' that I can't fault people for bein' who they always been, and if I wouldn't have put yo' snake ass in the position to bite me, I wouldn't of got bit."

"Gam-Gambino, what the hell you talkin' 'bout, I ain't ever did nothin' with that man, baby! I swear on our daughter! I don't know what that nigga said but he ly—"

"Bitch, stop lyin' to me!" Gambino's demand cut her lie in half. JuJu stared wide eyed at her, mouth agape at the soap opera playing before his eyes.

Bihh, what happened? he mouthed, with his hands up in question.

Tears blurred Monay's vision because she loved the man. What she and Pierre had was merely lustful fun to her, but at that moment, she knew she'd fucked up. She knew her baby's daddy was connected out there, and she'd had been hearing how lit Dunte was now. Trouble made people lie, so the threat of death had the potential to make a person do and say anything!

"Gambino, on my mama's grave, that nigga lyin'! I would never—"

"So, Dunte lyin' too, huh?"

"*Dunte?*" she asked, with a false sound of shock. "You know Dunte ain't never liked me, bae! You believin' them niggas over me? Over *me*, Gambino?"

137

***

Gambino frowned; his eyes lifting to capture his reflection in the mirror. Though the tears never fell, his eyes were bloodshot. He knew the bitch was a stone-cold lier, but men in prison had taught ʹ themselves the strange trick of believing their own lies.

"Mannnn," he drug the word before rubbing a hand over his hair. "Monay, don't play with me! If you—"

"Ridge!" The demand came from behind him and froze Gambino's blood in his veins. He was so caught up in his convo, he'd let the officer walk up on his cell. Spinning to face the CO, he quickly hid the phone behind his back.

"Wha-what's up, Lopez?" he asked nervously.

"Give it to me, Ridge, don't make me gas you, man, just"— CO Lopez paused to pull the can of chemical agents off his hip. He held the can of mace threateningly— "just give me the phone, inmate," he ordered, but Gambino knew in Texas, a cell phone in prison came with extra time. He wasn't hearing *none* of that!

"What phone, Lopez, I—" he attempted but— *Spisssss!*

Officer Lopez wasted no time emptying the can on him, and the can of MK9 instantly depleted the oxygen out of the air. He'd hit Gambino square in the face with the spray, temporarily blinding him, but all the gangsta could think about was how he was about to go all out to get rid of that third degree felony he held in his hands.

"Gambino? Can you hear me." He could hear Monay vaguely.

"Officer Lopez to all available staff! Help needed on G1-321, offender has a cell phone. Initiate ICS." He heard the corrections officer get on his radio. Shit was about to get stupid.

***

30 minutes later ...

"Bye-bye, Uncle Dunte, thank you for the ice cream," Khloe shouted before she disappeared into the apartment. Dunte paused on the top step, not moving to enter the apartment, and Monay's protective stance in the doorway was self-explanatory—*he wasn't welcomed*! Leaning against the door seal, she glared at him with eyes red from crying, eyes swimming with malice.

Dunte returned the heated gaze with equal dislike, but with an execution reflecting within his orbs. He contemplated downing her then. There. His trigger finger itched to squeeze the clit of that metal bitch he had stuffed down the front of his britches, but he knew the sin would eternally rob him of the love his niece held for him. Chuckling, he gave the lady a *temporary* reprieve, but still allowed her to get a glimpse of the rubber grip on the H&K USP.40 before he turned and made his way back down the stairs.

"You's a hoe-ass-dude, Dunte, I didn't take you for the gossip type, but you just like these bitches out here," Monay spat. Dunte paused midway down the steps, hand on autopilot as it rested on the ass of the burna. "Yeah, you heard me, nigga, you's a bitch! You didn't have to go up there and tell Gambino my business, now look"—she paused to let the jab set in— "he done got in trouble for that phone and—"

"Bitch!" Dunte growled menacingly before spinning to face off with lady. She could see the hurt in his eyes at the mention of getting his brother in trouble, but his gangsta was official. The fire appeared in his hand almost magically as he reclimbed three steps. "I'll blow your imagination onto my niece's night clothes if you spit on my name *one. more. time!*" he spat, staring with anticipation reflecting in his gaze.

Monay's vision fell to the grip he had on the iron in his hand, and impulsively, she took a step back. Dunte's bitter laughter made the hair on the back of her neck stand up.

"Crazy thang about it is, I know my bro *knows* you a punk hoe, but them walls got his screws loose and he doin' just like every other cat behind them doors and acceptin' fuck-shit from a nothin' ass bitch, just to have some company. See, a bitch ain't gotta lie about *her* pussy, so when one does, it reveals how sour the hoe is," he spoke through gritted teeth, before lifting the H&K until it was leveled with her facial. A slight tap of his finger caused a lime-green laser to omit from the tool and place a green dot on her forehead.

Renta

"Ole buddy you gave the pussy to is a slimey, snail-type nigga who deserves to have his shell cracked open, but *you*"— he spat the last word as if it were a swallow of spoiled milk— "you's the typa bitch who makes a man wonder what kinda nigga God is if he'd create a rotten bitch like you! But"— he eased his finger back and the beam disappeared— *karma* lurkin' in your future, mama." He smiled as if he knew a secret she didn't, and only after he turned and made his way down the rest of the stairs and hit the automatic start on his keychain, did she hurriedly slam the door closed.

Monay's hands shook as she engaged the locks before turning and placing her back against the door, doubling over, and struggling to breathe. A low moan escaped from her as her heart pounded against her chest. She *knew* Dunte would've downed her if Khloe hadn't been home. Sucking in a deep breath, she composed herself enough to rush to her phone.

"Calm down, girl, fuck that dude!" She encouraged herself before touching her finger to the screen. The last number she dialed illuminated before calling flashed across it. And as Monay waited, her leg nervously bounced.

"'Sup, lil mama?" the caller answered.

"Pierre, he just left!" she confirmed.

"Yeah, I see…but why you soundin' all nervous and shit? Just chill, baby, be cool, I got you," Pierre soothed.

"I just don't want nothin' to come back to *me*! You said y'all just gonna get the money, right?"

"Look, don't be on my jack talkin' reckless! Matter fact, I need to focus, I'll fuck with you later." He didn't ease her apprehensions, and when the line went dead, Monay pulled the phone from her ear and stared at the screen like it offended her.

"Really?" she mumbled.

***

In an unmarked car, backed into a parking spot not too far from Monay's apartment, Pierre sat watching as Dunte slid into the candy-green Buick before the machine came to life. As the trunk rumbled low from the muted bass, Pierre smirked connivingly, watching as the slab eased out of the parking space. Dunte was oblivious, never knowing that the wicked was on the lurk.

"What's good, bro bro, we gonna drill this boy *here* or what, I'm ready to step on 'em. Stand all in his chest wit' this shit like"— Spook, Pierre's relative, paused before easing a grey burna off his waist. Getting animated, he aimed the pistol, pretending to be standing over a victim, and mockingly pulling the trigger— "Bang! Bang! Bang! Talmbout givin' this boy the whole thirty to the face on some Mad Max shit, bruh, and then—"

"Spook, if we step on dude right now, how the hell we gonna know where he stashin' the fetti and work?" Pierre cut through his homicidal antics with a glare towards the passenger seat. Eyeing his family, he wondered if bringing him along on the play would come back to bite him on the ass? Shaking his head in mild irritation, Pierre knew Spook was a savage of the jungle, but he also knew that not all animals could think beyond eat, sleep, and kill mode. Spook fit the latter bill. Pierre watched as a thoughtful expression eased onto his younger relative's face as he considered the question, and without warning, the man burst into laughter.

"Ohhh"— he laughed with a slap against the leg. — "I ain't think 'bout that, kinfolk, you's a smart nigga, mane!" he praised. Again, Pierre shook his head, before easing the car out of the parking spot. He planned to tail Dunte like a Kamodo dragon does its prey, and just when he revealed his pot of gold, Pierre's homicidal intent would become the hand that rocked the cradle.

***

Nine p.m. ...

Walking out of the hospital into the frigid air of the night was refreshing to his aching body, and though they'd stitched him up and informed him that if the knife he'd been stabbed with had gone in just an iota deeper, it would have cut through his spinal canal, Nigil seemed as though he couldn't find the appreciation for the

141

second chance. As the exit doors shut behind him, the only thing on his mind was revenge.

"I'm gonna kill that whore," he swore, while pausing to glance around for Patrese. After the chaos, and after his deranged wife had fled the scene, Patrese had helped him to her car and rushed him to Houston's Ben Taub Hospital, but as he stood out in the chill of the winter's night, he'd realized she'd abandoned ship. "Dammit," he swore once more, concluding he'd have to call for an Uber. Patting his pockets for his phone, he frowned in frustration after remembering he'd left it on the dresser in his room— "fuck me, man, ain't this a"— he began, but paused when a jet-black Lincoln Navigator pulled to a halt in front of him.

Even before the five percent tinted window rolled down in the back, he knew the SUV belonged to the agency, and he wasn't disappointed when the familiar face smiled out at him.

"Hey there, Givens, need a lift?" Davis, his boss and the director of his region's Federal Bureau of Investigations, greeted.

Nigil nodded before making his way to the other side of the truck and getting in, He knew he had some explaining to do. As soon as he'd pulled the door closed behind him, the truck pulled off and that's when he noticed the stranger in the passenger seat. His vision trailed to his boss with question marks dancing in his eyes, but the man seemed in no hurry to make introductions. Instead, he pulled one of his favorite cigars from somewhere in his coat, placed the end between his lips, and lit its tip. With a quick puff of smoke, the sixty-year-old White man smiled to himself as he savored the taste of the foreign tobacco.

"You know, you're getting blood on my seats, but don't worry, son, I'll deduct it from your next check." He chuckled with an exhale of cigar smoke. "Rough night, Agent?" He probed. Nigil gave another gander to the tall, but polished gentleman in the passenger seat before returning his gaze to his senior.

"Yeah, just a little trouble with the wife, nothing I can't handle." He exhaled a breath before gingerly resting his back against the soft leather and laying his head against his headrest.

Davis chuckled mockingly before nodding his head knowingly. "One day the woman's gonna have it with being your punching bag and instead of a night in the emergency room, I'll be identifying your body at the morgue."

"I said it's nothing I can't handle, Boss, can we end it there? I've had a rough night as you can see."

"You look like shit," Morgan, Nigil's partner and the driver acknowledged. Nigil gave him the finger as Davis chuckled his sentiments.

"I won't tell you again, Givens, keep your hands off the woman, if you can't get your point across without putting your—"

"Dammit, Davis, I don't need a marriage counselor!" Nigil cut him off.

"Look here, you son of a bitch, *you don't need a marriage counselor*, my ass!" the director lost his control and reminded all present who ran the show. Pointing the cigar toward Nigil, he spoke his peace. "I will not sit back and watch you flush your career down the drain," he demanded, before regaining his composure. "Jesus, Givens, you're one of the best agents I have, man. To make matters worse"— he paused, leaned back in his seat, and allowed his vision to take in the passing scenery on the other side of the glass. Davis took a puff of his cigar before speaking— "you asked for this-this woman. Remember?" He asked before his orbs trailed to Nigil. The two men stared before Nigil's eyes drifted closed in remembrance …

2016 …

The night was a success. The good guys had kicked ass, and as a reward, the Mexican and U.S Federales celebrated at a classy club in Mexico City. Nigil sat at the bar nursing a cold brew, occasionally nodding his modesty to those who slapped him on the back in congratulations for his role in aiding the takedown of one of Mexico's most complex criminal organizations. Yet, the man's mind was galaxies away. All his life, all Nigil wanted was to climb the ranks

143

of law enforcement, to be just like his late father, and to make the old man proud.

At that moment he smiled melancholily— he truly missed his father, his hero who had died in the line of duty. He raised the cold bottle of beer and gave a silent toast to the man's spirit. "To you, Dad, for always being a tough son of a bitch." He saluted before taking a sip.

"Is this seat taken?" A feminine voice invaded his senses, and glancing up, Nigil's eyes feasted on the beauty of the woman who'd introduced herself as Oshaya. Gorgeous! The word floated through his mental like a blown kiss of the north wind, and he couldn't help but wonder what would become of the girl. Nodding to the empty chair, he took another deep swallow from his Corona as she delicately took a seat.

"What you drinking?" he asked her. Oshaya nodded her decline.

"Nothing, I don't indulge." Her voice was soft like the melody of the lyre, and for a moment after, they just sat in silence. Her staring at her hands in thought, and him gazing down into his bottle.

"Great job tonight, Givens, you're going places, man!" A fellow agent slapped him on the back in passing. Nigil took the compliment with grace and Oshaya smiled at him.

"You're quite popular," she acknowledged. Nigil's eyes trailed to her, shrugging his indifference.

"Just doing my job, that's all." He was ever modest. After studying her for a second of forever, he posed a question of his own. "What will you do now?" He could tell from the mixed expression on her face that, that was the million dollar question.

"I-I thought y-you bought me?" Her eyes were a strange mixture of sadness intermingled with loneliness. Nigil flinched in surprise and studied her to see if she was telling some sort of joke; however, seeing the absence of humor revealed the sincerity of the inquisition. He chuckled in disbelief, she frowned, not getting the joke.

"Pardon me, sweetheart"— he held up a calming hand when he saw he'd offended her— "it's just that, I see you still don't understand."

"Help me to," she demanded. Nigil composed himself before turning his chair to face her.

"Oshaya, I'm a federal agent for the United States. We were called to aid the Mexican Government and DEA in infiltrating the La Rosa Peligrosa faction. I was under deep cover tonight and have been for the past four years, posing as a wealthy, U.S drug dealer, looking to invest within the white slave trade. Tonight, I finally got the chance to confirm that the banquet presumed to aid the poor in Mexico, is nothing more than a cover up for White slavery. Human trafficking." He shrugged. "We called the operation 'Deadly Rose', and though our prime suspect has again evaded her just due, we were able to nab a few other big fish."

"So, "Oshaya began as her eyes searched, "where does that leave me? My friends ... the other girls?"

Nigil shrugged. "Your choice, Oshaya, their choice. You're free."

Free! Free! Free! The word echoed within the streets of Oshaya's mental.

"I mean, there will be some paperwork, and you and the other girls will need to answer a few questions, but after that?" Nigil again shrugged. "You can go back to your family." His revelation brought a strange expression to her face.

It seemed like a lifetime had passed since she'd seen her family, and though a part of her craved the reunion, there was the other side that made her too embarrassed to face them. She'd done ... she'd seen...too much!

"No, I can't face them right now." With a look of confusion on her face, she spoke more to herself than to him. Nigil frowned, just as confused. He didn't quite grasp the damage the traumatic experience could do to a young girl's psyche.

"So, what will you do?" he asked.

Oshaya's eyes traveled around the room, taking it all in, before they returned to him and briefly fell to his hand. Specifically, his ring finger.

"Are you involved with anyone, Nigil?"

"Huh? I-I mean," he stuttered in shock.

Though Oshaya was eighteen going on nineteen, she was more experienced with the femininity of a woman than women twenty years her senior. Nigil studied her curiously and allowed his eyes to trail from her wavy hair, and down passed her shoulders to where her velvet dress split at her breasts and teased his imagination. Impulsively, he ran his tongue over his lips because it had been too long since he'd shared the company of a woman, and though that particular one made the decision almost unethical, he smiled at her.

"No, sweetheart, I'm not involved." His response was universal. Oshaya smiled, she knew she'd use everything in her power to change her story and—

"And you asked me." Davis' voice pulled him back to the present.

Nigil's eyes cracked open, having to focus as he remembered he was in a truck with his boss.

"You asked me if I could bring her in and you vowed to make an honest woman of her and, dammit, you made her your wife!" Davis demanded, before taking a pull of the cigar. At that moment the passenger in the passenger's seat turned to face them.

"And that's where I come in, Mr. Givens." He extended his hand.

Nigil glared at the gesture and his eyes danced between his boss and the stranger.

"And who the hell are you?"

"Berkley, CIA." The man's intro knocked Nigil off his pivot. It had always been his dream to work with the Central Intelligence Agency. Reluctantly, he clasped his hand with the man's with curiosity evident in his features.

"And what do I— *we* owe the pleasure of this," he probed. Berkley responded by handing him a folder. Nigil opened it and began to examine its contents. Pictures of a tall European man, others of a light-skinned pretty boy, and a few other photos compiled within.

It was only after he'd studied each of them did Nigil glance up into the eyes of the other agent. The man nodded toward the folder with a serious expression.

"The European man is Tom Norris, a very wealthy oil tycoon. The man has his hand in some of everything and we suspect that he recently got in cahoots with Syrian extremists, and has also had his dirty hands in the ordering of very intricate assassinations. I'm talking the murder of very important men: Prime Ministers, Senators, Dictators, you name it, and we'll have reason to believe the man is very deeply connected to it." He gave a quick bio before nodding toward the other man. "Well, I'm sure you remember him." He chuckled.

Nigil studied the black-and-white photo until it dawned on him. ... *Gambino Mortay Ridge!* He gritted his teeth at the thought of the man who'd made a fool of the bureau. With the death of Malcom, their star witness, they had no proof of guilt. In the long run, his *state* charges were heavier than the weak case the feds had, so the man slipped through the crack.

Nigil nodded. "Yeah, I remember him, but what does this street punk have to do with this Norris character?" He was curious.

"Look at the last two pictures again," Berkley suggested.

Nigil obliged and that's where he found the photos that captured Gambino and Tom Norris conversing in the dark corners of the world. Nigil shook his head in disbelief, wondering how a street punk from the neighborhood of Fifth Ward had found company with such a man who was on the CIA's radar.

Berkley chuckled. "That's the million dollar question, isn't it?" He baited. Nigil replaced the photos before locking eyes with the man, then briefly glancing at his boss.

"Okay, gentlemen, let's cut the bullshit. What's any of this have to do with us?" He nodded from himself to the driver, his partner. "With *me*?" He cut to the chase. Berkley nodded his agreement to get to the purpose of the meeting.

"We've tried to get this son of a bitch, Tom Norris, for years, but the cock sucker is too slippery. Money too long. We need this other man"— he nodded towards the folder, indicating Gambino— "to be our bait," he revealed.

Nigil frowned in confusion. "I'm not sure I follow you, Berkley. Last I heard, Ridge had been sentenced to sixty-five years in a maximum-security prison. Besides"— he paused as his eyes trailed to his boss— "the man wouldn't help us even if we tried. We all know the man took the wrap for his team and spit in my face when I offered a deal for the remaining men. He won't talk."

"No"— Berkley agreed with a nod— "surely not to *us*, but maybe he *will* talk to one who has a softer approach," he spoke cryptically. Nigil frowned and suspicion blossomed across his face. Berkley chose that moment to drop his bomb.

"Your wife, Oshaya Givens, works at the Estelle Unit, right?" The question was loaded and as Nigil's mind wrapped around the implication, his heart dropped.

CHAPTER 13
Snakish

The cell door slammed in his face and Gambino could only stand there and glare as the officers turned to leave. "Enjoy your stay, Ridge, looks like you'll be staying here in "Hotel la Lock up" for quite a while," one of them mocked, as he made his exit. His partner, CO Austin turned to glance at Gambino before using his thumb and pinky to form a phone symbol.

"Call me," he, too, mocked before turning to make his way down the tier. Gambino gritted his teeth, not only in agitation, but also in pain. They'd refused him a right to a shower after he'd gotten gassed, and the chemical agent had his skin on fire!

"Fuuuuck! Aaarrrrgh," he growled in anguish. *BLAM!* He punched the wall. His entire arm went numb and reminded him that he might've cracked a few bones when he'd punched the wall earlier. In just his boxer shorts and barefoot, he began to pace back and forth in his cell.

"Look out, eight cell, who that is?" someone shouted from down the tier. Gambino wasn't in the mood for no friendly shit, and instead, he gritted his teeth against the pain—the *emotional* as well as the *physical.*

"This some hoe ass shit, mane! I can't believe I slipped like this," he chastised himself. "Dick sucka sprayed me, fam!" he hissed.

"Say, fool, I know you hear me! Who that just moved in eight cell?" The man was persistent. In the hole, dudes came in and out daily for all kinds of infractions. Some major, and some minor, but for the cats who had longer stays back there, they were constantly on the lookout for a familiar face.

Gambino paused before rushing to the iron bars. "Fuck you, boy, I don't owe you no explanation! That's the problem wit' you niggas, always on another nigga's dick," he raged, and the sound of his voice is what did it to him.

"Say, 44, that sound like Gambino!" someone shouted.

"Hell naw, Gambino *just* got out of lock up, I know bro ain't back *already!*" Another convict added his two cents. The run came to life with its usual chaos, numerous conversations at once, dudes speaking over each other to be heard.

"Gambino, bruh, that's you?" Old school V-Dub called over the ruckus. Gambino frowned, but V-Dub was his old timer and he rocked with him.

"Yeah, Dub, what it is, old head?" he gritted his greeting.

"G, nigga, what you got goin' on? Why you back here?"

"Mannn"— Gambino exhaled in frustration before plopping down on the steal bunk, resting his elbows on his knees, and burying his burning face in his hands. "SSSSS!" He sucked air through his teeth because the mere touch of his skin seemed to be reactive to whatever chemical the pepper spray was composed of. "I tripped out, Dub, fumbled the rock, fam," he shouted, so V-Dub could hear him.

"You sure did, dawg!" Tay's voice caused Gambino to flinch in surprise before pulling his hands away from his face. Tay was sweeping the tier *appearing* to be engaged in his janitorial duties, even though he was risking a disciplinary infraction for being out of place.

"Bruh," Gambino began. Even though he was fucked up about his own situation, he was happy his mans had pulled up to rock with him.

As if he was the opp, Tay glared at him before lifting a finger to tell him to chill. Gambino shook his head in disappointment as the man swept passed the cell. Moments later, he returned with a few bars of soap, a towel, and a fresh set of prison whites. Shaking his head in disappointment before tossing them through the bars, Tay went in.

"Niggaaa!" he spat, with a shake of his head. "What happened? Boys sayin' you asked the law for his math and he called it in on you! Word is, you dry *handed* the folks the jag, Bleed, but *I know* my dude ain't no lame?" The expression on his face was one of disbelief. Gambino laughed at the absurdity of the *make believe* people created with another mu'fucka's story.

150

"Tay, hellll naw, bruh, *you* know better!" he spat. "Them hoes ain't get shit off me, famo. I was just so caught up in checkin' this fuck boy and punk bitch, I was off my note. Lopez bitch-ass walked up on me and when I didn't give him the whip, he fired me up," he told the tale. Tay shook his head at the craziness as he watched Gambino make his way to the sink, sud up the towel, and begin to wash the gas off his face and body.

"SSSSS! This shit hottt," Gambino hissed. Just the meager touch of the towel made it feel as if his skin was peeling off. Tay burst into laughter at the sight of the gangsta hopping from foot to foot.

"Brooo"— he couldn't even get his words out because he was laughing so hard. Gambino glared at him— "a'ight, a'ight, brodie, you just lookin' like a real weenie right now, dawg!" He chuckled, trying to compose himself. "But I know that MK9 burrrn, bruh! That shit ain't made for no real nigga! They sprayin' boys with the same biz they use on *bears*, my guy!" He laughed so hard he dropped his broom.

"Fuck you, Tay! On God I ain't *never* felt no shit like this," Gambino *grown-man* cried. Tay nodded his agreement.

"I don't get it though, fam … how you let that boy see the jag?" He gave Gambino the '*you dumb*' look.

"Bruh, I told you I was checkin' Pierre and my BM," Gambino began, but his words trailed off. Just the mention of the two serpents in his garden twisted his heart in his chest. Tay frowned in confusion at the expression on his face, noting the mention of Pierre and Gambino's BM in the same sentence.

"What you mean? Pierre? Your baby's mom?" Evil was already beginning to swim through his veins as Gambino's eyes flickered to him before avoiding him completely. Tay spat on the ground in disgust.

"G, what you mean Pierre *and* your BM? Don't tell me that, Bleed"—

Gambino nodded in the affirmative— "Snakes, Tay, I let the snake in my garden, knowing my Eve was too weak to resist the forbidden fruit. They fucked over the kid, bro bro," he whispered, and Tay halfway believed the man was speaking more to himself than to him.

"Fuck boy! I ain't never like that boy, bro. I *told* you dude had that snake feel, dawg, and you still used to keep that boy close! Now look at this hoe-ass shit," Tay spat, mind racing, trying to figure which one of his people on the other side of that gate to send to get that boy's head! His angry eyes were fixated on his ace as he shook his head in disapproval. He couldn't understand how Gambino had allowed the serpent to slither into God's house. Gambino paused his wash off and his eyes locked with his partner in crime.

"Just thought I could charm 'em, fam. ...thought being real with dude would rub off on 'em." He shook his head, and his eyes revealed a tamed storm. *Real niggas get raw deals!*

Tays face balled up in anger. "Gambino, a charmed snake ain't no *changed* snake," he spat, before picking his broom up and resting it against the bars and stepping closer.

"See, *that's* where we, as street niggas, get the game twisted. Bro, we can *see* the slits in a mu'fucka's eyes and ignore that shit, like, just 'cause they bit *everybody* don't mean they'll bite us?" Tay was hot hot, and there was nothing more he hated than fuck shit! Pointing a finger at Gambino, he fed him righteousness— "Dawg, it's in a snake's nature to strike, even if you handle it with love. G, that's what makes snakes one of the most dangerous creatures in the world"— he paused to tap a finger to his head— "the serpent can, and always could *think,* and in the Bible we learned that people can be serpents as well, 'cause in the Bible, the serpent *talked* and *walked!*

"To top that off, the Bible revealed to us that the serpent had the rawest game known to man 'cause he had game *before* the man did. *Had to!* How else would he have known if Eve ate from the tree of knowledge she wouldn't die? *He* had to have eaten from that shit first!" Gambino chuckled at his boy's spiel, but Tay was as serious as a Monk!

"Fam, you can laugh all you want to, but dig"— he paused for the cause and held up a finger—"see, even in Genesis three, verse one, they say the serpent was *the most cunning!* Then, this when shit gets funky, if the serpent was the one that made Adam and Eve sin, *why* God kicked them out of the garden, but not the snake?" Gambino smirked but nodded because it was point seen, money gone! "Think 'bout this shit, Gambino … after all this, the snake became a symbol of *knowledge,"* Tay vibed. The expression on Gambino's face was one of disbelief, but Tay was determined to prove his point.

"When God sent Moses and Aaron to Pharaoh, He told them to lay down their staff and it would turn into what, Gambino?" he proposed.

Chuckling, Gambino nodded. "A snake!"

Tay nodded enthusiastically before holding up two fingers. "When it turned into a snake, Pharaoh's wise men and sorcerers followed suit, and their staffs turned into two snakes! That made *three* snakes, *three...* God's number. It takes *three* days to dehydrate. Jesus said he'd destroy the temple and rebuild in *three* days... The trinity is three entities … Jesus died and rose again in *three* days!

"Nigga, get back on topic." Gambino laughed.

"Yeah, you get what I'm talmbout." Tay chuckled. "Bruh, on that funny lookin' hat Pharaoh wore, what was on the front?"

Gambino thought until the mental image of the vile king, who once ruled Egypt, took shape within his mind. The golden-hued face, the eyeliner around his eyes, and finally... the *cobra-shaped* serpent that sat at its front. Tay, seeing that he got it, smirked.

"Yeah, nigga, a *snake*! And it was positioned at the front, where it would sit on his forehead"—he tapped his noggin and added—"the most vital part of a man!" Gambino laughed hard, but he was low-key appreciative of the game bestowed.

"My point is, fam, the snake has been a symbol for years, revealing to all *game* niggas and bitches that they're sneaky." He paused to retrieve his broom. "So, G, my question is why the fuck would you invite the snake into your garden when *you know* how crooked it moves?" He lifted a brow.

Gambino thought on it, never pausing his mission of wiping the gas off him. "Shid, some lessons come cheap, and some come hard, fam"— he shrugged— "it hurt, but *the game* protects me, Tay, and it'll spank 'em for me." He spoke it into existence.

Tay nodded his agreement. "So, what's up? We *can't* let that boy get away with no sin like this." Tay tasted blood. Gambino chuckled bitterly as his vision trailed to him.

"Don't lose no sleep over no creep, bro bro. I'ma have that snake's head cut off. His and the bitch he convinced to bite the apple," he added Monay.

Tay nodded. "Dig, these folks gonna try to crash you 'bout this case, so we gotta plot for rainy days, dawg. Look, I'ma holla at my dude who fucks with the major and see if we can smash this shit for the right price. You say they ain't get the horn, right?"

Gambino wagged a finger. "Naw, naw, unless they caught that hoe before it reached the sewage. I crushed and flushed it while that dick sucka Lopez was spraying me."

Tay exhaled in relief. "That's what's up, but I'm 'bout to get away from ya cell, daddy, this ain't even my shift. I snuck back here, and plus you hot as fish grease right now." He laughed. "But keep ya eyes peeled, you'll get a visitor tonight. Don't be askin' no questions either, Gambino." His statement boggled Gambino, and in return, he got a strange look from his boy. Yet, crooks knew not to put their noses in another man's aroma 'cause that was a good way to get a good whiff of a pile of shit.

Gambino waved him off but was still curious. "You always on some shit, boy, but what you talmbout?" he inquired, but Tay was gone.

***

I've cooked dinner, hurry before the food gets cold! The text played in his head as Dunte made his way into the building, hoping he was in the right place. Though he didn't recognize the number, nor was he sure it was the signal he was anticipating, he was willing to take the gamble of walking into a possible trap, if only in the name of securing the bag.

The woman behind the reception desk was a blonde haired beauty who studied him curiously. "Is there something I can help you with, sir?" she proposed, her gaze suspicious.

His all-black attire sent off alarms and he was sure the big bulge that imprinted his black thermal shirt gave off the wrong impression. Dunte frowned since he didn't even know what to tell the lady. The strange text didn't have a name, only directions. On second thought, that's when he figured his best response was no response. Instead, he took his phone out of his pocket and sent a text of his own:

D: Honey, I'm home, hope the food is still warm? He hit send and waited.

"Sir, I'm going to have to ask you to"— the blonde began, but the ringing of the phone on her desk cut her short. She'd seen him send the text, and with the same suspicious gander, she answered the call. "Yes..." She listened, and as the suspicion dissolved from her gaze, Dunte smirked arrogantly. "I see, and I'm sooo sorry for the inconvenience, Ms. Tapia. Uh-huh. Sure, I'll send him right up. Okay, ma'am, and my apologies once again." She was kissing ass before a strange expression eased onto her face. "Umm, hello? Ms. Tapia, are you still there?" She was speaking to a dead line. Dunte chuckled as she returned the phone to its place and gave him a fictitious smile. "My apologies, sir, I didn't know. The elevators are to your right and Ms. Tapia's place of residence is 821; she's anticipating your company." She'd lost her attitude. "And again, my—"

"Yeah, you Gucci, love, I understand that all Black people look as if we're going to rob you." He deaded her apology before heading to the elevators. He laughed at the dumb expression he'd left on the bougie bitch's face, but his most prominent curiosity was— *Ms. Tapia, huh? What's this all about?*

***

The car was dark as they shared a blunt. Pierre was alert as he passed it to Spook and exhaled a stream of smoke. He nodded his head to J-Dawg's "Back Trippin'" single.

"What's up with this boy? He doin' it up like this?" he mumbled to himself, wondering if Dunte lived at the condo or if he was just there visiting someone?

"Huh?" Spook inquired in a lazy drawl. "What you say, folk?"

"Talkin' to myself, wondering what's taking this dude so long. I think this his spot," Pierre revealed his thoughts.

"Shid, well let's crawl up in this thang, and take 'em down." Spook proved not to be a very good sound board. Pierre shook his head sadly.

"Spook, this a condo, bruh, this hoe got cameras and errythang. To top that off, we don't know what floor dude on. Stop being dumb."

Spook frowned. "Look, big cousin, I may not be smart like you, but I'm a steppa, bro. *Your* problem is you think *too much*, folk. Check this out"— he paused to hit the blunt before speaking over a lungful of dro smoke— "we can fall up in there, snatch up whoever at the desk, and get dude's info up out 'em. Shid... *everybody* talks when a gun is aimed at their top. Fuck the cameras, we gon' be masked up anyway!" His point froze Pierre who didn't expect his relative to *think*! Furthermore, *he* didn't have a better idea.

"Mannn," he said, but never finished his thought because that's when a knock at his window startled both men. They jumped in surprise. "Shit!" they shouted in union as a flashlight shined into the car.

"Sir, you need to move your car," an older police officer demanded. Pierre's heart fell as he thought of the heat they had on their persons, and when his eyes flickered to Spook, he knew shit was about to get spooky like a scary movie.

Spook was slowly easing his fire off his waist, and when Pierre's vision shot back to the officer, the man must've witnessed the demon dancing within his orbs. He cautiously stepped back and only then did Pierre fully take in the man's uniform. He wasn't HPD, but the hired security for the building, yet, he was armed and had a badge. *That was enough!* Pierre noted the man's hand fall to the butt of his gun, and at that moment, his instincts kicked in. Turning the key in the ignition, he nodded at the rent-a-cop. *Fuck it, now we know where this boy rests his head, we can just pull up at another time,* he thought, before pulling off. Only after they were free from holding court in the streets did Spook ease his grip on his burna.

"Sayyy, mane, I was 'bout to flip that boy's 157oupee!" He laughed away his nervousness. Pierre merely nodded his agreement. *For real though! I ain't ever goin' back to jail!* He thought, as he lusted about he and Dunte's next encounter.

***

"Señor, Dunte, welcome to mi casa." Christina smiled as she stood in the doorway. Dunte stood before her, his eyes molesting her petite stature. She'd answered the door in a sheer, black robe that stopped mid-thigh and her long hair was piled atop her head in a fashionably messy bun. Dunte's vision four-wheel drived down the hills of her geography, pausing at the twinkling diamonds in her ankle bracelet, before falling to her pedicured feet. Upon his climb back up her landscape, he had to fight against his nature. Impulsively running his hand over his lips, he wondered how Mexico could be so dangerously ugly, but give birth to something so wickedly beautiful. When their eyes clashed, a soft smile eased onto lady's lips.

"Tú persona grata." Her English was broken, but her intellect was expensive. Nonetheless, Dunte was merely a street nigga from the slums of *Liberty Road* in Fifth Ward, so he frowned at her word play. Christina giggled at his naïveté, but still found it cute. "Persona grata means you're *fully* welcomed here. In this case, in mi casa, so," she informed, before stepping to the side and waving him in.

Dunte frowned, frozen in place as his mental carried him back to the night he'd first captured her in his sight. The very night her father warned him away from her… *Off limits, Dunte, I'll castrate*

157

you and feed your balls to wild dogs! Hector Tapia's threat echoed throughout the corners of his mind.

"Christina, where's Hector?" he asked, *suspicious* of her intent.

"Will you come in or shall we discuss *business* here?" Christina's voice was soft but there was *something* just below its surface that propelled Dunte's feet to carry him forward.

"Mannn, lady," he began as he entered, shaking his head as his gut told him to run for the hills. "Mannn," he repeated, as Christina pushed the door closed behind him and *locked it.*

***

The sun had fallen asleep and his wife, "the moon", had decided to take a skinny dip within the vast sea of the Heavens. Her flesh, bright, illuminating the Earth with a powerful glow. Captured beneath its kiss, Monay stood as naked as a baby slipping from its mother's womb—beautiful beneath the moons luminous light as she strutted sexily through a vast garden, full and bursting with exotic fruit vines and trees. Lost in the night, her milky skin shimmered as if she'd been massaged with baby oil. Her breasts were succulent and capped with large, pink areolas, and her thighs subtly bulged from her frame. Her hair was wild like Chaka Khan's, but it was her waxed oasis that appeared to be a work of art against the wall of night.

She paused and studied a grape vine before gingerly plucking one from its place then, seductively, placed it in her mouth. "Mmmmah," she moaned, while savoring its sweetness. All around her, fruit trees stood enticingly, baring ripe fruit that she knew would be delicious.

As she made it passed the strawberry vines and sashayed beyond pear trees and a cluster of trees filled with hanging mangos, she came to a particular tree that captured her fancy. This one displayed vibrant leaves and soft white flowers, but in spite of its beauty, it was the hanging green apples dangling from their strong limbs that caused her to pause and lust.

She wouldn't partake, but still, the forbidden is often more enticing than the permissible. So, she merely gazed, wondering what was so special about this tree that God would forbid them from nourishing from it. She studied it, seeking answers, and it was as she did, that he approached.

"Damn, lil mama, I see that ass fat and you're gorgeous from your head to your feet, so that leads me to believe you're something with worth and not a playa in sight would deny you your fee. Titties right, hair wild like a freak, so tell me, sweet baby, why are you standing as if you're lost, staring at this here tree?"

His voice was as smooth as silk, and when Monay's eyes shot to him, her vision captured the snake! A bonafide playa, clad in a beautiful anaconda-skinned suit, complete with a pair of white, python skins covering his tiptoes.

"Boyyy, I'm just starin' 'cause I'm not gonna mess with this tree. God said if we ate of it we would die! I ain't in no rush to die, boo boo." Monay smiled mischievously and that's when the serpent slid up next to her with his eyes digesting her beauty. Smiling at her, Monay noticed the gold capped fangs and was intrigued; she'd never encountered a smooth talking playa like him. He chuckled.

"Die? I know ole God ain't told you no shit like that, love, and if he did, allow me to intro you so I can grow you," the snake jazzed before stepping forward and plucking an apple from the tree. He held it up so she could see. "You know why children will begin to place apples on their teachers' desk?" he inquired. Monay frowned, but nodded her ignorance nonetheless, and the serpent was happy to open her mind— "it's 'cause after tonight, this here apple will be a symbol of knowledge because of the shit I'm 'bout to open your mental to. "This shit is prophesy, ma. See, God doesn't mean you'll die "literally!" He just knows that after partaking of this here fruit, that thang between your legs will no longer be a mystery. And I ain't met a bitch yet who ain't tryna make history, so listen, baby, and vibe with our chemistry." He waved the fruit before her eyes. "God knows that after the veil is pulled from over your pretty eyes, he'll have to hold you accountable for being who you naturally are, bitch. So, why would you want to be stuck sleep walking through life when *you can change history with just one bite?" The snake paused and to Monay's astonishment, bit into the apple with relish. She stared with wide eyes as he swallowed the fruit, hissing in appreciation before extending the rest to her.*

"Uh-uhh, nigga, you might die later," she began, but the snake wasn't only cunning, he was also observant. He recognized the wild in her profile and he smirked.

"Bitch, I'm trying to open yo' eyes to the skies, but if you'd rather stand 'round this mu'fucka believin' Cinderella's carriage really turned into a pumpkin at twelve o'clock, then I'm gonna leave yo' lame ass standing here with one glass shoe on ya foot, waiting on a make believe Prince Charming to show up and rescue you from your ignorance." He was hard on a hoe, but Monay merely gave him the hand.

"Boy, boo! I don't know who you are but you can miss me with that slick shit." She rolled her eyes. The snake chuckled before getting real close and personal.

"Yeah, love, the truth always sounds slick to the ears of a mu'fucka who ain't got no grip beneath their feet, but..." He paused, and before she could protest his finess, the serpent's hand was between her legs, and his fingers danced over her clit as swiftly as Beethoven's fingers does across the piano keys.

Monay had never experienced pleasure because God had robbed her of carnal desire, and her first introduction to it was powerful enough to cause her to call on the devil in the church house! Her eyes grew wild, and an erotic moan escaped her, but just as he'd taken her to the top of the mountain, that cunning snake pulled away, leaving her suspended between God and Satan without the knowledge of how to climb back down.

"Uh-uhhh!" she cried, legs trembling as she eyed him evilly. "What the hell was that," she moaned in awe. The snake held up the apple with a smirk.

"If you had the knowledge of self, you wouldn't have to ask such foolish questions." His response was temptation. Monay's eyes fell to the bitten apple before reclaiming him. War-fire versus ice! God versus orgasm.

"You sure I won't die?" she asked, already choosing fire-or-gasm!

"Bitch, do "I" look dead? You just saw "me" eat of the fruit," he asked irritably.

"But you're the devil" ...

"No, Monay, I'm just a snake," he corrected, before extending the fruit to her. And without taking her eyes away from him, Monay ate. Eureka! With one bite, her mind opened, and at that moment, the woman became more powerful than man because she had the knowledge "before him."

Monay's eyes narrowed as she took the fruit and glared at the dude with a shake of her head.

"Boy, you's a snake-ass-nigga! Why-you-do that," she whined, but took another bite. With juice dripping from the side of her mouth, she smirked knowingly. "You too much, boy, but—"

"Monay, where you at, ma?" The sound of Gambino calling her frightened her. Her eyes grew wide in fear but the snake smirked a golden, fanged smile.

"Dig, give lil daddy a bite and test his might. After you open his mind take that there thang between ya legs and sit it on his dick and you'll have power over him," he schooled.

"Dick?" Monay didn't understand.

"You'll know when the time is right. I'll hide and—"

"There you are! Say, who you talkin' to?" Gambino came up from behind her.

"I- h-he," Monay stammered while pointing.

"He who?" Gambino was confused, and when Monay turned to where the snake had just stood, her mouth fell open. He'd vanished! Composing herself, she smiled to rob the moment of tension.

"No one, baby," she'd told the first lie.

Gambino studied her suspiciously, but being as green as a green bean, the distrust didn't last long. His eyes fell to the half-eaten fruit. "What's that?" Curiosity killed the lion. In response, Monay handed him the fruit.

"Eat," she encouraged him, and so he did. Man partook of the forbidden fruit from the hand of his rib which was bejeweled with

161

good game from a snake. Gambino ate and his mind was opened. At that moment, his nature rose as his mental wrapped around what had just happened. He glared at Monay, and seeing the heat in his gaze, she took a step back.

"You dirty, bitch, you fed me the forbidden fruit and now God's gonna be fucked up with me for listenin' to you." He took a threatening step toward her, but at that moment...

Sssssss! Threatening hiss gave him pause. Again, suspicion bled into his gaze as he studied Monay, but this time, he didn't see her in the same light 'cause the fruit had his game tight.

Qssssss! The hissing grew closer.

"Baby," Monay cried, as her eyes searched for the snake. "I swear I didn't mean to do this, I-I j-just let this funky ass snake whisper in my ear! The nigga is as slick as spit and told me to give you the fruit to devour... his slick ass even told me to put this pussy on you so I'd have all the power," she cried, just as the snake exploded from a rose bush.

Yet, the serpent had shed the clothes, and his powerful, languid body was a force to behold. He smiled, and his fangs glowed sharp beneath the glow of the moon... his tongue flickered, tasting the air as he eyed Gambino.

"Gambino, run!" Monay screamed at the top of her lungs, and as fast as a bullet, the serpent struck her. Gambino stood paralyzed as he watched the snake swallow her whole before fixating his gaze on him.

"What ya know good, young blood?" he greeted with a flicker of his tongue. "I'm sho' mighty hungry ... but let me tell you something nice so you can take it with you into the next life." He chuckled. "You should've ever let ya gal stroll while showing her pussy hole, and though it's too late, 'always' and I mean 'always', jewel ya bitch so she'll never relinquish your fate to a funky snake." He hissed before striking— teeth first!

"Arrrugh!" Gambino screamed, before jumping up from the hard mattress. His eyes were wild, and his breathing was heavy as he tried to figure out where the hell he was. Sweat tainted his flesh, and as he captured his bearings, the man had to shake his head in awe of how real the nightmare had been. "What the fuck, fam?" he mumbled.

"Damn, G. Bro, *whatever* you been smokin', I need some of that shit!" C.O Kennedy joked. Gambino jumped in surprise; he hadn't noticed dude standing in front of his cell until he heard his voice. First, he watched in confusion as the man glanced around to ensure he wasn't being watched. Then, he watched in curiosity as the cat reached in his pocket and came out with a *savior*.

"Here, this from your boy, Tay. He say he loves you and be on point this time," the CO relayed the message. He paused, and from the look on Gambino's face, he could tell he had some explaining to do. He chuckled. "We'll vibe another time, G, just get right," he assured, before hurriedly placing as much space as possible between him and the cell.

Gambino couldn't believe it. "This shit wild," he mumbled, as his eyes fell to the technology Kennedy had left on the bars. He hurriedly snatched it up before he found himself in another episode of *dumb and the reckless*. He saluted his mans Tay for keeping it a buck with him, but even with that third degree felony in his hands, he couldn't shake the nightmare he'd had. He wasn't on the superstitious tip but couldn't help but wonder if it were more of Tay's words that played in his subconscious, or if some *more* serpentine events were about to be added to his tale. He shrugged before powering the phone on— *if some more snakish shit on the horizon, I'ma be ready to cut the head off the snake with the machete!* he thought, while eagerly setting up the phone so he could see if his BM had been whacked yet.

***

"Have you ever dreamed, Dunte?" Christina asked. As she nursed a chilled glass of Merlot while gazing out at the city of Houston from ten floors up. The night was as black as a raven's wings, and the moon was high and full in the heavens. As she gazed up at the stars, her mind was aflame with possibility.

Dunte sat on her imported sofa and his eyes fixated on her as he wondered her intentions. With her back facing him, he was able to lust freely, so he allowed his gaze to explore her geography. The way her hair curled at the nape of her neck, the contrast of the black silk against her tanned skin, and finally, he wondered if her nice, little ass was natural or enhanced. The short robe ending just behind her sculpted thighs woke up a vulgar part of him and it dawned on him the woman resembled *a thicker*, but Hispanic version of the actress Zendaya.

"Why am I here, Christina? Is Hector on his way? Rosa?" he asked, ignoring her question entirely. Christina allowed a soft smile to touch her lips before taking a gentle sip from her wine.

"My question deserves *respect*, Dunte, and I don't like being ignored." She spoke, her English heavily accented. Dunte frowned, though she kept her back to him, he could see her demanding glare within the reflection of the floor-to-ceiling window. He chuckled to tame the animal, before sliding from the couch and stretching.

"Maybe that's *your* problem, lady, you're spoiled. And being *daddy's lil girl* has kept you out of the presence of a real nigga, so you not used to not gettin' your way." He shrugged. "Again, that's *your* problem. Now look, if Hector or Rosa not comin', or *business* not bein' conducted, I'm 'bout to mash out." He drew the line.

Christina turned to face him, heat dancing within her hazel gaze. "You know nothing!" she spat, pronouncing the word nothing— *noting!* "Sí, I'm my Papa's only child, but I *hate* the way he treats me … like, like I'm some fragile piece of fine China that will break easily," she fumed, before downing the rest of her drink. "You think you're special 'cause tú can kill, but you no dream? You will be nothing with no dream. Jus a vedy estúpido Amedican boy," she spat.

And before she could blink, Dunte was before her, that gangsta shit radiating from his posture. She took in his all black clothes, his freshly braided hair, and the bandana on his head.

"Naw, see, it's you and *you* who knows nothin'," he argued, fighting the urge to slap spit from her mouth. "*You* are too sheltered to know a fuckin' thing! You just the plug's daughter who *thinks* you know what time it is, but you in over your pretty lil head," he said in a raspy tone, eyes trailing up and down her anatomy.

Christina returned the glare. "I'm no ingénue, nor am I as ingenious as you may think. Dunte, I've *lived* beyond my Papa's watchful eye. So," she said and shrugged, "it's *you* who knows nothing!" She smirked with contempt swirling in her gaze.

Dunte chuckled. "You're nothin' more than daddy's lil girl,"— he returned the smirk—"that's *all* you gon' *ever* be, Christina, the plug's daughter." His words stung, and contempt melted and reformed as hurt on Christina's face.

"Fuck you!" she said in a raised tone. Her eyes began to mist. "You know what?" she began, before aggressively brushing past him. She rested her wine glass on the coffee table before disappearing down the hall of the spacious condo.

Dunte chuckled before turning to gaze out of the huge window. Though it was a *TGIF* night, the traffic down on the dark streets wasn't as bad as one would expect in the city of *Screwston*. As he admired the view, silent tears from heaven's eyes began to drizzle and pepper the window. The rain was light, but when a streak of lightening snaked across the sky, he knew it wouldn't be long before the drizzle became an outright downpour. The moon was half hidden and he loved the view, yet his appreciation of it was stolen when he heard movement behind him.

He turned to find Christina, *literally* lugging a heavy suitcase into the living room. Her heavy breathing and grunts told him she was having trouble dragging it, but he didn't move a muscle to help. Christina dragged it over to him before resting it on the floor. She paused to squat down and pop the clasp on it, and when the lid was lifted, Dunte's dick swelled. There, neatly stacked were freshly compressed bricks of Mexico's finest, and the Gulf's Stamp made it known that he'd finally arrived.

Christina lifted a block before turning to face him. "There's thirty kilos of coka here, your price is at eighteen a piece, and in you state, that can be sold for anywhere from twenty-six to twenty-nine grand. Here"— she tossed the brick to him and it slapped Dunte in the face before he caught it— "have our money or—"

"Bitch?" Dunte spat before tossing the dope to the side and rushing her. The animal was no longer tamed. His fingers found her neck and he squeezed enough to let her know it was official. "I'm gettin' tired of your mouth! I'ma gangsta and you will respect me or—" Christina's hand against his manhood froze his words. Confusion blossomed in Dunte's gaze. His fingers slipped away from her neck and he pushed her hand away. "Fuck is wrong with you," he demanded, but what happened next rocked his socks.

Christina stepped into his personal space and balled her small hand up in his thermal shirt, then she twisted it around her fingers to hold him still.

"Fuck you doin', girl?" he began, as she looked up into his eyes. Their stare-down was a stand-off like two gun slingers in the Wild Wild West— his, one of an uncertain lion—hers, one of a willing lioness.

"I haven't been fucked since mi came tú country, Dunte, *and*"— she shrugged indifferently— "Me gusta tú ," she whispered, but giggled when he frowned naively. "I like you," she translated, before lifting on her tip toes to kiss his neck.

Dunte was frozen, but his little man was on salute. Christina felt it and smiled. "You av mucho huebos, I likey el way tú stand up to mi family," she whispered, before nibbling his earlobe. Her hands undid his Medusa head belt buckle. Her tongue was wet as it slid down his neck, and her seduction was a powerful wave that fell over him like a waterfall. ...*off limits Dunte, I'll castrate you and feed your balls to wild dogs* ... Hector Tapia's warning oozed through the cracks of seduction's wall. Dunte gently pushed her back, *just a bit.*

"Naw, we can't rock like this, Christina. You beautiful, but your father will—"

"Coward!" she spat with a mocking glare. "The big bad Dunte fears mi father, sí?" She lifted an arched brow.

"I fear *nothin'*!" Dunte declared, his gangsterisms evident. *"Respect* is rare, and your pops giving me a seat at his table. He said you off limits, so…" He shrugged.

"You're pussy. I respected *you* more, but you're nothing more than another one of my father's *workers* and..." Her words died when Dunte's hand reclaimed her throat. This time with the hug of a python. She scratched at his hands, her eyes growing large in fear. "Air," she rasped, "can't-breathe..."

"And you won't if you *ever* disrespect me again. I'm *nobody's* worker," he demanded, as he considered ending her and running off on the plug. *Fuck you doin', bruh, you trippin'! This the cartel and you 'bout to whack the plug's daughter!* His gut screamed to his mental and he released her.

"Get out! You"— Christina fought for air— "you will die for this!" she cried, and at that moment, he didn't know if it was the thought of going to war with the cartel or if it was merely a ferine impulse, but he did the unthinkable. "Get. Out!" she screamed, water leaking from her pretty eyes.

Dunte did the opposite. To her surprise, he was as quick as a striking cobra when he took hold of the front of her robe and yanked her to him.

"Ahhh," she cried out, startled, but Dunte's lips upon hers silenced it. She fought against him in the beginning, but the dance of his tongue was magical to her. She moaned, surrendering to him. As they kissed, their hands pawed at each other's clothes. Hers freed his masculinity and his pulled the sash loose on her robe. "Mmmah," Christina moaned as their lips smacked, and the wrestle of their tongues poured gasoline onto their fire.

Her robe fell open to reveal a ripe set of breasts that sat up with chocolate chips topped at their peeks. When Dunte broke the kiss to step back and admire her, he ran his tongue over his lips in appreciation. Christina's lower island was beautiful with a manicured lawn. Slight fuzzy and fat, her lower lips glistened with her fruit juices. When her eyes fell to Dunte's engorged seven inches, she wondered if his girth would be too much for her. Yet, he was a thief, stealing the option of consideration from her when he invaded her personal space.

Reaching behind her, he slid his hand beneath her sheer fabric, running them up the back of her thighs, and only stopping when he cupped her bare ass cheeks.

"You're gonna get me killed," he prophesied, as they eye fucked each other.

Christina lifted her arms and interlocked them behind his neck. "Have you ever dreamed, Dunte?" she repeated her question from earlier. Dunte studied her before leaning down and burying his tongue in her mouth. His hands gripped her backside, and he backed her up until her back touched the glass window. The robe slipped from her shoulders and Christina aided to its decent to the floor.

Lifting her leg, she used her foot to push Dunte's unbuckled pants down, and they fell to the floor without resistance. Yet, when she went to lower her foot, he caught her leg and wrapped it around his waist.

Her eyes grew wide, vulnerability revealed. "Gentle, Dunte, please be"— she began, but Dunte ignored her.

Bending at the knee, his stroke inside her was so powerful, it lifted her up onto the tip toes of her balancing foot.

"Ssssss… Dun-tee," she purred, pleasure having a head on collision with pain. Her fuck-face was a mixture of pity and a frown of curiosity as Dunte pushed into the hilt. His sword sliced her open, filling her to the maximum before he eased out. Gripping her buttocks and stabbing her over and over again, killing the pussy with his thrusts.

"Uhhhhyyyiiieee!" she cried out, "me estas partiendo en dos peri no pares!" she cried seductively, telling him that he was tearing her in half, but don't stop.

"This what you wanted, huh? Huh?" he growled. The squeeze of her femininity took him to the top of Mount Everest and dared him to jump to a blissful death. "Arrr!" He roared like the king of the jungle.

"Myyyy Goddd," she moaned as he hit somewhere deep inside her.

"My-dre-dreams," Dunte grunted, "is to-to l-live like a king-pin!" he revealed. Pleasure was too great for her to speak, so reaching up and snatching the black bandanna from his head, Christina merely nodded her understanding. Their eyes never swayed as they became one, and behind them, a streak of lightening snaked across the sky, illuminating not only the street below, but also Christina's back and ass cheeks which were plastered against the tenth floor windowpane.

Renta

CHAPTER 14
Diamond Vibe

Next Night...

It had been twenty-four hours since Oshaya had stabbed her husband, twenty-four hours since she'd returned home to find the house deserted, and twenty-four hours since she'd last seen the blind man, Mirage. She'd returned to work and though the *Texas Department of Criminal Justice (TDCJ) franchise* gave good benefits to its workers, working in corrections just wasn't her cup of tea. *I'm so done,* she thought, concluding that she'd submit her two week's notice.

She stood in her kitchen slowly stirring a pot of Feijoada, a Portuguese stew made with beans, pork, and beef. Just the thought of the stew, poured on steamed rice with orange slices, made her mouth water. Comfortable in a muscle shirt and a pair of short-shorts, Oshaya rocked her hips to the tunes of the Caribbean singer, Buju Banton. "Batty Ride" was her jam and though she was merely using music as a distraction, her mental was a labyrinth of thoughts she couldn't find her way out of— *Where's Nigil? Is he dead? Is he with Patrese?* she thought, and just the memory of her husband fuckin' her bestie set a fire in her veins.

"Bitch," she spat, and at the same time her phone chimed. Placing her stirring spoon on a towel, she retrieved the device from the counter and noticed it wasn't a text, but a Facebook notification. She'd received a DM. Touching the icon, she frowned at the message:

🖤*I know this may be unethical and God have mercy on a real nigga, but I swear I fought against the urge as long as I could, but??? Shid, I got a jones for you, mama. Wud up?* It read. Her eyes flickered to the page name— *Mr. Tryin' to be yours.* Her heart sped up, there was only one person she knew to use that term and it was impossible for that person to have slid into her DM cause that person was locked up!

***

Gambino took a deep breath after sending the message.

"All I can do is wait now," he whispered to himself, while scrolling down her timeline. Lady was gorgeous to him. At that moment, an incoming call shrunk the screen and he accepted. "The business, my guy?" he answered.

"Shid, thuggin', but look"— Tay seemed in a hurry to say what he needed to say— "my lil relative gonna take care of that lil problem for us. Lil nigga a lunatic out South Dallas, and when he arrives in the H this weekend, he gonna hit you for the specifics." Gambino nodded as if he could be seen.

"What's dude's name?"

"OJ the Crooked."

"*The Crooked?*" Gambino smirked.

"Yeah, and lil bruh flatlinin' everythang in the city right now. Our friends won't even know the reaper there to collect until he's collectin' their souls but look"— Tay paused— "it's 'bout time for count time. I'll bark at you in traffic."

"Say, what's up with you and lil baby over there in high Security?" Gambino asked, but Tay had already disconnected. "Mark ass dude." He chuckled and then his phone vibrated. The Facebook screen had re-emerged and when he checked his DM, his eyes enlarged as a slow smile spread across his face— *"OG aka Oshaya Givens had responded!*

***

💬 *OG: Mr. Want to be Mine? Um, okay. So... you have a phone? Look, man, yes, this is unethical, and I'm not feeling you stalking me on Facebook, "but" ... I do find your persistence cute. So...phone?* As she sat with her feet tucked beneath her on the couch, Oshaya shook her head in disbelief. She couldn't believe she sent that message, but even more, she couldn't believe how much she was anticipating his response. Maybe it was all the BS she was going through at home, or maybe it was merely the truth—*he'd finally cracked her code.* Either or, she'd crossed the point of no return, and if she were to be honest with herself, the truth was, she'd *been* lusting for dude. There was just something about the light skinned gangsta that had her immersed within his gangsterisms, and when the iPhone vibrated in her hand, she smiled...

💬 *Mr. Wanna be yours: Naw, I don't have a phone, love, I'm texting you through telekinesis! :-) Yes, mama. This is my phone. Yet, feel me, I know your takin' a meeean risk with me, but I'm worth it!* She read at the same time a thought came to her.

💬 *OG: If this is really you, send me a picture!* She texted and waited. A moment passed before the word *loading* appeared and when the picture processed, Oshaya gasped before her hand flew to her mouth in shock. Gambino sent a picture in all his glory.

💬 *OG: I didn't ask for all that! :-{*

💬 *Mr. Wanna be yours: But that's how I'm comin'*

💬 *OG: What? Naked?*

💬 *Mr. Wanna be yours: Yeah! Except, more figuratively speaking. My flick wasn't to disrespect you but more so my way of showing you I have nothing to hide! This me, mami.*

💬 *OG: What do you want from me?* Oshaya was inquisitive.

💬*Mr. Wanna be yours: To convince you...* Oshaya read with a frown of confusion.

💬*OG: To convince me of what?*

💬*Mr. Wanna be yours: Of the impossible.* His response reminded her of the first kite he'd given her.

💬*OG: Okay, 346-642-8228, call me.* She did the unthinkable for the second time that night.

***

When she answered, Gambino got straight to the point— "*I'm possible, ma, and everything in life is a possibility until it's been through the fire. All I'm askin' is that you turn impossible into two words and allow me to walk through the fire to prove I'm possible.*" He cast fate to the wind.

Oshaya was silent for a moment, thinking.

"Why *me* though, Gambino? We're so different, what makes me so special?" She wanted to know.

"Have you ever heard *Big Poppa* by Biggie Smalls?"

"Yes, but what does that have to do with—"

"EVERYTHING," he cut her off. "Within his verse he states... *"A foolish pleasure, whatever/ I had to find the buried treasure, so grams I had to measure..."* See, niggas like me have believed in this perspective in every portion of our lives. With women, our hustle, life! It's crazy 'cause even after we've stumbled upon the *X* that marks the spot, we merely restart the campaign of finding *another X* that marks a different spot 'cause we're so use to hard luck, that in our minds...shid...we *anticipate* losing what we've found." He opened his chest to her and Oshaya digested it before responding.

"That's plain old crazy. That's what I don't understand about street dudes, Ridge, y'all—"

"Gambino."

"Excuse me?"

"My name is *Gambino*, but I'm listening." He smirked.

174

"Okaayy, Gambino." she giggled, loving the feel of his name rolling off her tongue. "As I was saying, what you just revealed to me is that you and most other brothas of the street culture, it's like you *begin* your journeys wanting to win, but dedicate your all to a way of life you already know the ending to." He could almost feel when she rolled her eyes! "So, in the end, it's like, if you already know the outcome of the game, and you still play, it's like you're *planning* to win, but *knowing* you're going to lose. An oxymoron! How does a winner like you play to lose, *Gambinoooo!*" She put emphasis on his name. It was cute, he chuckled. Glancing at the wall of his cell, his response was on auto.

"You're absolute, Ms. Lady"—

"*Mrs.*," she corrected.

"Yeah, we'll get to that in a minute, but to answer your question, most street niggas"— he paused to glance down the tier to make sure the coast was clear— "including myself, we, in a lot of ways, have a *cubic zirconia perspective.* We're so intrigued with the sparkle of a diamond, of our dream, *that's* all we see! The diamond is our visions of ballin'. We don't consider what *could* happen 'cause we gotta live for the day. We forgot that raw diamonds don't come out of the mud like that! Shining! We forgot that raw shit that we had to endure to dig for what one day will be a beautifully, cut stone. Shid, we just be happy we found the *X* that leads us to that mu'fucka." He chuckled. Oshaya understood even though she wanted him to see that while on the hunt for those diamonds, most men of the streets become so blindfolded by the perks *of the moment,* they begin to mistake *simulated* diamonds with raw stones.

"Gambino," she called, her tone saddened. "The crazy thing about it, and what you didn't mention is, it's only after the stone has been cut that its name changes. Then you can choose between a baguette, marquise, and even emerald cut. It's about the *type* of diamonds you're in pursuit of, 'cause a lot of men have spent their lives searching for treasures, only to wind up with a handful of cubic zirconias and fool's gold."

"Facts!" Gambino declared, loving her mind, her vibe.

"There's nothing more unattractive than a man who offers a girl *forever* but ain't got himself *a moment!*" She laughed. Then she heard a key being inserted in the door. Hurriedly ending the call, she was in time for Nigil to enter with his hands behind his back. He closed the door with his foot before leaning against it and allowing their eyes to connect. Oshaya studied him studying her.

"Nigil," she acknowledged by way of greeting. Nigil smiled sheepishly.

"Oshaya, how are you, baby?" His response left her mouth wide. It had been so long since they'd used pet names, and then, he did something that twisted her world upside down. Pulling his hands from behind his back, he revealed a beautiful bouquet of white roses. "These are for you." He smiled. Oshaya's eyes tangoed from him to the flowers, from the flowers to him before shaking her head pityingly.

"And I want a divorce," she spat.

Chapter 15
Ran Off on the Plug

Two Months Later...

Two months had passed since the faithful night they'd indulged within the forbidden, and though love had blossomed like a rose, their secret was still hidden. It was midday in the city of Houston, and the sun glared down upon the city with all it had. Yet not even the evening glare could rob Dunte or Christina of their happiness.

For weeks, Dunte had refused to allow her into his world, but Christina was adamant about seeing firsthand what his culture was made of. Dunte was hesitant because he knew she'd been sheltered her entire life. Bringing her into his world was not only dangerous, but the fact that her family had eyes *everywhere*, made the decision even more *reckless*.

"I'm not some little girl whose hand you have to hold, Dunte, you're acting like my father," Christina had pouted, so he cracked.

On that Sunday, he'd taken her on an expedition through *the bloody nickle*, Fifth Ward's moniker. He'd shown her Liberty Road, his block. Coke apartments, *Fifth Ward's Projects*. He'd even slid with her through the slab line, laughing at her wide-eyed fascination as the Lacs, Lincoln's, Rivies, and even a few Benzes, snaked through the city, gorilla pokas demanding space as they twisted and gleamed beneath the radiance of the sun. *"What's the rims? Why do all the cars have them?"* Christina was ever curious. He'd explained the city's culture and how if a car didn't have a set of 4s, 3s, or Gorilla's beneath them, in the city where DJ Screw once slung gray cassette tapes out his house, a mufucka wasn't considered lit! He'd exposed her to it all, and that's how they wound up at *Bert's,* an outside food joint that made the world's most delicious boudin. *Outside of the Pelican State!* They sat leaning against Dunte's car, smacking as they stuffed their faces.

"Ummm, this- is- so- good," she moaned, her accent making the word, *good*, sound like *guuud.* Dunte nodded his agreement before taking another bite from his seafood boudin ball.

"Umhmm," he mumbled, as he enjoyed the vision of the comings and goings of his hood. Christina placed her plate on the hood of the car before using a napkin to clean her fingers and dab at the corners of her mouth.

Though Dunte was fashionable, dripping in designer from the white Gucci original short set he wore, on down to the block Gucci kicks he rocked with the green-and-red Gucci tube socks pulled high on his calves.

She was vintage in a pale-yellow Celine sundress. The white sandals added to her down to earth vibe, and Dunte was loving it. He knew he was wrong for allowing things to run so deep, but his feelings for lady had become irrational. Yes, he was still cutting Mya! Yes, he was falling for the plug's daughter behind his back, but when Christina tossed the napkin and smiled at him, he knew he'd shoot dice with the devil if the gamble came with the possibility of making him and lady official.

"Dunte," she began, before running her fingers through her blonde streaked black hair, "I have something I need to tell you." The sudden serious look in her eyes caused him to down the rest of his food before giving her his undivided attention. She looked stressed—*worried!* Dunte frowned, wondering how she'd went from the happiest woman on earth to being at war with herself, fighting to find the words sufficient to express whatever was on her mind.

"What's up, Chris, why you lookin' like—"

"Dunte, I'm pregnant!" she blurted. Dunte's eyes grew to the size of silver dollars as his lips moved as if he were talking, but no sound came out.

"Wha-what?" he fumbled, but studied her to see if she was joking. She wasn't.

"I-I missed my period three weeks ago and-and I took a test. I—" She seemed at a loss as she again, ran a hand through her long tresses.

"Fuck!" Dunte spat, before beginning to pace. Things were just starting to jump for him. He had the north side of the city on smash and was even muscling into the tray. He, Hector, and Rosa had a good thing, and Christina being prego wasn't part of the deal. Running a hand over his braided hair, he thought of the three hundred bands he had in the backseat for Rosa, and wondered if he should just say fuck it and dip; they'd whack him off principal alone.

"Dunte, talk to me *please*," Christina pleaded. Dunte stopped mid stride and glared at her, but when she flinched, his expression softened. It wasn't her fault he couldn't control his dick.

"Damn, ma, what the fuck? I strapped up every time, how—"

"Except the *first* time," she corrected, and it was his turn to flinch.

BLAM! He spun and slapped the hood of his car, causing Christina's food to slip off and fall to the ground. "What is wrong with you! Tú act like me *wanted* this to happen," Christina screamed as a stormed converged in her orbs. Dunte placed his hands on the hood of his car, head down in thought.

"I'm sorry, baby, my fault. Just-just let me think for a second, a'ight?" His tone was low, and his mental was a tornado of scenarios.

Christina walked behind him and wrapped her arms around his waist before resting her cheek against his back.

"We can just run away. ... we have money and—"

"We *can't* outrun *the cartel*, Christina*.*" He deaded that. "I have to be a man and just step to this shit like a man. When we take this bread, I'll tell him the truth." He gritted his teeth.

"The truth?" She wanted to be clear. Christina knew how vicious her father and grandmother could be to those who'd betrayed their trust, and she wouldn't allow Dunte to become an example.

"Yeah, the truth," he clarified.

"Dunte, I don't think that's such a good—"

"Idea?" He cut her off before removing her arms and turning to face her. Dunte pulled her into his arms before using a knuckle to wipe away her tears. "Christina, I'm a gangsta *by law*, I won't run from no man," he swore, his animal staring out from his eyes. "This"—he nodded between them— "should've never happened." His words received a wounded look from her. "But"— he smirked— "I'm happy it did, you're my baby and I want you to have my child." His revelation brought a smile so big to her face, it overshadowed the sun. "But," he added, "I have to be a man and face your G-lady and father, let the chips fall where they may," he concluded, before placing a kiss on her forehead.

Releasing her, he slapped her on the ass before making his way to the driver's side and pulling the door open. "Let's get this shit over with." He nodded for her to get in the passenger seat. Watching her make her way to the other side of the car, Dunte could only hope he was making the right decision.

Skurrrt! The sound of the screeching tires snapped him out of his thoughts and his eyes shot to a brown Crown Vic that was sliding to a halt about ten feet away from them. His hand shot to the rubber grip of the H&K just as two goons jumped out, masked up on some stupid activity. Life slowed and played out in slow motion.

"Christina, get down," he shouted when he saw the sticks being aimed, and just as she heeded his words, the gunmen got active.

Bttttah!

Boom! Boom!

Both men fired different calibers of weapons. The first spray cut through part of the car where Christina had just stood. Dunte had no time to think as he turned to flee, receiving a wound to the shoulder in the process. He pitched forward and fell to his stomach from the impact of the bullet.

"Ahhh shit, mane!" he cried in pain. His tool slipped from his hand, but without having to think about it, he forged through the burning of his shoulder and reclaimed it.

The shooting had stopped, and as he crawled for safety, he heard a car door being snatched open. For the past month, shooters had been lurking and they had been on the prowl when he and Christina had loaded the black duffle stuffed with money, into the backseat.

"Got it, let's smash out, fam!" one of them declared as Dunte stumbled back to his feet. He frowned at the familiarity of the voice.

"Hold up, folk, let's finish 'em!" The other gunman shouted.

Dunte knew if he didn't get active, he'd be sleeping with the angels by the end of the showdown. He turned just in time to find

180

his shooter descending upon him with evil in his eyes, but this time he wouldn't flee from the reaper. Both men aimed and squeezed— *Boca! Boca! Boca! Boca! Boca!* Dunte was relentless with his work.

Boom! Boom! Boom! His intended killer sent fire his way with the pole. Dunte's thigh exploded at the same time the other predator's body jerked. Both men growled in pain, but the other killer must've realized he was fucking with a different type of animal, for he turned to flee.

"Uh-uh, fuck boy, where you goin'! Dunte growled through clenched teeth. He was beyond the pain—he'd tapped into his demon. *Boca! Boca! Boca! Boca!* He squeezed with the tongue of fire jumping out of the tools mouth with each squeeze of the trigger. *Boca! Boca!* He squeezed and—*bingo!*

"Arrrgh!" He heard the wounded cry of the fleeing soldier when the hollows ate through his back. Blood exploded from his shirt as the man flew forward; his weapon sliding across the asphalt. Dunte was now the hunter. He limped toward his prey while gripping his shoulder.

Skurrrt! Smoke rose from the back wheels of the Crown Vic as the driver deserted his partner and got away with the bag. Dunte made it to his prey just as the man had belly crawled, fingers grazing the glizzy— "Almost, pussy, but almost don't count," he spat, before using his foot to flip the man over.

"Arrrrugh!" his victim cried, bullets cooking his insides. Dunte knew time was of the essence and he needed to get to the business before the laws swarmed. "Pleee-please, dawg, spare-me," the wounded pleaded.

Dunte smirked through his own pain. "Who sent you fuck nigga, you shoulda thought about breathin' before you plotted on my bag! Now ya peoples left you to bleed out." He chuckled. He could see his words take root, the look in his victims eyes told the tale of being betrayed.

"It-it was Pi-Pierre's idea, I—" *Boca! Boca! Boca!* Three shots silenced him and knocked his dreadlocks out of the side of his ski mask. Dunte turned and moved as fast as he could for his car.

Pierre, huh? he thought, knowing they'd meet again, but first, *that hoe Monay "had" to put this boy up on me! She'll die first!* was his last thought before making it to his car.

***

"Divorce!" Nigil exclaimed. "Come on, Oshaya, baby, I have a problem! I know I went too far this time, but I'll do better. We can go to counseling. Therapy? He pleaded, but Oshaya was beyond working it out. She shook her head, declining all attempts.

"I've moved all my things to the spare room until I can find a place of my own. I've contacted a lawyer, Nigil, and there will be no more abuse. I'm done. She drew the line, and the look on her face was enough even if her next words had conveyed her new stance. "If you put your hands on me again, I'll kill you," she vowed. They eye wrestled and for a quick second, Oshaya saw the abuser in him surface but retract when he witnessed the resolution within her gaze.

"Alright, alright!" he relented with a raise of his hands. "Ouch," he cried in agony when he overexerted his stitches. When his eyes claimed her, they had such a fierceness that she flinched. "You're not such an angel yourself, Oshaya." He smirked. She frowned, wondering what the hell he was talking about.

"You ever heard of Gambino Mortay Ridge?" His question stole her cool, and guilt stained her face. How? she wondered. Knowingly, Nigil merely nodded, though she saw through his crushed ego.

"I don't—"

"No lies," he demanded, cutting her off. "We just need your help." The die was cast.

"Wha-what? We? What are you talking about, Nigil?"

"I'm speaking of you helping us turn Mr. Loverboy Gambino!

"Oshaya, girl are you okay?" Oshaya was summoned back to the present by Juicy snapping her fingers in front of her face. She jumped.

"Huh, what's wrong, Juicy?" she asked, bewildered.

Juicy studied her with a peculiar expression as if she was worried. "Girl, you just spaced out on us. I been callin' you for the past two minutes," she revealed. Oshaya's eyes grew in shock as she glanced around the hair salon. It was a full house, but too quiet, and as she made contact with a few of the girls, she realized the silence was due to her. She rolled her eyes. Andrea Styles was ever messy.

"Yes, I'm okay, Juicy, can't a girl *think*. Dang!" She sucked her teeth.

"Umph." Monay rolled her eyes.

"You sure, O?" Sissy asked.

"Oh, that bihh just dick deprived," Juju jested.

"I said I'm okay, damn y'all!" Oshaya was irate as she slid from her seat and made her way over to Carla's sink. "Carla, can you do my rinse, please?"

"Come on, girl, you know I got you. And don't pay these hussies no nevermind," Carla comforted, as she helped lead Oshaya's head beneath the water.

"Thank you, C," Oshaya mumbled.

"Oh, girl, don't mention it. I know how it is when you miss taking your happy *pill*. I take Zoloft, what you take, Oshaya?"

"Carla!" Oshaya cried from beneath the spray. The room exploded in laughter.

"Whaaat?" Carla asked with a giggle. "I'm just sayin'."

"Ayyyeee, y'all heard about Momo and Alula, that Taliban nigga off the southwest?" Sissy switched lanes and got the focus off her girl. All eyes shot to her.

"Uh-uh, what Momo's fast ass done did now?" Juicy was curious.

"Girrl, let me tell ya!" Sissy was extra as she stepped away from her client, holding up a finger. "Give me a second, Monica," she requested, before looking to Juicy. "Okay, so you know that crazy ass boy been killin' up everythang in the city, but somehow his pretty ass been gettin' away! Anyways, so his nut-ass done killed some boy on the Brae—in front of *everybody,* and get this"— she used her finger to twirl by her head, mimicking the *"he's crazy"* motion— "the crazy ass boy killed the man with a big gun, in broad day, and then took a handful of the poor man's dreadlocks for souvenirs!"

Juicy's mouth fell open, and, at the same time, the two women with their heads beneath the hair dryers reared back with stank expressions on their faces.

"Girl-get-ouuutt!" Juicy exclaimed, shaking her head in disbelief. "Okay, but what that have to do with Momo's triflin' assss!" She snaked her neck comically.

Sissy laughed. "Oh, boo boo, Ms. Thang is doin' the most! Alula got jammed a few days ago and now this hussy is fuckin' on pop, the man's homeboy!"

"Girrl, get ouuut!"

"Uh-huh, Juicy," Juju interjected. "That bitch is the *H* in thot! *I* almost had to snatch this hoe's bundles out when I caught her all up in Romeo's grill!"

"Biiitch!" a group of women shouted in union. Carla shook her head in disgust at the thought of Momo attempting to give up the goodies to a homosexual man.

"Ewwwwuu!" The woman in Juju's chair frowned in repulsion.

"Riiight!" Juju sucked his teeth. "Bitches are soo disrespectful these days, but the booga monsta ain't got nothin' on all this!" He turned sideways and slapped his own backside.

"Ju-Juuuuu!" the woman shouted.

"Girl, no he didn't!" Carla burst into laughter. Juicy shook her head at her friend, giggling at his attire. The petite, feminine man had his blonde hair done in a 90s finger wave, and the see-through button down shirt with only the middle button fastened was ideal to the fire-red, stretch pants. "Boyyy, where you get those boots, you killin' 'em!" Carla verbalized what Juicy and the other woman wondered.

"Girrrl, these old things!" He gushed as all eyes fell to his feet, and once he was sure he had their undivided, he pulled his pant leg up so they could get a good gander— "Monolo Blahnik, babyyy!" he sung and the women stared in envy.

"Tramp!" Sissy joked. Juju stuck out his tongue at her.

"I have a question for y'all," Carla announced, while helping Oshaya dry her hair. "We were just speakin' on Momo messin' with her dude's friend when he got locked up, and *that's* just down right triflin', buttt...," she sang the last word. "Is it really cheatin' if a woman gettin' her needs tended to while their man locked up? I mean, the nikka ain't got no business gettin' locked up no way. How can he expect me not to take care of my womanly needs?"

"Biiitch, riiight! I'm sayin'," the woman in Sissy's chair seconded.

"Like they want us to put the poonanny on ice til they get out!"

"Girrl, most of them men be havin' thirty and sixty years! You put that thang on ice *that* long, you gonna have that *ice aged* pussy!" Sissy joked.

"Bihh, ya goodies gonna be a popsicle by the time that man gets home!" Juicy added, as the room ignited with laughter and high fives. "No, but for real..." She calmed the room before using a comb to measure her client's bangs. "Be still girl, you don't wanna walk outta here with a George Jefferson," she advised, before carefully cutting her style. "*Yes,* "she spoke over her shoulder. "It's cheating *if* you and the dude are really rockin'. I mean"— she paused to make sure she didn't cut too much, and only after she was done did she resume speaking— "If you were faithful while he was home, why would you become unfaithful once he's down?" she proposed.

"Hell, 'cause the dick gone!" Juju answered.

"Amen! Baaabyy, *me* without some good dick is like Madea with that gun, girl. I'm too through," the girl in Oshaya's seat added.

"Youuu tooo," Juju exclaimed and went to high five the girl, but she gave him a funky look, like, *boy boo!* Juju reared back with a stank face of his own. "ICK, jelly, *much!"* He spat, and Juicy rolled her eyes with a giggle.

"See, *that's* what I'm sayin' about us women. You have to be *more* than what's between your legs. Dick is good, but if that's all your relationship is based on, what does that say about you as a woman?"

"That a bitch wanna nut!" Carla kept the humor strong. The ladies laughed, some nodding in agreement, and others shaking their heads, not so dick pressed.

"So, if God takes your vagina away, what will you be?"

"A miserable bitch," Sissy shot. Juicy shot her *the eye* when the laughter erupted. Sissy lifted her hands in surrender. "No, Juicy, I'm with you, girl— I just *couldn't* resist." She laughed. "But we're different type of women." She waved back and forth between her and Juicy.

"These bitches for the streets." She nodded to the girls who had been speaking.

"You just gotta have more respect for *yourself* than that, is all I'm sayin'." Juicy had become serious. "But I understand that every woman wasn't bred the same. *I'm* a real bitch and *if* I'm with a man, I'm with him! I can play with my own cootie cat. *My* nigga on lock, and before I stick a knife in his back, I'll play a random nigga *without* fuckin' him, and use his money to show my dude it's real. If all a bitch lookin' for is a wet coochie, the man you cheatin' on— 'cause yeah, *it is cheatin'*—he ain't losin' nothin' noway. Bitch, get your energy!" She rolled her eyes at the girl in her chair.

"Ugh, boujee much," the girl spat.

"Hey, y'all hear about that boy Dunte out the Fifth?" One of the girls switched lanes. Sissy frowned in thought before shaking her head.

"Uh-uh, what his crazy ass done got into?" she asked, and that's when Monay looked up from her client's hair. If anyone would have paid her any mind, they'd see the curiosity clashing with the fear in her gaze. But all eyes drifted to the girl as she rested her phone in her lap.

"I just got off the phone with my cousin and she said someone just killed Dunte and some girl and took a lot of money!" She was dramatic.

"Girl, uh-uhhh!" Carla couldn't believe her ears. The girl nodded sadly to confirm her story.

"Yes, and they saying Dunte was trying to run off on his plug!" She added her own twist to the mix. The hood always twisted and added their own flavor to another mu'fucka's tale. Juju's eyes shot to Monay, remembering the heated debate between her and Gambino, and the exchange didn't go unnoticed by Juicy.

"Monay, you sure been mute today." She smiled, dry being messy. Monay had a guilty expression on her face that seemed odd to Juicy. "Girl, what's wrong with you? Why you lookin' like that?" She wanted to know.

"Un-un, y'all not gonna play dig into Monay's cool air. What we need to be talkin' about is how this bitch done let that nothin'-ass nigga drive her crazy!" She pointed at Oshaya. All eyes shot to the woman indicated and Oshaya was done.

"Bitch, I'm tired of you always pickin'," she began, while pushing the hair dryer up. She shot to her feet, *on go!* Juju hurriedly restrained her.

"Oshaya!" Juicy demanded.

"No, bitch." Carla laughed. We need to be talkin' about how *you* fuckin' your baby daddy homeboy." She poured more mess on top of mess.

"Girl, shut up, who she fuckin'!" Juju jumped in. Monay gave Carla an evil glare. She'd confided in her 'cause they were tight, but not thinking it was a big deal, Carla was spilling the beans.

"She's doing the dude, Pierre, and—"

"Carla, shut up," Monay cut her off, but the cat was out the bag.

"Uh-hh, Monay, I know you didn't!" Juicy couldn't believe the drama. All eyes shot to Sissy, it was common knowledge that she still had feelings for Pierre, and before anyone could stop her, she'd went ape shit. Tossing her styling comb to the floor, she was up on Monay in seconds.

"Bitch. I'm. Sick. Of. You!" she spat, as she pummeled the girl.

"Bitch," Monay growled while dropping her head and swinging wild, and with a wild, desperate reach, she grabbed a handful of Sissy's bundles and things got crazy. She got in a few licks until— *BAM!*

"Uh-uh, bitch, let her hair go," Oshaya spat, before tearing into that ass. Both her and Sissy commenced to beating her unmercifully as the other women attempted to break it up.

187

Juicy stood back, watching. *The bitch deserves this ass whoopin',* she thought, as she began to mentally tally the cost she'd charge them for tearing up her shit.

CHAPTER 16
Facebook Messenger

A Week Later...

"Ridge, you have an attorney visit, be ready in 10 minutes," the CO shouted from down the tier. Gambino shot up in bed, surprise splashed across his face.

"Look out, fam, let me hit you back," he hurriedly spoke into the phone, before disconnecting without waiting for a response.

Slipping from the bunk, he stashed the device in his hideaway, all the while thinking ... *Lil bro came through on the lawyer. I love that lil nigga!* He smiled. *All I need is a time cut and I'll be Gucci with that,* he told himself. He hadn't heard from Dunte since his last visit, and though he'd been banging his line ever since he'd snatched up his new toy, *the phone,* he wasn't much worried about his younger brother not answering. He knew the pros and cons of being *the man* to see, and merely figured Dunte was getting it in with the Mexicans. By the time he'd gotten dressed, the officer was at his cell with his cuffs out.

"Ready?" he asked. Gambino nodded and turned to be cuffed.

"Ready as I'll ever be"—

***

Mirage stood out on the roof of his building, gazing out at the setting sun. Beside him was a drying canvas he'd just completed, and though he couldn't *see* it, within his mind he envisioned it perfectly. The canvas, the paint, the art! Upon splashes of red, he'd overlapped long strokes of gold, and dramatic slashes of African green, and with brown paint he'd created feminine and masculine *silhouettes* entangled within a vicious position of love making. Yet, in the background of the paint, he'd used an artist's pencil to intricately manifest a light outline of a roaring lion, its mane wild and its teeth sharp. The picture was beautiful, and to cap off its originality, just beneath the depiction of fornication, he'd used white paint to form three bold letters—*WAR!*

Seventeen stories above the earth, he stood barefoot in his favorite painter's jeans and an unbuttoned dress shirt. Mirage gazed out at what he couldn't see and allowed his mind to see for him. The sun was high above the city's skyline, causing the tall building to shimmer silver beneath its glare. As he turned to retrieve his saxophone from the futon he'd had installed up there, the man had the perfect melody for the mood.

Making his way to the ledge of the building where only a waist high slab of concrete was the only barrier between him and a seventeen story free fall, the wind was powerful at that altitude and there would be no survival of an accidental fall.

Yet, with the sun, glaring down upon him like one of God's eyes, he placed the single-reed mouthpiece to his lips and allowed his eyes to drift closed. Taking a deep breath, he blew his oxygen into the instrument, his fingers familiar with its anatomy. He blew a melody of a piece he'd composed, dubbed *"Where Passion Lies"*. The temp was reminiscent of Tank's *"Can't Make You Love Me"*, but more saucy as he made the sax cry.

Within his mind's eyes he could vividly see the painting he'd just manifested. Poetry in motion! Within his mental, the silhouettes came to life, waging passionate *war* as man and woman connected from their bottom halves. *War!* Man *fighting* to call down her lower storm, woman rotating her feminine *weapon,* determined to pull his soul from his sword and up into her womb. *War!* Swearing, two silhouettes battling for dominance, whomever came first would be the loser. Mirage blew his spirit into the golden saxophone as he envisioned the silhouettes become he and Oshaya… *at war!*

***

"That's our offer, Ridge, take it or leave it!" Berkley punctuated his point by sitting back in his seat and crossing his arms over his chest. Gambino sat on the other side of the table, staring at the auburn-haired, green-eyed man as if he had two heads. What they'd told him was an attorney visit had turned out to be a visit from someone he would've never expected—*the CIA!* The man had run his spiel along with the reasons for his visit, and as they faced off, two men from two different sides of the law, Gambino surprised the man. Bursting into laughter, tears came to his eyes, and he slapped the top of the table for emphasis. The look on Berkeley's face fed the fire, but the White man must've missed the humor.

"A'ight, bruh, a'ight." Gambino lifted a calming hand as he tried to regain his composure. "Look ..."— he sucked in a fresh breath before using the back of his hand to wipe the tears away— "you got the wrong man, my dude. I ain't never heard of no Tom Norris, who this boy is? *Chuck* Norris lil brother or somethin?" He tried his hand at comedy and though Gambino burst into laughter, Agent Berkley's face was as placid as a swamp before an alligator explodes from it in pursuit of its prey.

His green eyes were penetrating as he pulled a folder from his briefcase and slapped it on to the table. Gambino's laughter eased into a chuckle as the man flipped the folder open and slid five black-and-white photos from it. Sliding them toward Gambino, the agent nodded.

"Take a look, and then we can have a laugh *together!*" He smiled as Gambino's eyes fell to the photos.

"What's thi—" He started to say before his focus landed on the photo of him and Tom Norris standing in a parking garage in Paris. Another depicted him and *Tamia* making a toast at the charity event. Others were miscellaneous, but still frightening, because they weren't merely evidence of his familiarity with the European Tom Norris, but they were also *evidence* that he'd possibly been the last to see Tamia *alive.*

His heart raced in his chest, but he kept his face as stone as the faces displayed at Mount Rushmore. When his vision lifted to the agent, the man burst into *mock* laughter, slapping the table just as Gambino had done moments before. Gambino could tell the man was mocking him, and when his laughter suddenly died and he

191

stood from his seat, Gambino knew things were about to get funky like a donkey.

Berkley's eyes became slits as he placed his hands on the table and leaned forward. "Listen here you little punk. This isn't some sort of little game! We're CIA, not incompetent HPD who could only give you *a portion* of what you truly deserve. We're not the FBI whom you evaded! No, Gambino, we're much worse." He smirked wickedly before making his way over to Gambino's side of the table and taking a seat on its edge. "We know you were hired by Mr. Norris to do the *promiscuous* Tamia Amedeo. We know it was you and your people who pulled the job on her husband! Oh, we know it all, son, and—"

"If you know so much, fuck you talkin' to *me* for, playboy? Book me! "Gambino cut him off with a smirk before lifting his cuffed wrists. When Berkley merely stared at the steel brackets, Gambino chuckled while nodding his head. "Like I said, White boy, I don't know shit, and any further questions, let's get my lawyer on deck." He G'd up. Again, there was a stare off before Agent Berkley smirked and nodded.

"Suit yourself." He shrugged before gathering the pictures and making his way back to his side of the table. "It's sad," he said, "so much talent, so young," he acknowledged, before he gave Gambino a sad shake of the head. "You're *never* getting out for prison, son, and after you're finished with this sentence, we're going to get you, Gambino, and you've never been to a prison like ours. Twenty-four hour lockdown, son." He smirked as he gathered his briefcase. "Or"— he headed for the door— "you can help us and we'll get ya home in a few *weeks!*" That seemed to get Gambino's attention and he sat up a little straighter in his seat.

"Fuck you talmbout, *in a few weeks?*" He had to be sure he'd heard correctly. Berkley paused at the door, and though he didn't turn to look at him, Gambino could tell he had a smirk on his face.

"Yeah, if you agree to help us, we'll get you outta here in *weeks.*"

"How?" Gambino was curious. Agent Berkley chuckled.

192

"We're the CIA, Gambino. We have very unique ways of getting what we want. Think about it, son. We'll be in touch." The man smirked before exiting.

***

DUNTE AWOKE IN THE WORSE PAIN he'd ever felt in his life! His legs felt like they were on fire and his shoulder made him want to cry. "Where—"

"Baby," Mya cried out, before rushing over to him and smothering him with kisses.

"Arrrugh," he growled in agony when she'd aggravated his wounds.

"Oh, I'm sooo sorry, bae. I'm so happy you awake I completely forgot about"— she paused, and her eyes watered at the sheer thought of almost losing him.

They'd been on the outs for the past few weeks since he'd almost domed her, but her heart was his for the taking. So, when he'd stumbled upon her mother's porch the day he'd gotten stung for the duffle, her wall cracked down the middle and she allowed love to conquer her anger. Though she knew he'd only shown up there because her mother was an RN, Mya didn't care. She was just happy to have her dude come home.

Luckily, the two .40 cal. bullets hadn't hit any major arteries and they'd made a clean exit; otherwise, Dunte would've had to be taken to the hospital. Yet, he'd begged her mother not to call it in. He'd begged her to stitch him up and allow him to compensate her, and though the woman was a God-fearing woman, she loved Dunte like a son and felt his plight.

Now, a week later, here he was, healing from the wounds and blood loss. Mya watched everything come back to him and within his recollections, a look of utter horror splashed across his face. Mya frowned— "Bae, what's wron—"

"Where's my car?" He cut her off.

"Wha-what? *Your car*? It's outside, Dunte, where else wou—"

193

"Fuck," he muttered. He tried to sit up in the bed, but pain raged throughout his body causing him to fall back against the pillow. "RRRRugh!" he grumbled through clenched teeth.

"Dunte!" Mya was lost. "What the—"

"Help me up." Again, he cut her off. This time succeeding in sitting up but growling in the process.

"Dunte!" Mya demanded with some spazz in her tone. Dunte's orbs shot to her. "What-the-hell is going on! She wasn't trying to hear it. Dunte's eyes were dark as something evil evolved within his pupils.

"I gotta get out of here, Mya, it's not safe here," he exposed.

"What? What are you talkin' about, dude? *Why* isn't it safe *here?"* Mya needed understanding.

"'Cause if I don't get lost, the cartel is gon' find me *here,* and they'll whack every mu'fucka up in here"— he paused to try and slip from the bed— *"everybody* linked to me!" he revealed.

***

It was 10 p.m. and Gambino laid on his back, hands interlocked behind his head, deep in thought as he stared up at the ceiling. *"Help us and we can have you out in a few weeks—you're never going home, it's sad, so much talent, so young..."* The agent's words played in his mind like a mantra. Gambino had been a live wire his entire life, and he never even considered rocking with the opposite side of the line that divided crooks from the pigs.

He had been bred from the slums of *Liberty Road,* and he'd come up under some certified fifth wardians— Bo Eddie, Wolf-Man, LeLe, Randy T, and Big Hurb– all were legends, all were solid, and all were *conmen.* Yet, they were his guys, his mentors. *What would Wolf do?* he wondered, but before the answer could come to him, his phone vibrated beside him. He retrieved his peep-mirror and ensured the tier was clear before turning his attention to the device and bringing the screen to life. He smirked when his no-tifications alerted him to the Facebook Messenger message. He tapped the icon and read the DM:

OG: WYD? Oshaya's messages were simple but revealed so much to a playa like him.

Mr. Wanna be yours: Thuggin', just a lot on my top. He hit back.

OG: Yours too? Been a long week, need God to be a fence!

Mr. Wanna be yours: Lol! He responded with the praying hands emoji, followed by the wondering face emoji.

OG: What's so funny?

Mr. Wanna be yours: God being a fence… you're an old soul. He texted.

OG: So they say.

Mr. Wanna be yours: What's on your mind?

OG: A lot! :-(She revealed, and there was a brief pause before Gambino responded, but when he did, she frowned.

Mr. Wanna be yours: Where yo' husband?

OG: Ex-husband! And he's in his room, I think.

Mr. Wanna be yours: Ex? "His" room? I'm lost :-/

OG: Long story! Too long actually, but to sum it up, we're getting a divorce and we're now sleeping in separate rooms.

Mr. Wanna be yours: So you're in a room, alone?
His response received a roll of the eye from her. *I'm not sending this boy no coochie pic!* She'd concluded, not knowing that what Gambino had in mind was behind door number two.

Mr. Wanna be yours: ???? He DM'd

OG: Ummm, nosey much! Lol! Yes, I'm in my room "alone", Y?

Mr. Wanna be yours: Let me take ya stress away…
His next DM brought a strange look to her pretty face. *Hell?* She wondered.

OG: Negro, I'm not sending you any pics on that phone, nor am I sending any nude pics! Period!

Mr. Wanna be yours: Let me take ya stress away!
He reiterated, and after a brief pause, she fucked up. She asked *a playa* a question he could play with.

OG: How? She inquired. She stared at the screen, searing for the small dots indicating the other person was typing. But instead of that, she saw something much more demanding! *Incoming call* flashed across the screen, a green and red button flashed for the options to accept or decline the *video* call from Messenger. Her lips parted in a surprised *"O"*, in shock as her eyes fell to her attire. She was fresh out of the shower, curly hair pulled into a messy ponytail, and all she wore was an old button-up dress shirt and thong. The shirt was unbuttoned, revealing her juicy breasts and belly ring. "Oh my God," she groaned, as the phone stopped ringing. She exhaled a grateful breath, but the man was persistent!

The phone rang again and there was a decision to make. To her surprise, Oshaya hurriedly slipped beneath the comforter, and once her heart slowed its gallop, she hit the green button— *accept!* Gambino appeared on the screen—a real playa on deck! He smirked victoriously at the sheepish smile on her face.

"Oh my Goddd." She giggled. "Why'd you do this?"

Gambino chuckled. "I wish I could step into your mind."

She shook her head. "No you don't, my thoughts are ugly right now," she informed.

Gambino studied her face on the screen. "If I could, I'd tie a rope from your mental and slide down it until I reached the slopes of your heart."

Oshaya smiled. "And what would you do once you reached your destination, Mr. Ridge?"

Gambino's face was as unreadable as a book written in Chinese. "I'd climb inside it and disconnect whatever it is that keeps your heart and mind in alliance, 'cause the heart wasn't created to *think,* Oshaya, but when a mu'fucka *teaches* it to, it becomes the thoughts of a love gone wrong that makes you fear trusting in *chance* encounters.

"*Chance encounters,* huh?"

"If I would've never been on lock, and you hadn't got sent to this unit I'm on, we would've never met, and our lives would have led us in different directions. Yet,"— he shrugged before pointing at himself, then her— "our decisions led us to this intersection of *chance* and that's why our *encounter* is made for a nigga like me. Get it?" he asked, and received a seductive smile from her.

"Kinda."

"Meaning, we need to give our encounter a chance. *Chance encounter,* mama, an encounter that may lead to something promising if given the chance."

"Cute," she giggled. "But promises are easily broken. I've had enough broken ones to know." Her eyes were sad. Gambino G'd up for lady and hated to see a diamond in the hands of an undeserving man.

"Yeah, that's facts, *but* the difference between *a promise* and something being *promising,* is that a promise requires you having to place faith in *a person* to keep their word, whereas, something promising depends on the teamwork making the dream work." He smirked.

"You're too much, Mr. Ridge, but I don't think this is what you meant about taking my stress away?" she asked. An arched brow lifted curiously. Gambino chuckled before rocking her socks.

"Let me make love to you."

Oshaya almost dropped her phone. "Excuse me? Boy—"

"Let me make love to you," Gambino repeated.

Oshaya's lips moved, but no words came out. As she studied him, she could see his energy. Pulling the comforter up to her chin, all smiles were gone.

"Gambino, I like you, but I don't move like this, besides…" She paused, giving him eyes of uncertainty. Truth was, she'd felt this vibe for a while, and on a more carnal note, since the day she'd stumbled upon him taking a leak, she hadn't been able to erase the salacious image from her mind. "There's no way you can do such a thing. I'm not coming in no cell, I—"

"Take your clothes off." Gambino's interruption made her eyes grow wide.

"Wha-what!? Nigga you must be crazy!" She laughed until Gambino momentarily disappeared from the screen. There was movement but when he came back into view, Oshaya's mouth fell open. He'd propped the phone up against the bars so he wouldn't have to hold it. And standing up before her, as bare as a room without furniture, there he stood.

"Boyyyy!" was all Oshaya could mumble as she watched in fascination as the man began to stroke himself into erection. Without her consent, Oshaya's body betrayed her. Her nipples hardened against the fabric of the shirt and her ocean began to overflow. She became sticky, and as she watched the screen, she was lost within the act of erotica.

"Gam-bino?" she purred. He began to stroke himself faster.

"Take-off your clothes…," he gritted through self-pleasure. "Let me see that—"

"I cannn't," she whined, but her eyes were held prisoner by his gangsterisms. His dick had swelled to its full eight inches, and it was fat. Oshaya was done! Pushing the comforter away, she whispered, "I don't have any on." Then she revealed herself with a sexy smirk.

Gambino's eyes detoured her thickness, all five foot four of it. "Use the pillow to prop the phone up at the end of the bed," he instructed. She obeyed. "Take that shit off," he demanded, after she had the phone balanced perfectly and had scooted back until her back was against the headboard.

Oshaya shed the shirt before peeling the white thong down her thick thighs. Now as naked as a newborn, she reclaimed her position. Spreading her thick thighs, her flower was on full display. As

Gambino slowed his stroke to admire her frame, he had to fight against his urge to roar. Oshaya's shape was reminiscent of a *younger* Pinky, except her body was all one tone— *red*! Her nipples were chocolate and full, and when his vision captured her Garden of Eden, Gambino ran his tongue over his lips.

"Damn, ma," he groaned. His masculinity was as hard as the concrete that held him captive. Erotically, Oshaya bit down on the corner of her bottom lip, *too* familiar with the art of seduction.

"What now?" she purred, eyes half-mast.

"Massage that pussy for me..." Gambino was raw. Oshaya reached between her legs and slowly did as she'd been told.

"Like this?" She sounded like an innocent little girl. "Like-this, *daddy?*"

She moaned as she picked up the pace.

"Damn, baby," was all Gambino could growl as his stroke became feverish. Oshaya matched his speed and her fingers rotated as powerful as a whirlwind.

The pleasure was a roaring wave that fell over her like she was a surfer who couldn't outrun a giant wave of water upon the waters in Honolulu. With her head thrust back in ecstasy and her mouth ajar in a silent cry, Oshaya became a captive of the building volcano within her.

"Ouuu," she cried out, "Ahhh..."

"Look at me," Gambino's demand rose the wave of his own dance with that nut. "Watch this-this dick, Oshaya!" Oshaya had to fight to right her head, battling even harder to focus her eyes.

"Daad-dyyy," she cry-moaned, trying to keep her voice low.

"Faster!" Gambino demanded. "Work that pussy faster for me," he growled, as his stomach muscles tightened. Yet, he jacked faster. Oshaya watched. Watching his rapid pace, her pearl throbbed beneath her fingers. Her thighs shook. Her world shook.

"Ooooohhh myyyyyy!" She sounded hoarse as she bucked her hips up into her rotating fingers. Gambino watched her peach juice coat her fingers as thick as lotion. "I'm a-abou-about-to-cum-cum-cummm, papiiii!" She lost the war with focus as her eyes squeezed shut, toes balled up, and honeydew began to shoot out of her in quick squirts.

It fucked Gambino up and the vision led his spirit from his nut sack and it spilled all over the floor. Facebook Messenger is a savior!

CHAPTER 17
The Boy and the Pond

10 a.m. The Next Morning

"Ridge, pack your shit, you're going back to your old cell!" The C.O's order penetrated Gambino's slumber. His eyes cracked open, fatigue threatening to pull him back down into a dreamless sleep. "Ridge, did you hear me?" the C.O shouted from down the run, and Gambino fought through the fog.

"A'ight, man, yeah, I hear you," he responded, suddenly remembering he had a third degree felony in his possession. He fought to remember the night before, and when it came to him, he smiled. *That pussy had rocked him to sleep!* He slipped from the bed and took care of his hygiene before taking a morning leak. He didn't know why they were cutting him loose, but he was sure it had something to do with Tay's inside guy.

"Ready?" The CO appeared at his cell unexpectedly.

"Damn, Brown, give me enough time to pack my shit," he spat irritably.

The C.O glared. "You have ten minutes, motherfucker!" he demanded, before storming off.

"Gambino shook his head. "Dick sucka!"

"I heard that!" The CO shouted.

***

The sun had just awakened and stepped out onto its porch, but Oshaya had awaken moments earlier to watch it rise. Besides, that day, she hoped would be one of the happiest ones of her life. But, as she turned the Lexus down Colorado Drive in Spring, Texas, she allowed herself to be sucked down into a moment of melancholy... *You always think you better than somebody! I don't want to use your funky jump rope anyway,"* her sister had screamed on that faithful day.

"Girl, I'm about to—" Oshaya had taken a threatening step *forward to her, and the girl had taken off running toward their home, yelling for their father as if she'd been shot!* Pulling the car to the curb she'd spent her first sixteen years of life within, Oshaya smiled at the memory of the last time she'd been there. Since she'd been back in the United States, rescued from the life of White slavery, Oshaya had drove passed it, *wanting* to stop, but never having the Will power to do so.

Yet, that day would be different, so much different. And as she killed the ignition, her mouth dropped open! *This is not how I'd planned this,* she thought, at the sight of a middled-aged Caucasian woman who was out watering her rose bushes. She had auburn hair piled atop her head and she was just as beautiful as she'd been when Oshaya had last set eyes upon her.

Hearing the car pull to the curb, the lady paused her watering and glanced curiously at the beautiful car. Oshaya watched her from the other side of the tinted windows, before her eyes fell to her own attire. She'd opted for an off-white, chic pant suit, complete with a white-framed pair of sunshades, and white heels.

"Now or never Oshaya," she whispered to herself, before taking a deep breath and pushing her door open. The older woman watched with a raised brow as she slipped out of the car and closed the door.

Six years was enough time to change a generation, and as the woman studied the stranger in the expensive clothing, she wondered who she was and what she wanted. Oshaya walked up the driveway, seemingly confident, but internally she was a hurricane!

"Umm-hi," the white woman greeted with a wave. "May I help you?" she asked when Oshaya stopped five feet from her. "Do I know you?" she proposed, with a concerned expression on her face. That's when Oshaya pulled the large glasses from her face. The older woman studied her, staring into eyes identical to her own. The watering can fell from her hand.

"I would hope so." Oshaya finally found her voice. Tears baptized her vision, and at the same time, the older woman's curious expression melted away and shock slowly eased into her features as recognition began to seep in. First, her mouth fell open. "Hi, Mom, can't you-you recognize your own daughter? *Please,* remember me," Oshaya cried, suddenly feeling like that same sixteen year old who depended on her mother for everything. Salt water strayed from her face as the older woman's eyes became twin ponds, twin ponds that still reflected disbelief. Nonetheless, she took timid steps until only a foot separated them. And lifting a hand to the side of Oshaya's face, the woman remembered.

"Shayniece?" she whispered the birth name she'd given her child—the name Shay had abandoned in Mexico to become *Oshaya.* As her other hand touched the side of her daughter's face, she cried for times lost. She'd cried for her husband who died from a heart attack a year earlier, and finally, she cried because that's all she could do. Cry! They both cried. "My beautiful, child," she whispered. "I-I still have your sandal," she revealed. Speechless, Oshaya nodded her understanding. She knew she was speaking of the shoe she'd lost when she'd been snatched away. At that moment, the door to the house opened and out ran a beautiful little girl.

"Granma! Granma, look," she shouted gleefully, as she held up the cell phone her mother had gotten her. "It's new, Gran"—the child paused when she noticed the strange woman standing with her grandmother. "Who is she Granma?" the child asked, and to everyone's surprise, the older woman fainted. "Granma!" the girl cried, before her eyes shot to Oshaya. "What you do to my—"

"Khloe, girl, why you doin' all this yellin'? I told you I got a headache," the child's mother demanded when she appeared in the doorway.

When Oshaya looked to the woman with the oh-so-familiar voice, her mouth fell open and *she* almost joined her mother on the ground. With a black eye and puffy lip, the woman glared.

"What the fuck are you doin' at my mama's house, bitch! Oh, you came for the smoke?" *Monay* spat, slipping out of her sandals. *My mother's house! My-mother's house!* The words echoed within Oshaya's head. She shook her head in disbelief as she thought about her younger sister who she hadn't seen since they were children.

"Monay, I—" was as far as she got before Monay rushed her, wanting her revenge for the ass whoopin' she'd taken. So, Oshaya obliged, *while their mother was still napping beneath the kiss of the sun.*

***

"I'm cummming, niiigil, she screamed in ecstasy as Nigil pumped in and out of her with urgency.

"RRRugh," he growled, when his release surged from his scrotum. And just as his seed filled his penis, he exploded into the protective shield of the condom. "Fuuuck!" he roared. Patreses' legs appeared to be frozen in the *V* position, her toes throwing up gang signs as her orgasms raged through her. And only after the rage of the ocean fell into a peaceful roll, did she gaze up at her best friend's man. Nigil rolled away from her—satiated.

"Damn," he murmured. Patrese smirked seductively before reaching over and gripping his flaccidness.

"See," she smiled, before slipping the condom off him and stroking him tenderly. "No more stress!" She giggled at the strained expression of pleasure on his face as she massaged his tender member.

"You're ferocious, Treasey," he gritted as she felt his limp flesh began to refill with blood.

"So," she purred. "Why won't you leave her? I mean…"

She paused as she squeezed his dick head. "I cook and clean, and my pussy better than hers, right?" Her tone was seductive as she slid down his body until she was face to dick.

"Good Lord, womannn!" Nigil squirmed as Patrese began to lick her juices away from him. "Muthof"—

"You said you told her you wanted a divorce." Her lips wrapped around the head of his soldier. "Hmmm?" she mumbled over a mouthful of his flesh. Patrese had low-key *always* envied Oshaya.

She hated that Oshaya seemed to always be everyone's favorite, and she resented the fact that Oshaya, after all they'd been through, had incurred the house, the successful man, and even the Lexus! Patrese envied, period! So, when Nigil called that morning and revealed that Oshaya had left and he missed her, she wasted no time burying her insecurities between his and Oshaya's sheets.

204

As she swallowed him, his iPhone rang on the nightstand, and in attempt at discouraging him from answering, she sucked harder. She bobbed her head faster and allowed saliva to flow freer, but to no avail. As she performed, Nigil reached over and retrieved his phone.

"Damnn," he growled, as he gazed at the screen. "Wa-wait, baby, it's-my ... it's-my boss." He fought through her determination, but Patrese was relentless in her quest.

Her head bobbed quicker, causing his toes to curl, but Nigil still touched a finger to the *accept* button. "Yeah, umm, it-it's really not a g-good time for me," he spoke through clenched teeth. Whatever was being said, Patrese could tell he was trying to focus, and she smiled inwardly at the power she had over him— *bad bitches rock,* she thought, just as the veins in his nature swelled in her mouth. The throb of his release was demanding as she jerked it to the surface.

Nigil's explosion was so powerful, it shot in the back of her throat and damn near choked her with its thickness. She gagged before swallowing what she could while popping his flesh out of her mouth and jacking the remaining juice from his fountain. It was a mess, and whatever was being said on the other end of the phone, Nigil could only nod in response as if the caller could see him. Patrese smirked at a job well done before slipping out of the bed and gathering her clothes and purse from the floor.

Nigil was still nodding vigorously, toes balled up like the claws of an eagle, as she made her way to the bathroom.

***

"Now look here," Teresa, Oshaya's and Monay's mother demanded, allowing her eyes to bounce from one to the other. After she'd regained consciousness, to her horror, she found the girls brawling like two wild cats.

Now, as they all sat around the dining table, Oshaya at one end, Monay at the other, and their mother standing, there was much to figure out. Teresa's eyes were narrowed as she stared daggers into Monay. "This is no way to act in front of your daughter, Ashley Monay Jakes!" she demanded.

"That bitch started it when—"

"Watch your mouth in my house, young lady! I raised you better than that! And you," she began, even though her eyes softened when they captured Oshaya. "You're the eldest sister, and-and…" Her voice cracked and her eyes watered. She still couldn't believe, her first born, the beautiful little girl who'd been snatched from in front of their home at sixteen years old was sitting at the table they'd once sat at and ate dinner as a family. Oshaya had revealed to them what had transpired that faithful day she'd been abducted, and though Monay glared, Oshaya saw through to the little girl who cried her eyes out on that Fourth of July. "We missed you." Teresa found her voice.

"Umph, speak for yourself," Monay spat, with a roll of her eyes.

"Ashley Monay," their mother demanded. Monay sucked her teeth. Only family referred to her by her first name, hence, why Oshaya hadn't registered whom she was before that day. Teresa's glare rolled from her, and back to Oshaya. "Now, I'm sooo grateful you're back, Shayniece, but—"

"*Oshaya*, Mom, my name is *Oshaya* now. I haven't gone by Shayniece in years," she corrected. Teresa lifted a brow and realized her daughter had grown into a beautiful diva, and she was proud.

"You can call yourself whatever you choose, child. You're grown *now.*" She smiled. "But to your mother"—she pointed to herself— "you'll always be my baby, and *I* named you *Shayniece.*" She laughed when Oshaya rolled her eyes with a smile on her face— it was as if she'd never left. "Now, I don't know what happened between you and your sister, but I'm gonna give you two some space so you can figure it out. When I return, I want to see my girls carrying themselves like *sisters* and not like common hoodrats," she demanded, before making her way to Monay and hugging her. However, when she got to Oshaya, she paused. Uncertainty was evident within her gaze until her eldest daughter gave her a reassuring smile. Teresa was the happiest woman in the world as she hugged her before kissing her softly on the head. *Gerald, I wish you were here to see this, your child is beautiful!* She mentally vibed with her late husband. The girls smiled at her, but as soon as she made her exit, all pretenses were abandoned!

"Bitch, I should drag your red ass across this floor for how you and that tramp, Sissy, did me!" Monay half rose out of her seat. Oshaya didn't fear no ghost, but now that she knew Monay was actually the same little girl she'd once loved more than life, she couldn't bring herself to continue the war.

"Peace, little sister." Smiling, she held up the peace sign.

"Fuck you, bitch, my sister died six years ago!" Monay was stubborn.

"Maybe"—Oshaya began, eyes watering— "maybe that wouldn't have happened if you hadn't left me to go tattle to daddy." She knew it was a low blow but the girl was working her last nerve. Monay's mouth fell open in shock. Her eyes filled without her consent. Until that moment, she hadn't fully believed that the beautiful woman she'd grown to know as Oshaya was actually *her* Shay, but the words she'd just used were the only proof she needed.

"I-I didn't leave you." Her eyes finally melted salt water as she remembered the day her life flipped. The day those two popsicles melted on the ground. "I had popsicles for us, Shay, but they'd stolen you." She sobbed.

***

After she'd slipped the condom from his masculinity, Patrese had made sure to pinch the opening closed so there'd be no escape of his seed, and as soon as she had a chance, she fled to the bathroom. The shower ran hot, filling the room with steam as she lay naked on the tile floor, legs spread in a *V* position. She'd flushed the condom after using the turkey baster to suck up every drop of his seed, and that's why she found herself on the floor of the bathroom, skin damp with sweat as she pushed the instrument as deep as it would go into her womb.

"I love you, Nigil," she whispered, as she felt his juices fill her. Patrese wasn't naive, she *knew* Nigil loved Oshaya and never had plans to leave her, so her *Plan B* was in full effect. She giggled as she slipped the turkey baster from between her lower lips and brought it to her lips—sucking the remnants of Nigil's juice free.

207

"Please, God let me get pregnant with his child ... please!" She prayed.

***

C.O BROWN HELD THE DOOR open for him as Gambino made his exit from the cell. "Either you're one lucky son of a bitch, or you're a good snitch! I don't know how you beat—"

"Watch your mouth, dick sucka, before I crack your jaw!" Gambino spat, before stepping up into the man's personal. Gritting his teeth, Gambino dropped the little bag of personal property he'd been allowed to have in lockup. Totally disregarding the fact he had a felony in his possession, he reared back to slap fire from the man's face, but the morning janitor salvaged crack pride.

"Naw, young blood, tame ya flame until ya back up on ya game," someone gripped his wrist and warned. Gambino's eyes shot to Waco Shawn, a convict who had made his bones in and outside the prison walls. "Let 'em make it, daddy, the peon don't mean no harm." He saved the bar. Both men's eyes shot to the officer, the man appeared unshaken, with one hand down by his *bear spray*, but it's within a man's eyes that animals find the hearts of men. Dude had more pussy than the Kardashian sisters! Gambino reclaimed his cool and nodded to the OG who'd just saved him from making an already oppressing situation more *anti-playa*. Nodding his agreement, his eyes swollowed the lesser man, but it was Waco Shawn who spoke.

"I told ya, Brown, you can't be talkin' reckless to *everybody*, 'cause *everybody* ain't pussy. One of these young boys gonna tend to their bidness." He nodded toward Gambino. CO Brown saw that the beast had been calmed and he regained his *false* dignity.

"Well, I ain't scared, motherfucker, what you wanna do?" he challenged. Gambino's face instantly balled up into that warriors mask, but Waco Shawn chuckled with a calming nod.

"Let me talk to 'em, Brown. Give us a moment," he bargained for both mens' sake. *Visibly* thankful for the reprieve, the officer put some space between him and the threat.

"Yeah, just like I thought, you're nothin' but a coward!" he spat. "Ten minutes, Tillis, ten." The country bumpkin held up *seven* fingers. Gambino laughed, drawing the man's attention. "Talk to ya boy, Tillis, talk to him, 'cause I almost fucked him up," the CO declared, before going about his business. Waco Shawn chuckled as Gambino retrieved his bag.

"Emotions are a dangerous thang to a playa in the game, lil nigga," he acknowledged, before stepping into the cell Gambino had spent the last month plus, within. With a towel and spray bottle filled with liquid bleach, he began to wipe the walls and toilet down. Gambino respected the OG who was raised on Beto Unit under the set with OG Baby Cash.

"Nigga, I ain't got no feelin's," Gambino responded. Again, Waco Shawn chuckled.

"I said *emotions,* but feelings are all the same, and why niggas always actin' like they ain't got no *feelin's? Anger* is a feelin', my boy, and we just saw you almost become a victim to that. You ain't ever been sad? Anxious? Happy? In love? Been punched? All that shit is feelin's, Gambino."

"Yeah, well," Gambino began, as he watched the man strip the mattress. Waco Shawn glanced back at the younger brother, and Gambino shrugged indifferently. "You right, but my respect came too hard for me to let some fuck boy, or *anybody* come snatch it away. I'm a gangsta by law, Yard Style." He addressed brothaman by his *Beto Unit* name. Waco Shawn smirked, nodding his understanding.

"G, if these folks were to let you out *right now,* what's your plans, playboy?" The question caught Gambino off his note and though his answer was on auto pilot, it was typical.

"Ima get to the money, what else I'm 'pose to do?"

"But how? How you gonna get to it?" Waco Shawn pressed.

"I got my ways, Waco Shawn, but what's the bidness? I know you not twenty-one questionin' me just to pass time." Gambino studied him as Waco Shawn finished his task and leaned against the wall with an intense gaze.

"You right, Gambino, sho' ya right." He chuckled. "See, a lot of boys pray, prey, cry, and play for another chance at shining, but if given the chance, you know what they'd do, lil brotha?"

"Shid, probably fuck it off, niggas can't think." Gambino chuckled.

"And *you* can?" Waco Shawn's response semi-fried Gambino's fuse. He frowned, not knowing if the OG was talking down, or merely had a bigger piece of game to reveal. So, he gazed at the man eye-to-eye without blinking or needing to think.

"Fuckin' right I can think, OG, swift and sufficiently too."

Waco Shawn smirked. "So, if you can think so swiftly, *why'd* you just reveal your hand to me." He pointed to himself. "By revealing to me that you *can* think?" Waco Shawn chuckled as Gambino's face closed up, visibly becoming as unreadable as a book without words. "A true playa, a *thinker* knows never to let on to how deep their game runs, 'cause when a mu'fucka knows you swift, you—

"Become a threat," Gambino finished for him. He truly *appreciated* the game that had just been bestowed. Waco Shawn nodded his acknowledgement.

"Let me tell you a little tale, Gambino, and I want you to keep this gem tucked tight, my guy, 'cause all game ain't for all niggas, feel me?" Gambino nodded his understanding and that's how he learned the take of *The Boy and the Pond*. Waco Shawn smirked before he began ...

Once upon a time, somewhere deep in the country, there lived an elder couple and their seven-year-old grandson whom they loved very much. One day in the summer's heat, as the boy and his grandfather sat sipping lemonade out on the porch, the grandfather asked his grandson— "Grandson, where you wanna go when you're all grown up? What you want to be?"

The child glanced up from his glass. "Grandpa, I'm gonna be just liiiike you when I grow up! I'm gonna go all over the world and I'm gonna have a big house and everything, juuust like you, Grandpa," the boy vowed in a child's usual excitement. The grandpa chuckled.

"And how do you plan to do all this, boy?" he asked, and laughed when the boy frowned in thought.

The grandson finally shrugged his naivety. "I 'on know, Grandpa," he admitted.

At that, the grandfather smiled when a thought came to him. He rose from his seat and patted the boy on the head—they had a game they usually played, where they would make believe they were explorers.

"Come on, boy, follow ya grandpa," he beckoned, and the boy obliged. Grandpa led them to the back of the house where a large pond rippled from the slight breeze, and there at the edge sat a canoe and two paddles.

As the grandpa made his way over to the small boat, the boy watched curiously, as he pushed it onto the water before climbing in. "Come on, boy, let's take a few laps in the pond," Grandpa proposed, and gleefully, the little boy ran and jumped in the canoe. Grandpa used a paddle to push away from the bank, and the small boat rolled out deeper into the water. "Here, boy, take these here paddles and take us somewhere," he suggested, knowing his boy loved to do the paddling.

"Where ya wanna go, Grandpa?"

Grandpa shrugged. "Anywhere, boy, just get us there safe!" He began the game they'd dubbed "Anywhere"! It was a game where Grandpa would allow the boy to paddle all over the pond, pretending to go anywhere around the world, and so, that little boy began to paddle.

The grandson pretended they were going to Africa to see the pyramids, and he paddled with all he had. Up and down and 'round and 'round the pond he paddled, so many times, he became dizzy, and finally, with sweat pouring down his little face, the boy struggled to row the canoe back to the pond's edge.

"Whew!" he exclaimed, out of breath. "Grandpa, Iiii's tied, Grandpa! Africa is a long way away, Grandpa, and I'm too tired to get us there!" His revelation got a chuckle out of the old man.

"Sho' ya right, boy, let's get on outta this here boat," he offered, before climbing out and helping the boy onto dry land. Smiling *down at him, grandpa had another grand idea. "Boy, let's jog around this here pond to get a little exercise," he suggested. And though that boy was bone tired, he'd do anything to make his hero proud. So, they jogged and they jogged until the boy couldn't go around that pond not another lap!*

"Grandpa, mannnn, Grandpa, I's can't take another step around this pond or I'm gonna die, Grandpa, I'm tellin' you, I'm gonna die!" he swore, dramatically. So, chuckling, grandpa carried the boy back to the front of the house and they reclaimed their seats on the porch.

Chuckling, grandpa watched as the boy guzzled the rest of his lemonade before reaching for another glass. The chuckle turned into laughter as the boy drank his grandpa's glass as well.

"See, boy," Grandpa began, before patting the boy's knee. "That pond is like a man's wants, needs, and dreams. See, you "wanted" to go far, your "dreams" were big as you paddled, but no matter how hard, fast, or which direction you chose to steer that boat, it was only so far you could go, and only so much you could do. It's 'cause that pond had a "limitation!" Even when we ran around it with all we had, where'd we go, son?"

Grandpa paused the lesson he wanted to teach to gaze out into the distance of the land. He pointed towards the vast acres of land he owned. "What I'm teachin' ya, boy, is a pond won't lead you anywhere, what a man "needs" is an ocean to navigate! The ocean will always lead you somewhere, rather good or bad, far or near! Point is, you must always think bigger, if your thoughts or dreams are small enough for you to run around like you did that pond, they're too small! Make your aim bigger than a vast sea to cross in order to be bigger than you ever been. Always choose an ocean perspective versus a pond insight," he jeweled, before patting the boy's knee once more.

At that moment, the sweet aroma of baking cookies wafted from inside the house and the boy leapt from his seat and ran in the house. Moments later, he returned with a plate of freshly baked chocolate-chip cookies his grandmother had just baked.

Taking his seat, he began to devour the sweet confections, moaning in appreciation with each bite. Knowing that his wife made some of the world's moistest, most delicious chocolate-chip cookies, grandpa reached for one but the boy pulled the plate out of his reach.

"Can't I have a cookie, boy?" he asked, and to his amazement, the boy nodded his head no!

"Uh-uh, Grandpa, I told grandma what you said, and she said-she said 'if you want some cookies, you better stop havin' a pond insight and have an ocean perspective. 'Cause-'cause this here porch is like that there pond— no matter how long you sit on it, or talk on it, there's only so far you can go, and only so much you can do on it! It's 'cause this here porch has a limitation! It won't take you anywhere! What a man needs is a biiiig house to navigate!'"

The boy returned the jewel grandpa had just given him. "And she said, grandma said, "'you'" need to have an ocean perspective versus a pond insight and carry ya old ass up in there and get ya own cookies," Waco Shawn concluded with a chuckle. Gambino laughed hard, but the jewel was held sacred.

"Say, mane, where you get some shit like that?" he inquired, as they made their way out of lockup.

Waco Shawn chuckled. "It's this parable by this author named *Renta*, vibe with that boy books, the gems he drops is worth the pennies you'll pay for the them!

213

Renta

Part II: Power

After I pray to God, I praise the brothaman who's being oppressed by the other man for merely trying to get his family out the mothaland ... I'm not talking about Africa!

I'm talking about the ghetto, where mama cries 'cause innocence don't matter!

This one's from the crooked streets of Dallas! The cities of Denton, Screwston, Beaumont, PA, San Antonio, G-Town, Baytown, Murda Worth, New York, New Orleans, Baton Rouge, Baltimore, Compton, Miami, DC, and every other hood across America that I didn't capture ...

The struggle! All my refugees who's been stolen from their tribes and placed in concentration camps with football numbers or until ever after! The units of Beto, Telford, Coffield, Michaels, Estelle, Stiles, San Quentin, Georgia State Prisons, Colorado USP, Bloody Beaumont USP, all the way down to Angola, and back up to Rikers and where they're rioting for redemption on Attica! Black Power!

Negro, I walked through the fire and was disintegrated for my passions ...

What I do? I fought the good fight and allowed my spirit to dig its bloody fingers into the flames and rebuild my physical from the ashes! I'm from where the warriors clashing ...

Temperatures below zero and only the warriors braves it ...

This shit bigger than Nino Brown, and I'm just happy I made it out! Makes me wanna shout, 'cause I know a million dead men who are still livin' but didn't make it—out! The Jungle!

Where the paled-skin men invaded and Shaka Zulu couldn't save it ...

It's now where slaves hymns are sung at church and grandmothers pray for their babies!

The Jungle! Where the gorillas pound their chest, the hyenas have the strongest bite, and the lions never rest ...

'Cause the head of the pride always runs into a cub with pride that wants to put his roar to the test!

The Jungle! Where if you claiming to be a part of the tribe, that shit gotta be earned...

Trial by fire and when you're walking barefoot over those burning coals you bet not show that it burned!

Hunger! Can turn good niggas bad and bad niggas to a snake...

And after he strikes and poisons with his bite, he'll hiss and say, "no matter the love, my stomach was touching my back and you started lookin' like food, so I ate!

Heartache! Can 'cause a rainstorm to drip from the eyes of a warrior; you ever been stabbed in the back, warrior? Investigators showed you the written statement from ya main man's now you asking for ya lawyer?

Chance! It's somethin that we really don't give ourselves...

Yet, before we can do so, we first have to forgive ourselves!

Power!

CHAPTER 18
OJ The Crooked

Two Weeks Later ...

♪*There was an old lady sitting under a tree/ she called me over and she said to me/ my days here, may not be long, I wouldn't waste my time tellin' you nothin' wrong/ see love is like a flower, needs the sun and the rain ... ♪* Betty Wright's, *No Pain, No Gain,* played softly as Mama June sat at her dining room table with tears in her old eyes. She hadn't heard from her child in almost two months, and it wasn't like Dunte not to check in with his mama. As much as Gambino was a daddy's boy, Dunte was his mother's child. He'd never went more than three days without checking in. Ms. June loved both of her boys deeply, but ever since Gambino had gotten jammed, Dunte was all she had left.

"Where are you, chile?" she whispered, as she situated her notebook paper to write Gambino. She made it her business to write him twice a week, and since it was her week to have Khloe, she decided to write and let her grandbaby draw a picture to show their support. So, as Betty sang, Ms. June picked up her pen to inscribe:

Dear Bino,

You know what a mother's greatest fear is, baby? It's having to bury a child instead of that child burying her. As it should be. Gambino, I know I ain't been a model mama, but God knows I tried. See, ya daddy was a street nigga, and before him, my daddy was a bonafide hustla, so I always knew my offspring would be children of the ghetto. Why? How? That's easy, boy. I knew 'cause ya mama became a product of these same streets I watched kill ya daddy and sent my own pappy up the river to spend the rest of his life in one of the many federal penitentiaries of Amerikkka! Baby, don't ever think ya mama looks down on you or loves you less because ya situation is bleak, 'cause, Bino, a mother's love is more powerful than the black power fist! We love long! In and out of season! It's just that I see it in your eyes, Bino— the pain, the disappointments of my

217

addiction, and baby, it kills me to let you see this monkey ridin' my back.

You and Dunte are the best thangs a bitch done ever gave to the world, and without y'all and my grand baby, I'm nothin', Gambino, hear me? I'm nothin'! The sad truth is, baby, ya mama is dyin', and with the type of time you have, I'll never be able to hug you on this side of life again. Years, Bino. Tears.

I guess what I'm sayin' is, I'm worried, Gambino. I ain't heard from Dunte in two months, and that ain't like my baby. G, I'm not too old or removed from things that I don't hear what's goin' on in them streets. I heard somebody done killed my baby, Bino, but a mother knows! We know when a piece of us have been snatched from this world and I can "feel" it, Bino, my baby is breathin'! But...he won't be for long if he don't change his ways. Please, baby, talk to him. Can't you do that for an old woman? I love you, boy, with every breath I have left.

—Love Mama—

She had concluded the missive and it seemed as if pouring so much onto that paper had awaken a monster. Ms. Junes eyes drifted to the already filled syringe and without thinking, she reached for the belt lying across her legs. With track marks scarring her arms so deeply, finding a vein there was nearly impossible. So, she looped the leather around her thigh and pulled it as tight as she could.

♪*No pain, no pain, no gain, no...* ♪ Betty sang, as Ms. June took the syringe and spotting the perfect vein, she carefully danced with the devil. "Ahhh…" She inhaled a deep breath as the demon snaked through her system. The high was instant! As her eyes drooped and Betty's tempo changed with her classic, *The Clean-Up Woman,* Khloe entered the room. Her eyes were curious as they fell to the needle dangling out of her grandmother's thigh.

"Grandma, you taking your medicine?" she asked. It was all Ms. June could do to keep her chin from falling to her chest.

She nodded. "Yeaah, baby, gran-granny took her medicine." Her voice was scratchy. Khloe made her way over, eyes digesting the sleepy look on her grandmother's face, as she took a seat in the chair beside her.

"How it make you feel, granny?"

"Gooood, baby, it make ya-ya gran-granny feel good," Ms. June answered, before surrendering to the euphoria of her high.

***

"OK, sis, let me get back in here before these people fire me." Oshaya's voice came through the phone. Monay giggled.

"OK, girly, I'll talk to you when you get off work. We can go by mama's house and eat! She usually cooks chicken-fried steak, mashed potatoes with brown gravy, and cheesy seashells macaroni with some of the softest rolls. Girl, the woman can burn to be a White woman." She laughed as she ended the call with plans to meet up.

Resting her phone on the counter, Monay glanced up to find Juju and Juicy giving her a strange look. She sucked her teeth at them.

"Whaat?" She demanded. The salon was empty on Sunday, save for three friends.

"I still can't believe you and Oshaya are related. I mean, *how?*" Oshaya had been wrecking her brain trying to figure it out. She just couldn't put her finger on how two felines could go from civil war to becoming the Brady Bunch!

"Umm," Monay sassed with a roll of her eyes. "Nosey much!"

"No, bitch, there's the paranormal, the abnormal, and then there's the *can't* be normal!" Juicy counted off three fingers. "This new energy you and Oshaya got is really scary. Just a few weeks ago—"

"Uh-uh." Monay put her hand up to stop her before bringing her four fingers down to touch her thumb as if to say *hush it up!* "Don't go there, Juicy. If it wasn't for your messy bessy ass, it wouldn't have been no smoke, but—"

"Bihh," Juicy hushed her. "Shiiish!" She put her fingers to her lips for silence. "Forgive me if I'm wrong, but"—she paused, turning her attention to Juju—"I think the smoke came from this freak not being able to keep her legs closed, right, Juju?"

Juju rolled his eyes at Monay with a suck of the teeth. He hadn't spoken to Monay since the cat snuck out the bag about her goosing Pierre. "The bitch knows where the smoke came from, Juicy. I ain't got time for the T.T.O.T."

"*TTOT?*" Juicy asked with a raised brow.

"Girl, yass!" JuJu rolled his eyes once more. "That *tramp* over there!" He pointed at Monay. Monay had been catching the shade for weeks and was sick of it.

"Oh, bitch, you *still* throwing shade over that nigga? *Fuck* Pierre," she spat.

"Umph, that you did, slut."

"And fuck *you!*" The smoke was up. Juju had had enough and slid from his seat with a glare in his eyes.

"Juju," Juicy cautioned, but Juju gave her the hand.

"Bitch, your lip is getting old," he spat.

Monay wasn't dodging no smoke, stepping closer, she was ready for a smoke out! "And? You act like you mad *you* ain't fuck the lame."

"Hoe, I'll," Juju spat and took a step closer, but the bell over the door chiming blew a cool breeze over the tension. All eyes drifted to the handsomely rugged man who'd just entered the salon holding his hands behind his back.

"Which one of y'all is Monay?" He smiled charmingly before revealing what he held in his left hand. "I'm the gift bearer." His eyes twinkled as he held out a bouquet of white roses.

***

The Nigger Marriage

We breed two nigger males with two nigger females. Then we take the nigger males away from them and keep them moving and working. Say one nigger female bears a nigger female and the other bears a nigger male. Both nigger females being without influence of the nigger male image, frozen with an independent psychology, will raise their offspring in reverse positions. The one with the female offspring will teach her to be like herself, independent and negotiable. "We negotiate with her, through her, by her, we negotiate her at will." The one nigger male offspring, she being frozen with a subconscious fear for his life, will raise him to be mentally dependent and weak, but physically strong. In other words, body over mind. Now in a few years when these two offsprings become fertile for early reproduction, we will mate and breed them and continue the cycle. That is good, sound, and long range comprehensive planning.

"What you reading?" Oshaya's voice caused him to jump and damn near drop the book he was reading.

"Damn!" Gambino exclaimed.

She giggled. "Scary butt!"

"Watch out, Oshaya, don't be creeping up on—"

"Shush!" Oshaya put a finger to her lips. *"Here,"* it's C.O Givens!" She corrected him with a frown. Since she'd been back to work, they'd been rocking tough, and the man's charms had her doing some of the strangest things. Gambino chuckled.

"Yeah, you're right, *Ms. Givens,* but dig, you got that for me?" he asked, studying her. Oshaya nodded, glancing around suspiciously.

"Yes, and this the last time, Gambino"—she paused, rolling her eyes at the slip— "I mean, *Ridge."* She addressed him *professionally* before holding up a finger for him to give her a second. Being at the back of the tier was a gem for a playa, and as he watched lady turn and put her back to the wall so she could see anybody coming up the stairs, Oshaya hurriedly unbuttoned her pants, but paused when she caught him staring. "What, dang!" she pouted as she reached down and pulled out a small package from near her nether region.

Tossing it to him, she quickly fixed her clothes before facing him. "What were you reading anyway?" Her inquisition

221

contradicted the sacrifice she'd just made for him. Gambino held up the book so she could see the title.

"The Willie Lynch Letter and the Making of a Slave," he revealed. Oshaya frowned, and he took it as her being naive, so he jeweled her. "Willie Lynch was a British slave owner in the West Indies, but he came here in 1712 and gave a speech on the bank of the James River in the Colony of Virginia. Cocksucker was invited to teach slave owners his methods, and guess what?"

"What?"

"His methods are still in full effect til this very day! Every time you see a light-skinned brotha or sista who feels superior to a darker-hued brotha or sista? The reason a lot of Afro women may envy the next because her hair is"— he used his fingers to air quote— "*supposedly* better than hers, longer, and straighter. The reason bundles, tracks, wigs, and flat irons were created? Why a lot of sistas seek a smaller frame? It's all because of *this* very speech that was held on the bank of the James River back in 1712." His revelation caused her eyes to grow large.

"Boyyy," she began, but gave him a studious expression. "I've heard of the Willie Lynch Theory, but never really paid much attention to it. Yet, I still don't believe that he's the cause of all *that*. Hell"— she paused to touch her ponytailed hair— "I have some good hair, but I don't see myself as better than everyone else. All my sistas are beautiful to me."

"Yeah, but you're one out of seven billion! *I shall assure that distrust is stronger than trust and envy stronger than adulation, respect, or admiration.*" Gambino's words caused her to rear back with a stank face.

"Excuse me?"

He chuckled. "That's what Willie Lynch told the slave owners that night. His exact words were:

The Black slaves after receiving this indoctrination shall carry on and will become self-refueling and self-generating for hundreds of years, maybe thousands. Don't forget you must pitch the old Black male versus the young Black male, and the young Black female against the old Black male. You must use light skin slaves versus the dark skin slaves, and dark skinned slaves against the light skin slaves.

You must use the female versus the male and the male versus the female. You must also have your White servants and overseers distrust all Blacks. It is necessary that your slaves depend on us. They must love, respect, and trust only us. Gentlemen, the "kits" are your keys to control. Use them. Have your wives and children use them, never miss an opportunity. If used intensely for one year, the slaves themselves will remain perpetually distrustful of each other.

Thank You, Gentlemen."

He read the words of the book before closing it and tossing it on his bed. "To top off how great this pussy boy was to them, White folk named hanging our people after him—*Lynching!* The crazy part 'bout this man's strategy is he guaranteed, way back in 1712, that if done correctly, it would control our people for at least *300 years—2012!"* He enlightened, but Oshaya's attention had been stolen. Her eyes had fallen to his side, where he had a portrait tattooed with the word Khloe inscribed in cursive above it. *Strange!* she thought as she thought of her beautiful niece, and then her mental carried her back to a conversation she'd had with Monay. *Monay, you haven't told me nothing about you, girl, and as beautiful as my niece is, I know her daddy has to be fiiine!" She'd chided her sister. Monay had laughed before rolling her eyes.*

"That, he is, but the nigga got himself in some bullshit and found himself locked up with football numbers!"

"I'm sooo sorry to hear that! Girl, it must be hard raising that child on your own! Don't worry though, ya sis got your back!

"Givens, say?" Gambino's voice seeped into the recollection. Oshaya's eyes came into focus and slowly lifted to meet his. Her heart pounded so hard she could hear it! "Say, fuck wrong wit' you, you just zoned out on the kid, you good or what?" He seemed worried.

"Gam-Ridge,"she corrected. "What's your baby mother's name?" she almost whispered. The inquisition seemed so off the wall to him that Gambino took a step back.

"Fuck?" he mumbled, eyes falling to the tattoo of his daughter she'd just been so taken with. When his eyes lifted to hers, he couldn't quite put his finger on it, but he was sure he recognized fear in her gaze. "Wha-I mean, why? Why's that important?"

"What's. Her. Name!" Oshaya hissed through clenched teeth. Confusion was evident as it blossomed over his face, but rather than answering, he turned and got his photo album out of his locker.

"Look, I don't know your malfunction, Ms. Lady, but you need to check your tongue when you talk to me," he demanded, as he opened the photo album. Oshaya's eyes were locked on it and at that moment she found the truth within her cliché—*when it rains it pours!*

"Wait!" she demanded; her eyes as large as an owls. *Can't be!* she thought.

"What's good, mane, you spookin' me?" Gambino wasn't feeling her vibe but he complied.

"Go back a page," she requested. So, he did. "Oh-my-Godd!" she cried, before bringing a hand to her mouth in shock.

Gambino gave her a baffled expression before his vision fell to the pictures of him and Cat Eyes captured in the better days. His heart turned cold at the vision, but hers seemed to beat outside her chest! "How... I mean, I can't believe this. You know him?" She was flustered. Gambino frowned before his own heart began to pound. *Ain't no way!* His thoughts were doubtful. After so long, there was no way that woman could know his crime partner, the man he lusted on the thought of whacking for treason. "How?" Oshaya's eyes bounced from him to the picture and back.

"Oshaya, I need you to tell me something and be all the way solid with your answer. Okay?" His mouth salivated at the thoughts of revenge. "How do you know Cat Eyes?" His question got another expression of bafflement. *Cat Eyes? He told me his name was—* "Oshaya!" Gambino's tone was deadly, and it caught her attention. Their eyes danced; their minds raced!

224

"I-I have to go," she answered.

"Naw, you, Oshaya! Givens," he demanded, but she'd already speed walked away! "Fuck!" he spat, but he could've never imagined what that woman's mind was doing. Just beyond almost being certain that the woman who'd went from foe to family, being the mother of the man's child, she was falling for, Oshaya was stuck trying to figure out the connection between him and Mirage. Mirage—the man she now knew as *Cat Eyes!*

***

"Smmop!" Juju smacked his lips with a roll of the eyes before pointing at Monay. "There the bitch is. I don't know why she so special to niggas. She ain't got the only pair of lips that can suck a dick," he low-key hated. Juicy was the only one who didn't speak. Her eyes were suspicious of the man. It was true that image is everything, and the royal blue attire and the blue bandanna that hung loosely around his neck was a clear indication of his gangsterisms.

As Monay gushed as if she'd been crowned Ms. America, and Juju threw shade from across the room, Juicy's hood bitch's instincts were on fire as her eyes took in how the man held his other hand behind his back as if he still had gifts to reveal. *Chocolates? Jewelry? What?* She wondered what it could be, but even more, she wondered why her intuition was screaming for her to run. There was just something about how the man's smile didn't reach his eyes. The Rick Ross beard only seemed to add to the wickedness in his appeal, and at that moment, she decided to follow her feelings.

"Girl, them flowers are beautiful!" She gushed. "I'm going to get a vase to put them in," she acknowledged, before excusing herself.

Monay smirked with conceit—*Yeah, these bitches got a reason to be jelly now!* she thought, while making her way toward the man. She just knew the roses came from Pierre. She hadn't heard from him since the day she'd set him on Dunte's trail, and she had some shit she needed him to digest. He was fun, but her love for Gambino ran thick and she felt like shit for doing him like that, so... she was gonna dead things before feelings evolved on either side. *But then this,* she thought as the man extended the flowers. Monay cut her eyes at Juju, who had envy written all over his face as she accepted the flowers and made a big show of closing her eyes as she inhaled their fragrance.

"Tell Pierre I said thank you sooo much and that this was sweet but we need to talk," she said all this with a smile on her face.

"You tell 'em," the strangers deep voice caused her eyes to flutter open, and a perplexed expression to paint her pretty face.

"Huh," she began, but the man's hand was a blur when he brought it from behind his back. And before Monay could scream at the sight of the Glock .19, he fired— *BOCA!* The slug pushed her stomach in and almost folded her.

"Huuuuuu!" Monay sucked in a deep lungful of air as her eyes grew wide in a mixture of shock and horror. The stranger laughed when Juju fainted. Monay stumbled backward, and the flowers tumbled to the floor as she gripped her stomach, and the man wasted no time with the business.

"You can tell the fuck boy yourself, 'cause when I catch 'em in traffic, y'all can explain to the devil why y'all there!" he gritted, before squeezing the trigger once, twice, three times, *face time!* The last bullet and death blow splashed lady's noodles against the mirror behind her. Monay coincidently fell crooked into her beautician's chair, one eye open, the other half closed, as her soul slipped from her lips. "Betrayal!" the man declared, before turning to make his exit. "Tell 'im OJ The Crooked sent you."

CHAPTER 19
Fatal Attraction
12 a.m. ...

"I'm going with you, Dunte, and that's all there is to it, nigga. You not about to just up and leave me. Period!" Mya wasn't trying to hear it. She pulled the car to a stop light on the street of Little York before glaring at him as he stuffed bullets down into the fifty round magazine of a M4 he'd been dying to play with.

"Twenty-one..." he paused his count at the twenty-first bullet before his dark eyes slowly trailed to her. The night was as black as the fur of a black cat, and the interior of the slab was slightly aglow from the cars amenities. "Mya, you're going *home,* I'm dipping far away from *the H* to keep everythang I love safe. I love you, ma, but I won't be able to think *and* worry about your safety. This shit ain't no game and—"

"But, what about *me,* Dunte? *Us!"* she declared, unconsciously rubbing her slightly bulging belly. She'd finally told him she'd been carrying his seed for the past six months and the revelation rocked him, terrified him; had him thinking some unseen force was toying with him!

Dunte didn't know if losing Christina and their child only to regain Mya and their little world was a sign of the Gods or what, but he wasn't into subliminal messages. When tears leaked from Mya's eyes, frustration dived into the pool of his stress and swam straight to the deep end! The streets seemed deserted at that hour and a slow drizzle fell.

"Fuck, mane!" He cursed before glancing back at the duffel bag in the backseat. Two bricks of white and two hundred and fifty bands was all he had to his name, but that was enough for him to skip town and start anew. Falling back against his seat and resting his head against the headrest, Dunte blew a long whoosh of air. "Ai-ight, Mya, you can"—

SKURRRT! The screeching of tires sliced through his spiel. Dunte's mouth fell open as a black van slid to a stop in front of them, but instincts were instant. He fumbled to get the clip in place

227

as the side door slid open on the van and a group of machine gun wielding Mexicans jumped out and took aim.

"Oh my God!" Mya screamed in shock.

"Bitch, put the car in reverse and drive!" he spazzed, spittle flying from his mouth. Mya did just that and stomped down on the gas, but—*SKURRRT!* The sound of burning rubber snatched Dunte's attention behind him just as they smashed into another van. And before he knew it, they were boxed in on all sides and the type of artillery that was trained on them had the power to dismantle the entire car.

"Fuuuck!" Dunte shouted, defeated. He knew it was the cartel and even the M4 would be useless—Pisssh! His window exploded from someone rushing over and smashing it with the butt of an assault rifle, causing glass to rain down on him. Just over the loud demands spoken in Spanish, his greatest fear came to pass— *BOOM!* A single gunshot splattered Mya's thoughts across his shoulder. Instinct kicked in and Dunte wanted his lick back, but just as he went for his weapon, the butt of the rifle rocked him to sleep.

***

Oshaya sat in the driveway of her home, gripping the steering wheel so tightly her knuckles turned white. *Why can't I just be happy, God? Why does my life have to be filled with so much drama!* she thought, with tears of anger filling her eyes. The night was absolute and as heaven's tears softly fell against the windshield, she'd realized Nigil's truck wasn't in its usual spot. *Thank God for small blessings!* she thought, before retrieving her purse and phone from the passenger's seat. She frowned because she'd been trying to call Monay since she'd gotten off work to tell her she wouldn't be able to make it, but the girl wouldn't answer the phone. She knew Monay was a live wire, so she'd chalked it up to her having other plans.

"Let me hurry on in here before it starts raining cats and dogs!" she told herself, before exiting the car and hurrying to the front door.

Upon entering, she tossed her purse on the couch before shivering from the chill of the night. "Could've sworn I left the heater on…," she wondered aloud, before turning the dial to adjust the lighting in the room. Oshaya's phone vibrated in her hand as she made her way to the room. Seeing that it was Gambino, she felt conflicted… *How do you know Cat Eyes, Oshaya, I need to know. You'll never know how long I've been trying to find this nigga. Let me ask you something… have you ever loved a mu'fucka? Sacrificed it all for them on some real shit, and got ya throat sliced for it?* The text aroused her curiosity, and though earlier while in front of his cell she couldn't deal, after calming down and thinking it over, the woman honestly wanted to fit the pieces into their rightful places. So, she responded.

I apologize for the way I acted earlier. It was just tooo much, but I'm woman enough to admit I owe you an explanation. Yet, you owe me one too! So… since I asked you first, how about you answer my question, and then I'll answer yours: what's the mother of your child's name? A second passed before his response rolled in and it almost made Oshaya drop the phone.

Monay! The name turned her world upside down, but not as much as when she entered the room and turned the light on. "Girrrl!" she cried out, but this time she did drop her phone. Hand flying to her chest as her heartbeat slowed its gallop, Oshaya's laughter was strained as she eyed Patrese sitting on her bed Indian style. The girl's eyes seemed unfocused and as they studied each other, Oshaya's initial shock melted away along with her smile. Frowning as her *ex* friend's betrayal swam to the forefront of her mind, she took a threatening step toward her.

"Bitch, what the hell you doin' in my house! In my mofo bed?" She lost it.

Patrese smiled evilly. "You mean, *my* house, *my* bed that I fucked *my* soon-to-be husband, and father of my child upon not even six hours ago, right? *MINE* Oshaya! And when you're out of picture, we'll be a happy family. Just-what-*I've*-always deserved!" The girl sounded possessed, but Oshaya was ready and willing to perform an exorcism up in that place.

"Bitch, *what,*" she spat.

And just when she was lunging for her, Patrese lifted the Glock 9 Nigil usually kept on the top shelf in the closet—*BOOM!* The gun exploded, the bullet grazIng Oshaya's arm, and spinning her, nonetheless.

"Ohhhh!" she cried, as she crashed into her bureau. Her perfumes and nail polishes crashed to the floor as she landed on her knees, almost in a football hiking position. Patrese rushed from the bed and stood over her, gun aimed for a headshot.

"*Mine*, bitch! He doesn't want you, but *you* won't let him be happy. You won't let him leave!" she screamed at the top of her lungs. Oshaya leaned back on her heels, tears of pain in her eyes as she held her burning arm.

"Why are you doing this, Patrese? Over, *Nigil?*" She cried in disbelief as she studied the psychopathic wildness in the girl's eyes.

"Yes, Nigil, *and* because you've always thought you were better than me, besides"—Patreses' eyes seemed to come back into focus— "Tabitha told me to do this." She spoke in a child's voice before her facial features transformed into a deadly grimace. "Shut up, Tabitha!" she exploded, as her eyes briefly went to the space inside her. As she aimed the gun at Oshaya, she looked beside her as if there were someone there. "Just shut up! It's because of you we hurt Nigil!" she shouted at thin air before her eyes reclaimed Oshaya.

And it was then that Oshaya remembered their time in Mexico, during the times Patrese feared for her life, she had created a best friend. *An invisible best friend named* Tabitha no one else could see except her. Tabitha was her polar opposite—the part of her with courage! Oshaya's eyes grew wide at the mention of Nigil's name, and though she knew they could no longer be, she still loved the man. Her mind raced for a way to find out what the deranged bitch had done to him, but the wait was short lived.

"Patrese, Tresey, what have you done to Nigil?" she asked. Patrese cocked her head to the left and studied her curiously before a wide smile eased onto her face.

"Oh, Nigil, I almost forgot!" She'd suddenly became gleeful. "No, Tabitha, we can't kill her yet... No!" she demanded, a quick look to where Tabitha was supposed to be standing. Glancing back to Oshaya, she glared. "Get up," she requested. And though Oshaya was struggling to her feet, her pace wasn't fast enough for the other woman. "GET UP!" Patrese screamed, veins bulging in her neck and across her forehead. Oshaya hurriedly complied and once to her feet, Patrese waved the gun toward the closet. "Move!" she demanded. So, holding her arm, Oshaya made her way to the closet, all the while praying for Nigil. Patrese snatched the closet door open, and it was there, staring wide-eyed and attempting to talk from behind his gag, they found Nigil. He bled from a gunshot wound to his shoulder and was in bad shape. Somehow, Patrese had bound his wrists and ankles with belts and sashes from their robes. As Oshaya glanced to the girl she once protected, she knew she'd be dead in moments. Patrese nodded. "He wouldn't shut up!" She shrugged. "So Tabitha and I shut him up." She giggled. "No, Tab, I don't think that's—"

That's as far as she got before Oshaya went for the gun.

To Be Continued...
Ski Mask Money 3
Coming Soon

231

Renta

Lock Down Publications and Ca$h Presents assisted
publishing packages.

BASIC PACKAGE $499
Editing
Cover Design
Formatting

UPGRADED PACKAGE $800
Typing
Editing
Cover Design
Formatting

ADVANCE PACKAGE $1,200
Typing
Editing
Cover Design
Formatting
Copyright registration
Proofreading
Upload book to Amazon

LDP SUPREME PACKAGE $1,500
Typing
Editing
Cover Design
Formatting
Copyright registration
Proofreading
Set up Amazon account
Upload book to Amazon
Advertise on LDP Amazon and Facebook page

***Other services available upon request. Additional
charges may apply
Lock Down Publications
P.O. Box 944
Stockbridge, GA 30281-9998
Phone # 470 303-9761

Submission Guideline

Submit the first three chapters of your completed manuscript to ldpsubmissions@gmail.com, subject line: Your book's title. The manuscript must be in a .doc file and sent as an attachment. Document should be in Times New Roman, double spaced and in size 12 font. Also, provide your synopsis and full contact information. If sending multiple submissions, they must each be in a separate email.

Have a story but no way to send it electronically? You can still submit to LDP/Ca$h Presents. Send in the first three chapters, written or typed, of your completed manuscript to:

LDP: Submissions Dept
Po Box 944
Stockbridge, Ga 30281

DO NOT send original manuscript. Must be a duplicate.

Provide your synopsis and a cover letter containing your full contact information.

Thanks for considering LDP and Ca$h Presents.

NEW RELEASES

HEAVEN GOT A GHETTO by RENTA

SOSA GANG 2 by ROMELL TUKES

KINGZ OF THE GAME 7 by PLAYA RAY

SKI MASK MONEY 2 by RENTA

STRAIGHT BEAST MODE III

De'Kari

KINGPIN KILLAZ IV

STREET KINGS III

PAID IN BLOOD III

CARTEL KILLAZ IV

DOPE GODS III

Hood Rich

SINS OF A HUSTLA II

ASAD

YAYO V

Bred In The Game 2

S. Allen

THE STREETS WILL TALK II

By Yolanda Moore

SON OF A DOPE FIEND III

HEAVEN GOT A GHETTO III

SKI MASK MONEY III

By Renta

LOYALTY AIN'T PROMISED III

By Keith Williams

I'M NOTHING WITHOUT HIS LOVE II

SINS OF A THUG II

TO THE THUG I LOVED BEFORE II

IN A HUSTLER I TRUST II

By Monet Dragun

QUIET MONEY IV

EXTENDED CLIP III

THUG LIFE IV

By **Trai'Quan**

237

Renta

THE STREETS MADE ME IV
By **Larry D. Wright**
IF YOU CROSS ME ONCE III
ANGEL V
By **Anthony Fields**
THE STREETS WILL NEVER CLOSE IV
By **K'ajji**
HARD AND RUTHLESS III
KILLA KOUNTY IV
By **Khufu**
MONEY GAME III
By **Smoove Dolla**
JACK BOYS VS DOPE BOYS IV
A GANGSTA'S QUR'AN V
COKE GIRLZ II
COKE BOYS II
LIFE OF A SAVAGE V
CHI'RAQ GANGSTAS V
SOSA GANG III
BRONX SAVAGES II
BODYMORE KINGPINS II
By **Romell Tukes**
MURDA WAS THE CASE III
Elijah R. Freeman
AN UNFORESEEN LOVE IV
BABY, I'M WINTERTIME COLD III
By **Meesha**

QUEEN OF THE ZOO III
By **Black Migo**

238

CONFESSIONS OF A JACKBOY III

By Nicholas Lock

KING KILLA II

By Vincent "Vitto" Holloway

BETRAYAL OF A THUG III

By Fre$h

THE MURDER QUEENS III

By Michael Gallon

THE BIRTH OF A GANGSTER III

By Delmont Player

TREAL LOVE II

By Le'Monica Jackson

FOR THE LOVE OF BLOOD III

By Jamel Mitchell

RAN OFF ON DA PLUG II

By Paper Boi Rari

HOOD CONSIGLIERE III

By Keese

PRETTY GIRLS DO NASTY THINGS II

By Nicole Goosby

PROTÉGÉ OF A LEGEND III

LOVE IN THE TRENCHES II

By Corey Robinson

IT'S JUST ME AND YOU II

By Ah'Million

BORN IN THE GRAVE III

By Self Made Tay

FOREVER GANGSTA III

By Adrian Dulan

GORILLAZ IN THE TRENCHES II

239

Renta

240

HEARTLESS GOON I II III IV V

A SAVAGE DOPEBOY I II

DRUG LORDS I II III

CUTTHROAT MAFIA I II

KING OF THE TRENCHES

By **Ghost**

LAY IT DOWN **I & II**

LAST OF A DYING BREED I II

BLOOD STAINS OF A SHOTTA I & II III

By **Jamaica**

LOYAL TO THE GAME I II III

LIFE OF SIN I, II III

By **TJ & Jelissa**

BLOODY COMMAS I & II

SKI MASK CARTEL I II & III

KING OF NEW YORK I II,III IV V

RISE TO POWER I II III

COKE KINGS I II III IV V

BORN HEARTLESS I II III IV

KING OF THE TRAP I II

By **T.J. Edwards**

IF LOVING HIM IS WRONG…I & II

LOVE ME EVEN WHEN IT HURTS I II III

By **Jelissa**

WHEN THE STREETS CLAP BACK I & II III

THE HEART OF A SAVAGE I II III IV

MONEY MAFIA I II

LOYAL TO THE SOIL I II III

By **Jibril Williams**

A DISTINGUISHED THUG STOLE MY HEART I II & III

241

Renta

LOVE SHOULDN'T HURT I II III IV

RENEGADE BOYS I II III IV

PAID IN KARMA I II III

SAVAGE STORMS I II III

AN UNFORESEEN LOVE I II III

BABY, I'M WINTERTIME COLD I II

By **Meesha**

A GANGSTER'S CODE I &, II III

A GANGSTER'S SYN I II III

THE SAVAGE LIFE I II III

CHAINED TO THE STREETS I II III

BLOOD ON THE MONEY I II III

A GANGSTA'S PAIN I II III

By J-Blunt

PUSH IT TO THE LIMIT

By **Bre' Hayes**

BLOOD OF A BOSS **I, II, III, IV, V**

SHADOWS OF THE GAME

TRAP BASTARD

By **Askari**

THE STREETS BLEED MURDER **I, II & III**

THE HEART OF A GANGSTA I II& III

By **Jerry Jackson**

CUM FOR ME I II III IV V VI VII VIII

An **LDP Erotica Collaboration**

BRIDE OF A HUSTLA **I II & II**

THE FETTI GIRLS **I, II& III**

CORRUPTED BY A GANGSTA I, II III, IV

BLINDED BY HIS LOVE

THE PRICE YOU PAY FOR LOVE I, II ,III

DOPE GIRL MAGIC I II III

By **Destiny Skai**

WHEN A GOOD GIRL GOES BAD

By **Adrienne**

THE COST OF LOYALTY I II III

By Kweli

A GANGSTER'S REVENGE **I II III & IV**

THE BOSS MAN'S DAUGHTERS I II III IV V

A SAVAGE LOVE **I & II**

BAE BELONGS TO ME I II

A HUSTLER'S DECEIT I, II, III

WHAT BAD BITCHES DO I, II, III

SOUL OF A MONSTER I II III

KILL ZONE

A DOPE BOY'S QUEEN I II III

TIL DEATH

By **Aryanna**

A KINGPIN'S AMBITON

A KINGPIN'S AMBITION **II**

I MURDER FOR THE DOUGH

By **Ambitious**

TRUE SAVAGE I II III IV V VI VII

DOPE BOY MAGIC I, II, III

MIDNIGHT CARTEL I II III

CITY OF KINGZ I II

NIGHTMARE ON SILENT AVE

THE PLUG OF LIL MEXICO II

CLASSIC CITY

By **Chris Green**

A DOPEBOY'S PRAYER

243

Renta

By **Eddie "Wolf" Lee**
THE KING CARTEL **I, II & III**
By **Frank Gresham**
THESE NIGGAS AIN'T LOYAL **I, II & III**
By **Nikki Tee**
GANGSTA SHYT **I II &III**
By **CATO**
THE ULTIMATE BETRAYAL
By **Phoenix**
BOSS'N UP **I , II & III**
By **Royal Nicole**
I LOVE YOU TO DEATH
By **Destiny J**
I RIDE FOR MY HITTA
I STILL RIDE FOR MY HITTA
By **Misty Holt**
LOVE & CHASIN' PAPER
By **Qay Crockett**
TO DIE IN VAIN
SINS OF A HUSTLA
By **ASAD**
BROOKLYN HUSTLAZ
By **Boogsy Morina**
BROOKLYN ON LOCK I & II
By **Sonovia**
GANGSTA CITY
By **Teddy Duke**
A DRUG KING AND HIS DIAMOND I & II III
A DOPEMAN'S RICHES
HER MAN, MINE'S TOO I, II

CASH MONEY HO'S
THE WIFEY I USED TO BE I II
PRETTY GIRLS DO NASTY THINGS
By Nicole Goosby
TRAPHOUSE KING **I II & III**
KINGPIN KILLAZ I II III
STREET KINGS I II
PAID IN BLOOD **I II**
CARTEL KILLAZ I II III
DOPE GODS I II
By **Hood Rich**
LIPSTICK KILLAH **I, II, III**
CRIME OF PASSION I II & III
FRIEND OR FOE I II III
By **Mimi**
STEADY MOBBN' **I, II, III**
THE STREETS STAINED MY SOUL I II III
By **Marcellus Allen**
WHO SHOT YA **I, II, III**
SON OF A DOPE FIEND I II
HEAVEN GOT A GHETTO I II
SKI MASK MONEY I II
Renta
GORILLAZ IN THE BAY **I II III IV**
TEARS OF A GANGSTA I II
3X KRAZY I II
STRAIGHT BEAST MODE I II
DE'KARI
TRIGGADALE I II III
MURDAROBER WAS THE CASE I II

Elijah R. Freeman
GOD BLESS THE TRAPPERS I, II, III
THESE SCANDALOUS STREETS I, II, III
FEAR MY GANGSTA I, II, III IV, V
THESE STREETS DON'T LOVE NOBODY I, II
BURY ME A G I, II, III, IV, V
A GANGSTA'S EMPIRE I, II, III, IV
THE DOPEMAN'S BODYGAURD I II
THE REALEST KILLAZ I II III
THE LAST OF THE OGS I II III
Tranay Adams
THE STREETS ARE CALLING
Duquie Wilson
MARRIED TO A BOSS I II III
By Destiny Skai & Chris Green
KINGZ OF THE GAME I II III IV V VI VII
CRIME BOSS
Playa Ray
SLAUGHTER GANG I II III
RUTHLESS HEART I II III
By Willie Slaughter
FUK SHYT
By Blakk Diamond
DON'T F#CK WITH MY HEART I II
By Linnea
ADDICTED TO THE DRAMA I II III
IN THE ARM OF HIS BOSS II
By Jamila
YAYO I II III IV
A SHOOTER'S AMBITION I II

BRED IN THE GAME

By S. Allen

TRAP GOD I II III

RICH $AVAGE I II III

MONEY IN THE GRAVE I II III

By Martell Troublesome Bolden

FOREVER GANGSTA I II

GLOCKS ON SATIN SHEETS I II

By Adrian Dulan

TOE TAGZ I II III IV

LEVELS TO THIS SHYT I II

IT'S JUST ME AND YOU

By Ah'Million

KINGPIN DREAMS I II III

RAN OFF ON DA PLUG

By Paper Boi Rari

CONFESSIONS OF A GANGSTA I II III IV

CONFESSIONS OF A JACKBOY I II

By Nicholas Lock

I'M NOTHING WITHOUT HIS LOVE

SINS OF A THUG

TO THE THUG I LOVED BEFORE

A GANGSTA SAVED XMAS

IN A HUSTLER I TRUST

By Monet Dragun

CAUGHT UP IN THE LIFE I II III

THE STREETS NEVER LET GO I II III

By Robert Baptiste

NEW TO THE GAME I II III

MONEY, MURDER & MEMORIES I II III

247

Renta

By **Malik D. Rice**

LIFE OF A SAVAGE I II III IV

A GANGSTA'S QUR'AN I II III IV

MURDA SEASON I II III

GANGLAND CARTEL I II III

CHI'RAQ GANGSTAS I II III IV

KILLERS ON ELM STREET I II III

JACK BOYZ N DA BRONX I II III

A DOPEBOY'S DREAM I II III

JACK BOYS VS DOPE BOYS I II III

COKE GIRLZ

COKE BOYS

SOSA GANG I II

BRONX SAVAGES

BODYMORE KINGPINS

By **Romell Tukes**

LOYALTY AIN'T PROMISED I II

By **Keith Williams**

QUIET MONEY I II III

THUG LIFE I II III

EXTENDED CLIP I II

A GANGSTA'S PARADISE

By **Trai'Quan**

THE STREETS MADE ME I II III

By **Larry D. Wright**

THE ULTIMATE SACRIFICE I, II, III, IV, V, VI

KHADIFI

IF YOU CROSS ME ONCE I II

ANGEL I II III IV

IN THE BLINK OF AN EYE

Renta

THE BRICK MAN I II III IV V
THE COCAINE PRINCESS I II III IV V VI VII
By King Rio
KILLA KOUNTY I II III IV
By Khufu
MONEY GAME I II
By Smoove Dolla
A GANGSTA'S KARMA I II III
By FLAME
KING OF THE TRENCHES I II III
by **GHOST & TRANAY ADAMS**
QUEEN OF THE ZOO I II
By **Black Migo**
GRIMEY WAYS I II III
By Ray Vinci
XMAS WITH AN ATL SHOOTER
By Ca$h & Destiny Skai
KING KILLA
By Vincent "Vitto" Holloway
BETRAYAL OF A THUG I II
By Fre$h
THE MURDER QUEENS I II
By Michael Gallon
TREAL LOVE
By Le'Monica Jackson
FOR THE LOVE OF BLOOD I II
By Jamel Mitchell
HOOD CONSIGLIERE I II
By Keese
PROTÉGÉ OF A LEGEND I II

LOVE IN THE TRENCHES

By Corey Robinson

BORN IN THE GRAVE I II

By Self Made Tay

MOAN IN MY MOUTH

By XTASY

TORN BETWEEN A GANGSTER AND A GENTLEMAN

By J-BLUNT & Miss Kim

LOYALTY IS EVERYTHING I II

Molotti

HERE TODAY GONE TOMORROW

By Fly Rock

PILLOW PRINCESS

By S. Hawkins

Renta

<u>BOOKS BY LDP'S CEO, CA$H</u>

TRUST IN NO MAN

TRUST IN NO MAN 2

TRUST IN NO MAN 3

BONDED BY BLOOD

SHORTY GOT A THUG

THUGS CRY

THUGS CRY 2

THUGS CRY 3

TRUST NO BITCH

TRUST NO BITCH 2

TRUST NO BITCH 3

TIL MY CASKET DROPS

RESTRAINING ORDER

RESTRAINING ORDER 2

IN LOVE WITH A CONVICT

LIFE OF A HOOD STAR

XMAS WITH AN ATL SHOOTER